16 & Pregnant

MTV 16 & Pregnant

A NOVEL

BY LALA THOMAS

MTV Entertainment BOOKS

NEW YORK LONDON TORONTO SYDNEY NEW DELHI

Entertainment
B O O K S

An imprint of Simon & Schuster Children's Publishing Division
1230 Avenue of the Americas, New York, New York 10020
First MTV Books hardcover edition January 2023

Jacket illustration by Bex Glendining
For information about special discounts for bulk purchases, please contact Simon & Schuster Special Sales at 1-866-506-1949 or business@simonandschuster.com.
The Simon & Schuster Speakers Bureau can bring authors to your live event. For more information or to book an event contact the Simon & Schuster Speakers Bureau at 1-866-248-3049 or visit our website at www.simonspeakers.com.
Interior designed by Tiara Iandiorio
The text of this book was set in Adobe Garamond Pro.
Manufactured in the United States of America
2 4 6 8 10 9 7 5 3 1
Library of Congress Cataloging-in-Publication Data
Names: Thomas, LaLa, author.
Title: 16 & pregnant : a novel / by LaLa Thomas.
Other titles: Sixteen and pregnant
Description: First MTV Books hardcover edition. | New York : MTV Books, 2023. | Audience: Ages 14 and Up | Summary: Best friends Erykah and Kelly have their junior year planned out, but everything changes when Erykah finds out she is pregnant, and as Kelly tries to support her throughout the pregnancy the two girls learn some harsh realities about the world and are forced to make some huge decisions.
Identifiers: LCCN 2022030395 | ISBN 9781665917278 (hardcover) | ISBN 9781665917292 (ebook)
Subjects: CYAC: Pregnancy—Fiction. | Best friends—Fiction. | Friendship—Fiction. | High schools—Fiction. | Schools—Fiction. |African Americans—Fiction. | BISAC: YOUNG ADULT FICTION / Social Themes / Pregnancy | YOUNG ADULT FICTION / Social Themes / Friendship | LCGFT: Novels.
Classification: LCC PZ7.1.T4627 Aae 2023 | DDC [Fic]—dc23
LC record available at https://lccn.loc.gov/2022030395

To every Black momma in America.

You matter.

Erykah

I'm here to tell you that turning sixteen aint always sweet. And I'm not trying to ruin anybody's dreams or nothin' like that, because I get it, everybody's different, but I never thought I'd fall into the not-so-sweet bunch. I thought my sixteenth birthday would be one of the happiest days of my life, but instead it turned out to be . . . well, let's just say, it turned out to be more of a wake-up call. Not because I didn't get a dope-ass party or my driver's license like most kids my age. Nah. Matter of fact, I wasn't even expecting none of that. Instead of me celebrating my special day with my boyfriend and best friends, I was hovering over a toilet seat, sweat beading down my forehead, as I slowly watched my life change on a stick. All I could do was watch every one of my dreams and goals swirl down the drain right along with the puke that spilled from my gut. For me, turning sixteen was supposed to be the start of my "It Girl" year, not the moment where every dream I'd ever worked toward was yanked from me in a flash. I guess I never thought something like this could happen to me. And now, instead of me prepping for the ACTs or scheduling my driver's test, I'm on my way to an appointment that I never thought I'd have to go to, especially at sixteen.

CHAPTER ONE

Erykah

"Ma, can you please slow down?" I scrunch in my seat, clenching my stomach for dear life.

We ride over the bumpy road, bouncing up and down like her car has hydraulics. She rolls over a pothole and then comes to a stop, shaking her head at the creaky gate that is taking forever to open.

"This is supposed to protect folks from getting shot at in the jets, huh?" She arches her eyebrow at the sign.

I lean back with a shrug, cause I'm thinking the same thing. How's a shabby gate supposed to provide safety for one of the worst project buildings in Lynwood Heights? I guess after Lil Mark died last year from that drive-by, the city came up with the idea to have a security gate installed to "protect the residents," but I'm sure a few metal bars aint stopping nobody from bangin'. Momma pushes through, even though the gate is still rattling open, then mumbles something under her breath. Something about how we're running late, but I just press my earbuds in and mellow out to Ari Lennox. The inside of this car feels like a freakin' sauna. I probably shouldn't have worn this hoodie, but when we left this morning, I had the chills. Momma said it's probably my hormones or my anemia. Regardless, I just wish it wasn't so damn hot already. It's not even eight a.m. and my phone says that it's 92 degrees outside. Unfortunately for me, Momma refuses to blow the air, talkin' bout it eats up her gas, but damn, I thought that's what gas was for.

I would think she'd have more consideration being that I'm already uncomfortable as hell, but her car, her rules. She pulls up next to a candy-red Oldsmobile that belongs to one of the OGs from around here. It's hella fly, making Momma's car, a 2009 Altima, look basic as hell. The sun is beating our ass from the sky, and even though her hair lays like a second skin over her warm brown cheeks, the most she does to beat the heat is lower the back windows, like that's gone do something. I press my sweaty water bottle against my neck and think about how much more my life is about to change within the next few hours. I'm starting to feel like we should just turn around, so I can think about this some more, maybe even convince Momma that I don't need to go through with this, but there aint no turning back. I mean, I do want to see my boyfriend Miguel and all, but I'd rather be getting dropped off so me and him can chill, not because my momma is taking us to an abortion clinic.

Momma keeps saying that me and Miguel are too young to

raise a child and this and that, but that's just because she doesn't like him. I don't think she likes any of my friends, except for Kelly. Lots of girls my age survive through teen pregnancy. My momma had me at nineteen, but she says it's not the same as my situation because she had her diploma and her and my daddy were married. At first I thought having an abortion just might be the best thing, but as each day goes by, I can't help but think of how I'm getting another chance at having a real family again.

"Erykah, call that boy and tell him to hurry up or I'm driving off without 'im." Momma eyes me down while her fingers tap the leopard-cloth steering wheel. I told her the only way I'd go to this appointment was if Miguel could come. I pull out my phone just to make her happy.

> Me: Can u plz hurry? Moms is trippin'.

> Miguel: Be down in a min. Cleaning this oatmeal off Mitzi.

> Me: Awwww. Give her kisses 4 me.

Miguel's daughter, Mitzi, is two years old and looks like a little chocolate baby doll with a head full of thick curls. She mostly lives with her mom, but Miguel watches her every now and then. Momma doesn't know that Miguel has a little girl. She doesn't need to know. She already calls him a thug because he sags and lives in the roughest part of Lynwood Heights (Miguel moved in with his sister, Lita, after he had a falling-out with his mom). She says I shouldn't even be focusing on boys right now, but if I had a girlfriend, she'd probably say the same thing.

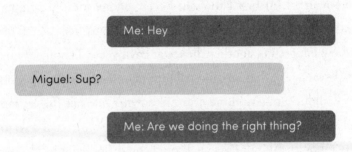

Me: Hey

Miguel: Sup?

Me: Are we doing the right thing?

I stare at my phone as the three dots appear next to his name, but then they disappear, without a response. *Maybe we should've just left his ass at home.* I lay my phone facedown on my thigh and take a few sips of warm water, which I want to just spit out of the window. Finally, he responds.

Miguel: You gone be straight. Stop worryin Ma.

Easy for him to say, just like it is for everyone else. I keep asking myself if I'm really making the best choice or if I'm just doing what everyone else wants me to do. Six months ago, I was planning to do extra hours toward the business program that I'm studying at school. It's one of the reasons why I wanted to go to

East Prep, so that I can learn the basics of what it'll take to own a beauty salon, but lately all I do is obsess over YouTube, searching videos like, *What does abortion feel like?* and *Can I have kids after abortion?* When I told Miguel I was pregnant, he didn't speak much on it, just said he was gone "be a man about his" and that he's down for whatever I want to do. Part of me feels like he's not ready for another child, but I keep telling myself that it's just my hormones making me overthink everything.

As we sit in front of Miguel's building, Momma looks at me with beads of sweat rolling down her forehead. I prop my seat up a bit and shrug, before sending Miguel another message about how he needs to hurry up.

"See? This is the stuff I'm talking about. This boy is not responsible, and you thought you wanted to have a baby with him? How much you wanna bet he's gone cause you to miss your appointment?" She glances at the time, then looks at me with her deep, hazel-brown eyes.

"He said he's coming, dang."

"Watch your mouth, Erykah. I'm not the one who got you pregnant." She waves her finger. "Of all the things I would rather be doing, *this* was not on my monthly agenda."

Umm, it wasn't on mine, either.

I suck through my teeth and clench the water bottle tightly to avoid saying some shit that will probably make Momma wanna just leave my ass stranded.

Let me be clear.

I didn't get pregnant on purpose.

This wasn't supposed to happen.

But it did.

A really heated night turned into a moment of irresponsibility. It wasn't our first time not using a condom. Matter of fact, we did use one that night . . . but not the following morning. Miguel took me to get the Plan B pill, but we had to wait almost a week to buy one, since he hadn't gotten paid yet. The box said it's best to take it within seventy-two hours. I knew something was up when I started gagging at the smell of Takis two weeks later, and I *love* Takis (chili dynamite flavor, to be exact). So glad that's no longer a thing, because now I crave them like crazy.

I took three pregnancy tests at my bestie Kelly's house instead of turnin' up for my sixteenth b-day like we had planned to do and got a triple reminder that my ass had slipped up, but TBH, I was just in denial. I swear the pink lines on the last test were glowing, rubbing it in my face even more that my ass was not experiencing stomach bug symptoms like I had told my momma the night before. It took a heart-to-heart talk with Kelly's mom to make me realize that even though having a baby might not be easy, it's not the end of the world. But my momma's reaction was a whole 'nother story. She basically gave me two options: get an abortion or get out. Momma even threatened to send me to stay with my dad, but he's living his best life with his new family on the other side of town, and I doubt he'd be all open arms taking in his pregnant and estranged sixteen-year-old daughter. Last I heard from him was Christmas, when he sent me and my little brother, Jayden, a sorry-ass card with two twenty-dollar bills in it.

Momma said that she can't afford to feed one more mouth and that me having a baby at sixteen would be a huge mistake. Sometimes I just wish me and Kelly could swap moms. I mean, Mrs. Lancaster is super into church and stuff, but not the kind who blasts Kirk Franklin on Sundays or who has pictures of Black Jesus all over the house. She's the one who told me that no matter what I did, God would still love me, and that I should let my heart help me decide if I wanted to go through with my pregnancy. She really is like a second mom to me. I aint gone front. I feel like she gets me more than my own momma sometimes.

"His sister is still bringing you home after your procedure, right? I wish I could bring yall back, but I'll be late for my shift." Momma looks at the time on her phone.

"Yeah, she's supposed to."

I stare down at my phone, waiting for Miguel to send me an OMW text.

Momma's eyes are posted on a group of teenagers who are huddled on the sidewalk, sharing a blunt. I low-key inhale the musky scent, which would normally make me gag, but for some reason, it's making me feel less nauseous. I wish she would try to be a little bit more compassionate. It's like she can barely even look at me when she talks, and even though I know she's hurting, she has to understand that I'm hurting too.

Things had been really good between Momma and me ever since I transferred to East Prep Career and Technical Academy last year. Kelly's mom, who's one of the principals there, helped me to get accepted. It's literally the best school in our district, so Momma was all for me transferring, especially because she knew that would separate me from Miguel. I can't front, it'd be cool to be with Miguel at the same high school for his senior year, but he probably won't even be there that much since working and taking care of his family are his priorities. Before I got pregnant, Momma had been bragging to everybody about how I'm on the honor roll and how I was going on an all-expense-paid Black College tour for rising juniors this summer. Me and Kelly were hella excited about it too, but after I told Momma that I was pregnant, she said there would be no way in hell that she was letting me go on that trip. I'm supposed to be there right now.

"Foolin' round with yall, I'm a be late for work," Momma mumbles while rolling her finger up her phone screen. "I need to call Manny just in case, because I know he's looking for a reason to write my ass up," she continues, talking to herself.

Momma's been cleaning rooms at the Palm Desert Casino for the past five years. It don't pay much, but it gets us by. Even though we could use the extra help, she would rather work a double shift than apply for food stamps, not to mention the long-ass drive to the Vegas Strip and back. She always says that being a Black woman makes you realize how strong you are, but I think you get extra points when you're a good-ass Black

single mother. It's not like I want to be in that category, cause as much as Miguel acts stupid, he aint going nowhere. But if my momma can kill this parenting thing, I'm for sure that I can.

A loud ding blazes from my phone.

> Bestie: Mornin' even though it's almost noon here.

> Me: GM BF :/

> Me: How's DC?

> Bestie: Ughh I kinda don't wanna come back to NV LOL

Kelly sends me a few pictures of DC and one of her and Ray, all hugged up in front of what looks like Howard University. She said they're visiting Virginia State, which isn't too far away, next. She's out there living her best life. Meanwhile, I feel like I'm getting a contact high from the thick skunk-like smell that's creeping through the car's vents while waiting on my turtle-ass boyfriend and praying I don't throw up my breakfast quesadilla.

> Me: Yall got to visit Howard?

Ever since Kelly and me watched the classic movie *Drumline*,

we've wanted to go to an HBCU. That's another reason why I was so hyped about going on the summer college tour, because I know being there in person is like a whole different experience.

Bestie: Yeah! The campus is huge. I wish you were here 😕

Bestie: Are you there yet?

Me: Waiting on Miguel. But we'll be there soon. And yeah, wish I was there too

Bestie: Is Ms. Monica still trippin' or she good? Sucks that she can't be there the whole time.

Me: Miguel's gonna be with me

Bestie: Yeah but he's

Bestie: NVRmind, E. Just want U to be Ok :).

When I had my online consult with one of the counselors at the abortion clinic, she told me to make my decision based

on my heart too, even if that meant going against Momma and Miguel's wants. Sometimes I feel like I know what he wants and sometimes I'm hella confused. Part of me wonders if me and Miguel will ever have this chance again. I know legal abortions are safe and that it won't make me like sterile or anything and I'm not against abortions, but my heart doesn't sit right when I think about missing out on the chance to not only love a piece of myself, but for that piece to love me and Miguel back. The week I found out I was pregnant, me and Miguel had the "what are we gonna do" conversation in the back of his homeboy Dre's truck. We had just come back from chilling at a little pool hall spot, something that his homies threw together. Now that Miguel's eighteen, he can basically do whatever he wants, unlike me, who has two more years to go. I still remember how warm and breezy the night was. We talked about keeping the baby and abortion, as well as adoption, but I just couldn't imagine living without our child. And that night, it seemed like Miguel felt that way too. I mean, he didn't say much, but I could tell by the way he held me that night, the way his hands were trembling when he gripped mine, that he wanted a family with me too.

If someone were to ask me what I'm feeling right now, I'd say torn. Torn because I don't know if I'll be able to live with a bunch of regrets. I mean, I'm actually about to step foot into an abortion clinic and will come out no longer pregnant. Like what if this baby is here to piece my family back together or maybe even make this world a better place? My baby might be the next Angela Davis or John Lewis. And if it's a girl, she just might be the first Black female president of America. This isn't like me deciding whether I want to wear box braids or faux locs. Nah, this is way more serious, and even though I'm pretty good at making decisions, I still feel like whatever choice I make, I'll still be unsure of my fate.

"Erykah, I'm not gone wait too much longer." Momma starts the ignition.

I nod, while sending both Kelly and Miguel texts.

> Me: Listen, I'm a be okay. I just wish my momma would stop being so, grrr!!

> Me: Miguel, my momma's about to dip

> Bestie: LOL! Don't do Ms. Monica! Ur mom really loves U.

> Bestie: Hey, bus is loading. Going to the National Mall today! Txt me as soon as U get there. 143.

> Me: 143

When we were in sixth grade, me and Kelly did this project on nineties pop culture and learned that 143 was a code people used to send to each other's pagers to say, *I love you*. Corny, right? But we both thought that was pretty dope, so it became our bestie code.

Momma grips the steering wheel with both hands, then turns toward me. Her face softens a little. Damn, she's looking like she's about to cry.

"Erykah, I don't want you to think I'm making you do something you don't want to do. This is serious, I know, but I just can't watch you mess up your life and ruin all your dreams for some clown. I know I had you at a young age. . . ." She balls her calloused hands to her lips.

I wish she didn't have to work so hard. I remember when I was little, Momma stayed with her nails slayed, but that was when she worked for that fancy lawyer's office and before Daddy dipped.

"But taking care of a baby is not easy. It's more work than you think, and at your age, it's the last thing you should have to deal with. I can't support another child, and neither can you."

"Okay, but I'm only like three years younger than what you were. And I got Miguel, Ma."

Momma squeezes her eyes shut and lets out a breath like she's tryin' not to go off on me, then reaches over to pull open her glove compartment. She fingers through stacks of envelopes, some falling to the floor.

"This is just one of the many bills that's kicking my ass every month." She waves the thick envelope in my face. "I'm fighting to keep my hours steady so we all can have insurance, and I done borrowed so much money from Ms. Benita, it don't make no sense. Now, do Miguel have insurance for you and this baby? He got money saved up for all the co-payments? Is he gone take you to every damn appointment and back? This boy probably don't even know left from right. Hell, he couldn't even wear a condom like he was sposed to."

Actually, he did, but whatever.

She acts like Miguel is the most incompetent person on earth. And I'm pretty sure it doesn't cost that much to go the doctor's. The lady at the clinic said there's government programs that help single parents who don't have a lot of money to pay for stuff like that. I really wish she would just chill out.

"I'm not like most of these mommas."

Damn right, she aint. Most mommas wouldn't be so damn preachy.

"I want you to have the things in life that I aint have, and repeating the cycle is not gone get you them things. I know it seems hard right now, but once you realize the mistake you almost made, you'll see that your momma was right."

Ouch. A mistake? The only mistake I'm making right now is listening to this bullshit. She has some nerve to think that me having a baby would be a mistake. She had me at a young age and I turned out to be okay, so why does she think that I can't raise this baby and do the same? The only mistake I've made so far is telling her that I'm pregnant.

I fold my arms across my chest and look out the passenger

window. Weeds and dead grass replace what was once, I imagine, a beautiful lawn with sweet-smelling flowers. Right now, I feel like one of those weeds in Momma's eyes. It seems like nothing I do is ever right, especially since she had my little brother Jayden seven years ago. She praises him and treats him like he's the golden child. She says it's because he's the baby, but I think she just loves him more. The only thing I ever get credit for is when I'm babysitting or if I pick him up from school on time.

I watch Miguel make his way down the stairs, galloping like he's glad to be outta that apartment. I want to curse him out so bad for making me and Momma wait, but I'm afraid of what Momma will do to me if she hears me. He pauses midway as he chugs a can of Arizona tea. His shiny do-rag is stuck to his head. He pulls his baggy jean shorts up before sliding a black tee over his wifebeater, then heads toward us. Right now, he's looking so good, he's making me want to get pregnant all over again.

"Please, after this, let that boy go," Momma says. "You still got plenty of time to fall in love. He looks like he can't even raise his voice if he tried, let alone a child."

She makes a sour face in Miguel's direction. He's slapping hands with a guy who has jet-black skin and is rockin' some dingy white Forces. The dude slides Miguel a twenty-dollar bill, then shuffles to the group of old dudes who are hanging out on some steps. Yeah, Miguel has his little hustle on the side, but weed aint even illegal no more and working at a drive-thru window don't pay him much, so I don't see no harm.

Miguel leans through my window with a wide grin on his face, smiling at me like he's just meeting me for the first time. His blinged-out bottom grill shines like it's still in one of them display cases at the swap meet. Even though the diamonds aint real, it still gives him mad swag. He reaches for two frozen water bottles that are stuffed in his back pocket. He's been teasing me about how I went from wanting room temp to ice-cold water overnight, but I feel like I have to drink hella bottles a day. I stay thirsty and peeing.

"Sup, Ms. Smith." He sucks his teeth before handing me the frozen bottles.

Momma gives him a sharp stare. "Hey," she says dryly, then continues searching for a playlist to listen to from her phone.

Once we're on the road, we hit every pothole and bump again, feeling like we're at an amusement park. *Damn, is she doing this on purpose?* I roll the window all the way down to let in some air so I don't pass out from heatstroke. After thirty minutes of cruising down the I-15, a sign assures us that Las Vegas is ten miles away. The hot breeze whips my face as I scroll through my Instagram feed. Most of my friends are posting memes about what people be like when they have to return to school or the last moments of their summer breaks at places like Splash Mania Water Park or the Circus Circus Amusement Park. I wonder how many likes I would get if I posted a pic of my positive pregnancy test?

I look onto the deserted highway as we pass the mass of sandy mountains and dried shrubbery. I let my brain roam free and my heart explore new destinations as the city becomes closer. Momma drags out riffs while singing to Lauryn Hill's "Ex-Factor." I can see Miguel through the side mirror, bobbing his head with his AirPods hanging from his ears.

Everybody seems to be a vibe, except for me.

There's a queasy feeling deep in the pit of my stomach. I'm not sure if it's from the pregnancy or the realization that I need to keep it real. I lean back and take deep breaths.

It's gonna be okay.

You're making the right choice.

But am I? *What if Momma is right? What if Miguel leaves me? What if my life changes for the worse?* I weave my fingers together, taking another deep breath. I gotta remember to quit listening to anything but my heart.

"You okay, baby?" Momma winces at me.

"Yeah, just thirsty."

I hold up my water bottle and let the chilled water soothe my dry throat. Momma reaches over and gently grasps my hand. The warmth of her grip is so soothing, but not enough to soothe these emotions away. I can feel my eyes starting to water, but I quickly rub the tears away with my sleeve.

I should probably just tell Momma and Miguel now.

Tell them how I really feel.

But we're literally almost there.

The GPS dings, directing Momma to exit. I take a few more sips of water and clench my stomach, while mentally preparing how to tell them I'm not getting an abortion.

CHAPTER TWO
Kelly

It seems like all I do these days is imagine myself kicking back, without always having something to do. Always having to study, always having to go to practice, always trying to be the best girlfriend, and an even better best friend. Always having to maintain my GPA, but never really taking the time to look out for myself. Mom says that self-care is the best care, which I guess is true, and I thought this trip was gonna give me a chance to escape from the norms of life. But as the bus driver rolls over the potholes and bumpy roads of these DC streets, I still feel like there's an expectation I'm supposed to be upholding, even though all I wanna do is lock hands with my boyfriend Ray, rest my head on his shoulder, and stare off into the gloomy sky. Listen, being Kelaya Lancaster does require some skill. I know I should be grateful and count my blessings and all that stuff the older folks in my neighborhood always say, but for once, I'd like to just chill in my room, pop in my AirPods, hang at the mall or the city pool, and worry about planning my future some other time, but that's not how valedictorians are made. I have the highest GPA in my graduating class, and my parents are like my number one fans. My parents couldn't go to college until a few years after I was born. Had to wait for my dad's military benefits to kick in, so that they could afford it. I get his benefits too, but it probably won't cover the cost of everything, which is why I'm hoping to get a few scholarships.

My dad has been more excited about me going on this trip than I have. He even gave me an extra hundred-dollar bill so that I can buy him some Howard University gear from their gift shop. I reminded him that he could easily just buy the same stuff from Amazon, but he said it wouldn't be authentic if he did. I'm just glad Mom and him didn't volunteer to chaperone. That would've been so cringy. I thought this trip was gonna be boring, but it's been alright. We even got to experience a subway (which was way less scary than I imagined). And even though this trip is not so bad, I still feel bummed, because the one person who I wanted to share this experience with is about to make the hardest decision of her life and I'm not by her side. Being on this trip without her feels weird. E told me that things have been so heated between her and Ms. Monica and that she's still not sure what she's going to do. I told her that whatever she decides, I'll support her and help out the best way I can. I'm just glad that we live in a state where abortions are still legal and available.

But even though E isn't here with me, I've been surrounded by "the best and brightest from East Prep." That's what our National Honor Society advisor, Ms. Naiter, calls us—who, by the way, is getting on my nerves, but that's a whole other story. Most of the people on this trip are alright, except for Blaise Hampton, who has one more time to flirt with my man before I go off.

I check my phone for the twentieth time. No new messages from E. No missed calls. I lean my head against the warm glass as we zoom past a row of tall houses that are so close together, they look like they're hugging. This is the perfect opportunity to make a reel, just because they're way different from the cookie-cutter houses that are in my neighborhood.

#DC #Rowhouses #Blkcollegetour #summervibez

Ms. Naiter is announcing something from the front of the bus. Her orangey-reddish bangs need a serious trim. She keeps pushing them to the side as she mumbles into the microphone. I take out one of my AirPods and bump Darrion's shoulder.

"What she just say?" I ask.

"Something about a famous Chinese arch we're about to pass." His eyes are glued to his phone.

Halo Infinite. That's all I'm gonna say. I flip through a brochure I snagged from the hotel lobby, looking for this famous arch.

The Friendship Archway, located in DC's Chinatown, was built in 1986 to celebrate the friendship between Washington and its sister city, Beijing, China.

Makes me think of E even more. She's like my sister and my best friend. The night that Erykah found out she was pregnant,

I was there. When she stared at those two pink lines, as that long white stick trembled in her hand, I was there. When she practiced a million times how to tell her mom, I was there. And even when she told her stupid-ass boyfriend that she didn't have the stomach flu, I was right by her side. But today she needs *me* more than anyone, and I'm two thousand miles away.

A breathtaking archway with curved rooftops and beautiful Chinese-style art shifts my attention. I switch to portrait mode on my phone and try to get the best angles, before sending some pics to my parents and E. After I delete the blurry ones, I lean into Darrion, with the three lenses staring at us.

"D, look up," I say.

He pauses his game and throws up a peace sign with a slick smile. Darrion's been like a brother to me since third grade. His dad is the pastor at the church my family goes to, and our parents are thick as thieves. I scroll through filters before finally picking the lo-fi one, which accents the deep brown hue of my skin.

#roadtrip #DC #HBCU #day3

Posted!

In the corner of my eye, I can feel Blaise giving me a stank face. If I didn't care about my ratchet status, I would get up and smack all that thick-ass foundation off her face. I constantly remind myself that she's not worth it. She and Ray were assigned to sit together. On the plane *and* on the bus. It's like Ms. Naiter did that shit on purpose, and even though he's been texting me nonstop and is barely even checkin' for her, I still feel a way. I mean, she is one of the more popular kids at our school and used to be Ray's sneaky link. Blaise swears they were a couple before me and Ray got together, and she's been telling everyone that I stole her man, but they were never official. Plus, I aint got to steal nobody's man. As far as I'm concerned, she got the term "friends with benefits" mixed up with a relationship. I should just set her straight right now, in front of everyone, but I decide to text E instead.

> Me: Hey. Haven't heard from you. Everything good?

I send her the best pic I took of the Friendship Archway.

> Me: Took hella pics just to get the right one lol. Wish u were here ;(

Why isn't E responding? My insides feel like they want to burst into a million pieces. Maybe it's just my nerves because I'm so worried for her, or maybe I'm just exhausted because I stayed up late doing Mr. Morgan's AP Stats homework. That's the one thing I hate about AP classes. Why can't they begin in late August, like every other class does? I scroll through TikToks of WNBA players doing the three-pointer challenge. So far, the only one who's been able to do it is Ty Young, of course. She's my favorite WNBA player. Last year, Dad got us courtside tickets to see the Vegas Aces play. It was ten times better than watching it on TV. As I continue to thumb through, I pause at a post from Ms. Jayde, a teen influencer, who gives all the best mental health advice and whose purple locs are fire! I wish my mom would let me dread my hair out. Jayde is talking about the five ways to know you're an empath. I literally feel like she's talking directly to me as the signs flash across the screen.

You're the advice giver.

Check.

Vibes matter.

Check.

You take on others' emotions.

CHECK.

You can sense lies easily.

Double check.

You sometimes feel people's physical illness symptoms.

Check. Check. Check.

Is that why I threw up my organic chia-watermelon smoothie last night? Could I be feeling E's symptoms too? My mom said that when she was pregnant with me, my dad was the one throwing up the whole nine months. Since Miguel is a deadbeat loser, the universe probably deemed me the father.

We come to a sudden stop that jerks us so hard, it looks like I'm making out with the back of my seat. I peel myself off of it and glance out the window: the National Museum of African American History and Culture. I never thought I'd be so happy to see a museum, but I'm actually hyped about this one.

I did some research before this trip, and Michael Jackson's fedora is on display here. Like the actual hat that he wore in his "Smooth Criminal" video. Definitely going live for that one.

#MJistheGOAT

"Okay, everyone, we're going to get off the bus soon." Ms. Naiter stands at the front of the bus, waving a clipboard to get everyone's attention. "I just need to check us in—I'll be right back."

Everyone either has AirPods stuck in their ears, their eyes glued to their phones, or are knocked TF out. Most kids at East Prep are the epitome of swag. See, there's two sides to Lynwood Heights. The South (better known as Black Hollywood and where I live) and the North (which is where most of the news activity takes place). E lives in the North side, which my parents probably wouldn't even let me go to if it wasn't for her. The South side is filled with successful Black-owned businesses, nice houses, and East Prep, the best school the Heights has to offer. It's like a little Black Mecca. It was even mentioned in *Ebony* magazine as one of the top ten places for Black people to live in America.

> Ray: Ask Darrion to switch partners w/ U so we can be together inside babe

> Me: U sure U don't want to go on a tour with ur boo lol? JK

Ray: Man, stop playin'. I'm bout to come over there.

Me: K

Darrion agrees to switch with Ray, thank God, cause I don't want to have to slap nobody. Blaise is looking like she's about to sweat her twenty-two-inch lace front wig off, but who TF cares? I check my phone again to see if there's any update from E, but it only has one service bar. *Damn. Seriously?* Ray slides into the seat, instantly giving me chills down my spine. Yes, he is that fine.

"You good, Snugglebutt?" Ray pulls me closer.

Okay, I know, I know, the nickname is kinda corny, but it's cute to me. Not gone lie, every time he calls me that, my heart beats faster than Usain Bolt when he raced at the Rio Games. Ray has this twinkle in his gray-blue eyes that reminds me of how lucky I am to have such a fine-ass boyfriend. He's definitely my MCM every day. People say he looks like the pop star Ozuna. Yeah, I can see that. Actually, he's like ten times more fine and all mine. We met in AP Biology class—he started off as my tutor and we just couldn't resist each other. I truly am the luckiest girl in our school.

"My phone barely has any service, and I'm buggin' cause I don't want to miss E's texts. I'm so mad my mom switched us to crummy-ass Speed Mobile from AT&T." I roll my eyes.

"That shit should be called Turtle Mobile," he mumbles.

We both laugh. Ray's phone buzzes, interrupting our vibe.

"Damn." He stares at the screen.

"What?" I ask.

He doesn't take his eyes off his phone.

"Nah, just something Marsaun sent me." He places his phone facedown on his thigh, then presses his head against the seat, smushing his sandy-brown dreads, which are tucked in a man bun.

I look back at Marsaun Green, who's standing in the aisle flirting with Effia, the exchange student from Ghana. She's laughing at everything he says, but I don't think she's laughing with him. I notice Blaise glancing our way with a smirk on her face, almost as if she knows what Ray was just sent.

"Something Marsaun sent you?" I arch my brow.

"Yeah, but umm . . . it's nothing." He stuffs his phone in his pocket.

I feel like he's not telling me something, and I'm really tempted to make him show me what Marsaun sent, but I don't want to be *that* girl. What if Marsaun has a secret he made Ray promise not to tell, just like E made me promise not to tell hers? She made me swear I wouldn't tell anybody about her pregnancy. Ray is her close friend too, and he wouldn't tell a soul, but if she wanted him to know, she would've told him. I lean on his shoulder, taking in the scent of Axe body spray.

"You sure everything's okay?" I look up at him.

He holds a thumb up, then kisses my forehead.

I turn my phone off and back on to see if it helps with my service, but now it's just saying that it's searching for a signal.

"What if E's been texting like crazy and I'm not responding, and she thinks I'm ignoring her?" I sit up.

"*Or* maybe she hasn't and you wildin'," Ray laughs.

I smile faintly. Ray probably thinks I need an edible or something, the way I'm freaking out about my best friend, who he thinks is riding to work with her mom to earn community service credit. Every kid that's in the National Honor Society has to do so many hours of extra credit to stay active in the organization. I finished mine right before school was out and so did E, but Ray doesn't know that. It's a terrible lie, but it was the quickest one I could come up with so that Ray doesn't get too suspect. He doesn't know the real reason she couldn't come on the trip. I stare out the window, gazing at the Washington Monument; it's not as big as the internet makes it look, but it's still photo worthy. I zoom in and take a few pics, since that's the least my phone can do.

"Maybe Erykah and her mom are just busy at her job, and she hasn't taken a break yet," Ray says as he starts playing *GTA*.

"Yeah, you're right. It's just, E and her mom are barely back on cool terms since her mom found out about her pr—"

Ray's eyebrows meet.

"Pre . . . ACT scores. Scores were horrible." I nod uncontrollably.

I'm not a very good liar.

Ray just stares at me like he's got something on his mind, then puts his arm around me. I flatten my PopSocket and slide my phone in my pocket. Hopefully my service returns once we get inside the museum. Ms. Naiter lets us know we're free to go outside, and everyone pours off the bus. I take in the earthy damp smell, but my peace is interrupted by Ms. Naiter, who is assigning us partners to walk through the museum. She's really getting on my nerves with all these assignments. Technically, this is still summer break. I bet she's even trying to give us a grade.

"Okay, yall, listen up," Ms. Naiter says, enunciating the *yall* a little too much, while cheesing all hard.

I lower my head because that was so cringy to hear. For some reason she thinks she has to use AAVE when talking to Black kids. She's been embarrassing us for the past couple days. Like yesterday, when we ate at a Black-owned restaurant for dinner, she asked the server if the fruit punch was real or if it was Kool-Aid.

She stands at the front of the bus, surveying the group. No one is paying her ass any attention, except for me, maybe two other kids, and Effia, even though Darrion's trying to show her something from his phone. Blaise is looking jealous as hell because, TBH, Effia is pretty, and the guys are giving her the attention that Blaise usually gets. Effia turns and waves to me. I give her a quick wave, then use my hand as a visor since the sun is starting to peek out. I thought Vegas weather was crazy, but DC definitely has it beat. We've experienced cold, rain, humidity, and heat all in one day.

"Remember, there are no electronics while we're in the museum, or they will be confiscated. And stay with your assigned buddy. No switching up with the homies," Ms. Naiter snorts.

Wait, what? How am I gonna make sure that E is okay? Ms. Naiter is seriously tripping.

"But Ms. Naiter, what about emergencies? My parents told me to have my phone on me at all times," I say.

She pauses for a moment. "Emergency phone calls only." She waves a finger.

I give her a smile and turn around. If E calls or texts, I'm answering, period.

"Okay." Ms. Naiter claps. "Partner time!"

"Ay, yo, Ms. N?" Marsaun yells from the back of the line.

I don't even know how he was allowed to go on this trip. Last I checked, you had to have a 3.5 or higher to attend. But he's a star athlete, so I'm sure Coach Banks pulled some strings.

"Yes, Marsaun?"

"Why we gotta have partners? I thought yall sposed to be preparing us to be independent or whatever, so why can't we just do our own thang?" The rest of us agree, causing Ms. Naiter to blush.

"What I'm hearing is that you're concerned about having your freedom," she says with air quotes. "But for everyone's safety, we need buddies." She shrugs.

"You just think we gone be in there stealing," Daraysha Jackson blurts out.

The rest of us burst into laughter, and Ms. Naiter is now bright red. She asks us to settle down several times before telling us who we're going to be paired up with. Yet *again*, Ms. Naiter pairs Ray and Blaise. I'm put with Effia.

My stomach drops into my lap. Blaise is grinning from ear to ear, her long rhinestone nails clinging around her hips. At least Ray's eyes sink with disappointment. Effia taps me on the shoulder, with a bright grin.

"Kelly, I am so glad we finally get to . . . link up."

Damn, she seems sweet as hell, but this is some bullshit. I notice Ray waving at me from a distance.

"Can you excuse me for just a sec?" I squint at her.

She looks between me and Ray, puzzled, then gives an *aha* expression. I meet Ray near the front of the museum.

"What's up?" I tilt my head.

"You want me to see if Ms. Naiter will let me switch with Effia?"

"Nah, it's cool. Not like yall are sharing a room together." I wave him off.

Inside, I really want him to switch. I don't trust Blaise as far as I can throw her, and I'm really starting to think that Marsaun wasn't the one who sent Ray that text on the bus.

"You sure?" Ray arches his brow.

"Was that text you got on the bus really from Marsaun?" I fold my arms.

Ray rubs the back of his neck. That's his thing when he's about to tell a lie. My heart sinks into my stomach. *Why would he try to keep something like that from me?*

"Maan, Blaise AirDropped everybody a pic of her in her summer bikini." He pulls me closer to him. "I deleted it off my phone. I'm not checking for nobody but you."

He leans in for a kiss, and I can't help but give in. It's not Ray's fault that Blaise is thirsty as hell, and at least he's not trying to deny anything.

"Excuse me, lovebirds, please get with your partners," Ms. Naiter tells us.

She really irritates me.

Ray sneaks in another kiss before heading the opposite way. Blaise is holding out a snack bag for him, but he isn't even paying her no mind. He walks right past her and is slapping hands with some of the guys from his basketball team.

Effia returns with our snack bags.

"Thanks," I say, frowning at the crinkled brown sack.

"Yeah. It's no problem. You okay? I know you'd rather have your boyfriend as your partner," she says, peeling an orange.

"Oh, yeah. I'm fine. I'm glad to be your partner." I smile.

"I wonder what kinds of displays they have inside." Effia stares at the large museum.

"Lots. I researched it before we got here. I'm hyped about the Michael Jackson display." I peek inside my bag. This school has got to be kidding me. Two hard, glazed doughnuts, a carton of chocolate milk, a green apple, and a tan-colored sausage patty. I'm about to march to the Department of Education instead of inside this museum. This snack bag has got to be unconstitutional.

"My mother wants me to take pictures of some display about a guy named Prince." Effia looks confused.

Okay, Prince is way before our time, but he was dope as hell too. Most kids my age don't have a clue about him, but when you're an old-school R & B and pop fan like me, you know that Prince was a legend. The ones who get it, get it.

"Your mom has good taste," I say as I toss everything but the apple into a nearby trash can.

When we get inside, I try to keep my cool, but it's hard.

I swear Blaise's skirt just got like two inches shorter, and she's standing *waay* too close to Ray. I see her leaning over Ray's shoulder, whispering something in his ear.

This has got to be one of the worst days ever. Like, I can't communicate with my bestie, and now I'm being forced to watch this hoe flirt with my boyfriend right in front of my face?

I check my phone again to see if E has hit me up, but still nothing. What if she's having a full-blown panic attack right now? If it were me, I know I would be. Having an abortion sounds scary as hell, even though every method is pretty much safe. Me and E researched the two types of abortion methods and found out that serious problems after either procedure are rare. If E decides to go through with the procedure, I understand her

100 percent. I can't imagine E being a single mom when we've barely even got this teenage thing down.

I pull out my phone again.

Still, nothing.

Effia looks at me with her glistening brown eyes.

"Everything okay, Kelly?" she asks.

"Mm-hmm." I force a smile.

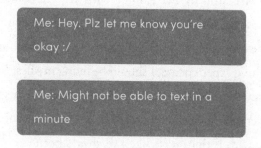

Me: Hey. Plz let me know you're okay :/

Me: Might not be able to text in a minute

I put my phone in my pocket, trying to ignore the grumble in my stomach. I take a few bites of my apple, which is surprisingly satisfying.

There's a buzz in my pocket and this time it's an actual message.

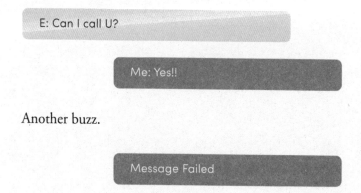

E: Can I call U?

Me: Yes!!

Another buzz.

Message Failed

Shit. This cannot be happening! Effia nudges me as the rest of the crew enters ahead of us. I follow along with the group, but everything is a blur. E needs me, and I'm in some museum. I'm barely looking at the exhibits, just sneaking my phone out to check for service, but I can't get a good signal. As we venture into the next exhibit, Effia pulls me by the wrist suddenly.

"Look! It's what you've been waiting for." She grins.

We stop at the exhibit with MJ's fedora, and everyone is crowded around the display. I should be living this up, taking the most pics and bragging on social media about how dope this whole experience is. I should be living my best life right now, and I should be squeezing hands with Ray, but instead, my mind is everywhere but here, and all I can think about is how I'd rather be with E right now, like I've always been.

CHAPTER THREE

Erykah

The clinic is nothing like what I expected it to be. There are no people surrounding the building with signs and megaphones to discourage me from being a "child killer" or to "repent" before it's too late. I mean, I was at least expecting some sweet old lady to be shoving an antiabortion brochure in my face. But there's no one in sight. Momma parks, turns the car off, and then takes the keys out of the ignition. She sits for a minute, looking straight ahead with her hands still gripping the wheel, before she turns to me.

What the hell?

"Why are you parking? Aren't you gonna be late for work?" I ask.

I look back at Miguel, who is still bobbing to whatever, his arms spread out across the top of the seats. Momma turns to me, then gently grabs my hand.

"I'm gonna stay with you, Erykah."

What?

She can't stay. If she stays, that could cause some issues. The last thing I need is for her to know that I'm not getting an abortion, just so she can go off on me about how I wasted her time and made her miss out on work. I'm waiting for her to say she's just playing, but her face is giving serious. I can feel my stomach churn as my heart races like I just finished running uphill. I turn to Miguel again, who's still in his own world. I slap his knee and he jumps, pulling out one of his pods.

"Fu—I mean, dang, bae, what you hittin' me for?" He leans forward, rubbing his knee. He's starting to make Momma seem like she knows what she's talking about.

"Miguel, can you tell my momma that Lita is picking us up and we don't need a babysitter?"

The inside of the car is starting to feel like an oven again. Momma is looking at Miguel like he'd be wise not to say shit. He runs his hand down his face and looks away.

"Uhh, we good, Ms. Smith. Lita's gonna pick us up once we're done," he mumbles.

"You can call your sister and tell her never mind." She smiles, but it's not friendly. "I'm going to call out today. I want to make sure you at least have *my* support." She looks between me and Miguel.

Shit. I try to say something, but my mouth is so dry, my tongue just sticks to the roof of my mouth. I squeeze my eyes shut and let out a groan.

"Problem?" Momma tilts her head.

Yeah. We have a big problem. You were supposed to drop us off and dip. I suck my teeth and shrug, not giving Momma any eye contact.

"I hope your attitude is better by the time we get inside," Momma warns.

"I'm good, Ma," I mutter.

Momma's car door lets in a warm breeze. She scoops up her keys and her knockoff Michael Kors bag. Miguel and I lock eyes. Mine are begging him to save us right now, but I know he can't, because he doesn't know the plan has changed. Miguel yanks my door open and leans toward me.

"After this, you can chill at my spot if you'd like. Lita been up here a few times, so she'll help take care of you, bae."

Yay, just the words I've been wanting to hear.

Miguel and I follow Momma to a tiny office. A girl with fiery red hair and another with blue and black box braids are sitting along the wall. The girl with the box braids grabs a magazine from the coffee table and gives me a nervous smile. She looks like she really doesn't want to be here either. The office is decorated with soft colors and smells like warm vanilla. I frown at the smell. It's probably not even that strong, but to me, it smells like they gathered a bunch of vanilla beans and crushed them into the carpet. Momma takes a seat across from the other two girls, then watches as I sign in. Miguel sits next to her, though he leaves the seat between them open for me.

I lightly tap on a silver bell that's sitting on the outside of the receptionist window. There's a sign that reads, IF YOU CHOOSE LOCAL ANESTHESIA FOR MEDICAL ABORTIONS, YOU CAN DRIVE YOURSELF HOME OR USE UBER, LYFT, OR ANY PUBLIC TRANSPORTATION. I'm not even supposed to be getting anesthesia, I don't think, which is why Momma should've just dropped us off like she said she would. I told her I was going to do the pill method, which means I do the abortion from home instead of going through surgery. The window slides open, and a woman with bright blue eyes in a scrub top with wildflower patterns picks up the clipboard I just filled out.

"Erykah Smith?" she says. She sounds like the lady I spoke with on the phone, the first time I called up here.

I nod.

"Do you have your ID, hon?" She smiles. Her blond hair is brushed into a neat bun that complements her plump face.

"I have this," I say nervously, digging my school ID out of my bag.

"Aww, aren't you darling!" she says as she looks at it.

I can't help but smile. I low-key like this picture. I did a cute silk press on my hair, and my lashes were on point. My lip gloss was still shiny and everything. Mama says I look like the baby girl she used to know in this picture, whatever that means.

The receptionist runs my ID through a scanner, before handing it back.

"Will you be paying with cash or a card?"

Neither, is what I want to say. I look back at Momma, who's got her nose deep in an *Essence* magazine. Miguel is sitting next to her, tapping away on his phone. I cup my mouth and lower my voice.

"What if I'm not sure about what I want to do?"

She pauses, then smiles. "Of course. We can just do the initial exam to start with, but there's still a fee." She rests her hands under her chin.

"Um, my momma gave me this." I slide the insurance card underneath the glass. The receptionist takes the card and gives me a nod. She turns her seat around and begins to sift through some folders in a filing cabinet. She pulls one out and flips through it.

"So, it looks like you have private insurance, but they were only willing to cover a portion of the procedure. You're still about forty dollars short."

Forty?

The lady must see the look of concern on my face because she adds, "That's pretty good, considering abortions usually cost three hundred fifty to four hundred dollars."

"Erykah, what's going on?" Momma asks.

"Umm . . . I'll be right back," I say to the receptionist, holding up a finger.

I walk toward Momma and stand next to her.

"Is everything okay?" Momma looks at me curiously.

"The lady said I'm forty dollars short." A part of me is hoping so badly that Momma just takes us home, since I know she aint got an extra forty dollars to spare.

She folds her hands in her lap, then turns toward Miguel, who's bobbing away. I signal for him to take his earbuds out.

"Everything alright?" he asks.

"I need forty dollars to pay for the visit," I say, praying that he can tell that I don't want to go through with the abortion. But instead, he fumbles through his pockets and pulls out four ten-dollar bills. Momma shifts her mouth to the side like she wants to talk shit but leans back with a satisfied look and flips through her magazine. I give Miguel a hard, mean mug before snatching the money and paying the receptionist. After processing everything, the receptionist hands me a receipt. *Damn, this visit alone cost $150!* I guess Momma was right about how expensive this shit is.

Before I can sit down, I hear the door across from us open. A pretty Black woman in a white coat motions for the girl with the box braids to follow her.

"Bree, I'm Jill. I'll be doing your assessment today." The woman gives her a comforting smile, before closing the door behind them.

I flop into the empty seat between Momma and Miguel. I can feel my heart rate rising, and even though there's barely anyone in here, I feel like there's a million people watching me. Judging me. I can't pretend no more. Who am I fooling? I don't want to do this, and I need to keep it real and just let Momma and

Miguel know that I'm not going to. Momma puts her hand on my thigh and leans in.

"Do you need me to go in there with you when they call your name?" Her voice seems so surreal, even though these are the words that most girls in my shoes would wanna hear.

I shake my head slowly. "No." My voice trembles. I try to stop my leg from shaking, but I can barely control myself.

Miguel sits up straight with a worried look. He scoots closer to me and squeezes my hand.

About ten minutes later, Jill appears again and calls back the girl with the red hair. I hear the girl ask if everything went okay. I guess she was here to support someone who just had their procedure. After confirming things with the girl, the woman looks at me and smiles. *God, I wish Kelly was here.*

"Erykah?" Jill's voice is as gentle as the receptionist's. She grips a thin manila folder that is tucked under her arm. "My name is Jill. I'll be assisting with your care for today."

I rise from the creaky seat and look between Miguel and Momma. I can feel tears forming. I don't know if it's because I'm hormonal or because I've disappointed my momma for the hundredth time or because I gotta find a way to walk out of here without making another big mistake. *Wait. My baby aint no mistake.* But getting pregnant was. I wish we would've waited a few more years, but shoulda, woulda, coulda. Momma's bottom lip slightly pokes out as she looks at me.

"You're doing the right thing, Erykah. I'll be right here if you

need me," she says. Why couldn't she have said that three weeks ago? Those were the exact words I wanted to hear then. Miguel stands up and wraps his arms around me.

"I got you, babe," he whispers in my ear as he kisses my cheek.

I squeeze him real hard, then look deep into his eyes. I'm tempted to ask him to go back with me, but Momma might suspect something. That churning feeling creeps back into my stomach and throat. It's like I'm at the top of the highest roller coaster in the world and I'm about to drop. Miguel reaches for my hand, then tells me that he loves me. I tell him the same, then head behind the door with Jill.

CHAPTER FOUR

Erykah

"I'm not having an abortion," I blurt out.

The words flow effortlessly even as I blink uncontrollably. *Damn, did I just say that out loud?* I hope nobody on the other side of the door heard me. Nurse Jill turns toward me, causing her hoop earrings to swing a little. She rests her hand on my shoulder.

"You don't have to make any decisions today. If you don't mind following me to the exam room, we can talk about it some more." Her eyebrows lift and so does her smile.

I'm frozen to this spot, not sure what to do.

"It's only a few doors down. There's snacks in there if you're hungry."

Nurse Jill's warm brown skin makes it hard to tell whether she's Momma's age or younger. She waits patiently, before I nod. I follow her to a room toward the end of the corridor. She removes a heavy lanyard from her neck and taps the doorknob with a fob key. Her work badge reads JILL-MARIE HOLLINGSWORTH, NURSE

PRACTITIONER. That's what Kelly says she wants to be. She says it's almost like being a doctor, just a different career path.

The room is cold and tight. Nurse Jill motions for me to have a seat while standing near a table that's covered with medical instruments. I wonder if those are used during an abortion. There's a diagram on the other side of the room that explains each stage of pregnancy. I focus on it as I slowly enter the room.

"You can make yourself comfortable on the table."

The examination table is neatly lined with white tissue paper, and I don't want to mess it up. I was expecting for this room to look way different. Like those surgery rooms you see on TV with the life-support monitor and the bright light above the hospital bed. The shifting of my body causes the paper on the table to crunch. Nurse Jill sits on one of those circular chairs with no back and rolls toward me, handing me a pack of Oreos and some Doritos.

"I'm sorry if I was rude, Nurse Jill. It's just, everyone wants me to do what they want, and I don't want to make another . . . mistake." I bite my lip.

The word "mistake" stings my mouth. I can feel warm tears rushing down my cheeks. Nurse Jill takes a pack of tissues from her front pocket and pats my face gently. I get a whiff of sweet essential oils as she continues to pat my sorrows away.

"Erykah, it's okay. I'm not here to judge you or make you feel pressured to make a decision today."

She leans toward me, her toffee-colored eyes peering into

mine. "There's no rule that says you have to get an abortion."

I smile a little, because she's right. There's no law or anything written in stone that says a sixteen-year-old must get an abortion if they accidentally get pregnant. Why did I let everyone (except for Kelly) get in my head and try to convince me otherwise?

"Okay?" She looks at me with a pained expression.

"Okay." I sniffle.

"Do you still want to get examined? We can do a sonogram, which will tell us how many weeks you are. And then we can talk about next steps so you can decide what's best for you."

"A sonogram? Is that the same as the ultrasound?"

"Mm-hmm." Her gold and black braids sway a bit from her high ponytail.

"Will I get to see the baby?" My voice cracks.

"If you'd like to." She smiles. "Do you have any other questions for me?"

So many, but I also want her to get started so I can see what my baby looks like. I know the baby doesn't have that many features, but just to see a visual of who is growing inside of me makes me feel like this could all be worth it.

Nurse Jill tells me to lay down and relax while she goes to grab some things for the ultrasound. After a few minutes, she returns with a probe in one hand and a tube of gel in the other.

"When was your last period?" She connects the probe to a monitor.

"Umm . . . like a month and a half ago." My voice cracks again.

I try to count the speckles in the tiled ceiling while she squeezes the goo on the bottom of my stomach. I thought it would be freezing like this room, but it's actually not. Reminds me of the warm lotion Momma used to massage me with before bedtime when I was little. I can hear my phone randomly buzzing, breaking the silence of the room. It's probably Momma wanting to know what's going on. *Oh my God, how am I going to tell her that I'm not having an abortion?*

I catch my breath.

"You okay?" Nurse Jill asks.

I nod, even though I'm definitely not okay.

She explains how the ultrasound thing works. Basically, she rubs the probe over the gel on my belly so she can get a good look inside. It's uncomfortable but not awful. She moves the probe around with one hand while tapping the keyboard like she's trying to find something. I lift my head a bit to see what's on the monitor, but it's turned all the way toward Nurse Jill. My heart is racing so fast, I feel like it's going to burst from my chest. What if she doesn't have good news, like it's twins or something? I mean that's not terrible news, but I'm still coming to terms with being a mom of just one.

"Is everything alright?" I ask nervously.

Nurse Jill winces at the screen, still tapping like crazy. She turns to me, gripping the many badges and keys around her neck.

"As far as I can see, everything looks fine . . . but there is one concern," she says.

My heart sinks. How can everything be okay, but she's concerned? Make it make sense. She gives me a towel to wipe the gel off my stomach and helps me to sit up, then sits back down on her rolling chair. I feel like I've been called to Principal McClarkson's office out of the blue. What is she so concerned about?

"Erykah"—she places both hands on her thighs, using a serious tone—"according to your measurements, you're nine weeks and three days, which means you'll be in your second trimester in a few weeks."

Wait. Almost what? I barely found out I was pregnant a few weeks ago. Nurse Jill has to be wrong. I can't be this far with my pregnancy.

"No, I'm pretty sure I had my period six weeks ago. I remember because I couldn't go swimming with my best friend. I was cramping so bad that day and I didn't bring a tampon and . . . how can I be that far along if I had cramps and everything?"

"It's not uncommon to have cramps in your early weeks. Lots of women experience a period or period-like symptoms," she says.

I look up at the pregnancy diagram, which shows how developed my baby already is. "So, I'm . . . already two months?" I extend my neck.

"Yes. I know you said you're no longer interested in an abortion, but if you were to change your mind later down the road, you may have to get the surgical procedure. We don't do the pill method after eleven weeks." Jill holds the chart to her chest.

"I'm not going to change my mind," I mumble.

"How do you feel now that you know you're further along than you thought?" Jill asks.

"Honestly?" My voice trembles. "I'm scared."

Jill pushes herself off her seat and sits beside me.

"What's scaring you, Erykah?" Her voice is soothing, like the picture of the ocean that hangs above the sink.

I stare down at the tiled floor and just let the tears flow, fighting to get words out, but Nurse Jill tells me to take my time. She pats my back, then hands me some tissues.

"Just wasn't expecting to hear that. I barely found out not too long ago that I'm pregnant, and now I'm finding out that I'm in my second trimester. Right?" My voice trails off.

"Almost." Jill nods with a smile.

"This explains why I've been so sick. I've been throwing up like crazy and I'm tired all the time," I continue.

"How are you feeling today?"

"Nauseous." I lower my head.

"Those are all pretty common symptoms. They're signs that your hormone levels are rising. Hopefully your symptoms will start to ease in a couple of weeks. It's a good thing you came here today so that you can start taking better care of yourself and the baby."

I give her a faint smile. I appreciate her kindness and all, but I need more than just something to cure my nausea. What about something to take all the stress away of having to drop another bombshell on everyone?

"Are you taking prenatal vitamins?" she asks.

I shake my head. Damn. Vitamins? I stopped taking those after fifth grade. Momma used to have to crush them into the pancake batter, I hated them so much.

"It's okay." She grins. "I'll get you started with some prenatals. It's very important that you take them every morning, because these are nutrients that you and the baby will need during your pregnancy."

"Okay," I say.

She writes something on her chart before turning to me. Her scent is a mixture of sweetness and essential oils. They don't make me nauseous, like most scents do. I could just inhale those smells all day.

"This is a hard decision to make alone. Do you have support?"

"My boyfriend and my best friend Kelly," I mutter. "Miguel, that's my boyfriend, he said he'll be here for me and the baby no matter what. He was happy when I told him about being pregnant."

Or more like content. He definitely wasn't upset and he hasn't ghosted me like some guys do the moment they find out.

"Do you think your boyfriend will keep his word?"

"Yeah. I mean, he already has a kid that he takes care of."

Jill just nods. Not like she's judging, but like she's processing what I just said.

"What about your parents? Is that your mom out there?"

"Yeah, she thinks I should get the abortion. She says we can't afford a baby, and that it's gonna mess up my life. But I don't feel that way. Lots of girls my age go through worse and still achieve their goals." I shrug.

"Sounds like Mom just wants what's best for you and your future. Most mothers do," Nurse Jill says.

Why do grown folks always agree with each other?

"But this isn't your mom's choice. It's yours, Erykah. Mom's right, it won't be easy. I won't lie to you, but it's very possible to have your baby and still achieve your goals. Where do you see yourself three years from now?"

She reminds me of my National Honor Society advisor when she asks this. She's always encouraging us to think about the future, even though the answer is always the same. Graduation, college, and my own place.

"At Howard University studying business. I'm gonna manage my own salon one day."

"Impressive," she says with a smile. "What will your salon's specialty be?"

"I want to specialize in Black hair care. I'm really good at braiding, but I want my salon to be more than just that. I want Black women to come there and leave feeling like celebs."

Nurse Jill shakes her head at me, leaning to the side. She has that *you go, girl* look on her face. I'd know that look anywhere because Momma is always giving me the same one when I show her my report cards.

"Well, let me know when the grand opening is so I can get some services." She pats the back of her braids.

"Will do," I say. "Do you think I can still go to an out-of-state college with a baby?"

She looks down at the floor, then at me.

"It depends on your support system and if you have any family in DC who can help you. Going to school full-time is a lot of work. There are some schools that provide childcare for a cost, but you can always consider going to UNLV instead. You'd still be getting a good education."

She gives me a quick smile, then hops off the table. "Do you have a doctor in mind you'd like to see during your pregnancy?"

"You can't be my doctor?"

She shakes her head. "Unfortunately, I don't deliver babies. My specialty is more focused on prenatal care and women's health, but I can refer you to a maternity doctor that accepts your insurance," she assures me.

My heart tanks again. Even though I just met Nurse Jill, her whole vibe makes me feel comfortable . . . normal.

"I was kinda hoping I'd have a Black doctor, like you. It's just, I feel like you get me."

She looks at me, her arms folded across her chest like a proud mom.

"Thank you, Erykah. Tell you what, I have a friend who specializes in maternal care. We went to school together. Her name is Dr. Richards. You'll like her. She's from Lynwood Heights. I'll put her info on your discharge sheet, and you or your mom can schedule your next appointment. Sound good?"

"That sounds good," I lie. I can't schedule anything with Momma, because she's not gonna know that I need a doctor to care for me and my baby.

Jill leaves to grab the vitamins and the images from the ultrasound. After she steps out, I feel a new wave of emotions. Scared. Confused. Lost. How's Miguel gonna react when I tell him I'm almost two and a half months pregnant? Or even worse, how's he gonna react when I tell him I didn't get the abortion? I grab my phone. There's hella messages from Kelly, wanting to know if I'm okay. I text her back so at least she knows I'm good, but I don't want to give her the details until we actually talk. I slide back on the table and try to make myself warm. The room still feels like a freezer, but it's not the reason I feel so numb. Jill returns with a white paper bag that has everything in it. I'll have to hide the picture from Momma, but right now that's the least of my worries.

"Okay, you're all set." Nurse Jill reaches her hand out to help me off the table.

We walk down the hall together; the echoes from her shoes are all I hear. When we reach the door, Jill turns the knob, then turns toward me.

"Erykah"—she uses that serious tone again—"talk to your mom."

CHAPTER FIVE

Erykah

9 Weeks

Later that night, I lock myself in my bathroom at home. I've been waiting all day for a moment alone, but Momma and Jayden have been keeping me busy. I carefully unfold the paper bag Nurse Jill gave me. I stare inside of it, before pulling out the big bottle of prenatals. I really wanted Miguel to be here with me, but I couldn't tell him in front of Momma that I decided to keep our baby or that I was already nine weeks pregnant. I texted him once we dropped him off. His reply said, damn 4 real?, and that's literally all he said. Maybe he's just shocked. Yeah, that's all it is. Miguel loves me just as much as I love him. Our baby is important to him, too. He's probably just tired from working this week and taking care of Mitzi. Momma was acting nicer toward Miguel after the appointment. She even asked him if he wanted to get a bite to eat before we dropped him off, but he made some excuse that he had to hurry and get ready for work.

I check my phone to see if he's got anything more to say, but my phone is drier than the Mojave Desert.

I grab the bottle of prenatals and run my finger across the directions. I shake the bottle, before popping the top off.

"Siri, is it okay to take prenatals on a full stomach?" I whisper into the phone, since I ate some leftover spaghetti when we got home. She sends me a list of websites that have different opinions. One website says it's fine, but another says I should take them on an empty stomach in the morning with only water. The internet is so damn confusing these days. I'd probably do better searching for the answer on TikTok. The large white capsule sticks to my sweaty palm as I try to come to terms with the fact that I'll have to swallow these horse pills every day for the next several months. I drag to the sink and halfway fill the cup next to the faucet with some water, before dropping the pill onto my tongue and forcing it down my throat with a chug of water. It feels like I just swallowed a AA battery. The aftertaste is chalky and gritty, and I gag. Almost instantly, I start throwing up all over the sink. Noodles and red gravy splatter the walls. I press my hand to my mouth to make it stop, but it keeps flowing until there's literally nothing left to throw up but spit. I grab the two decorative towels Momma has hanging above the toilet. I know Momma will probably kill me for messing up her good towels, but I kinda have no choice. Tears rush down my cheeks as I try to clean up the disaster I just made. I can feel my throat burning from the acid of the tomato sauce. I lean against the wall, with the towels balled up in my hand, breaking down just like the mess that's all over the sink.

"Erykah? Baby, you okay?" Momma taps on the door.

I don't answer, just stare at myself in the mirror.

"I have a heating pad if you need it. I know the lady you did the consult with said the cramps could get pretty bad," she says.

Momma thinks that I'm feeling the effects of the abortion pills that I never took. Before we left the clinic, I showed her the bag and told her that I already took the first pill to start the process. Thank God she didn't do a meds check, or my ass would've been busted.

"I'm okay, Momma," I moan. "Just cramping, that's all."

"You really shouldn't be in there all by yourself, Erykah."

"I'm okay, Ma. Really." I slide down the wall, scooting myself into the corner, and cry as quietly as I can. A part of me wants Momma to be here with me, to console me, to tell me everything's gonna be okay, that it'll all get better. That this won't last much longer and soon I'll have a beautiful healthy baby. But I know that's not the reaction I'll get if Momma really knows why I'm in here suffering.

I pick up the crumpled bag and pull out the envelope with the ultrasound pictures. I stare at it for a sec and then slide my finger underneath the seal. It feels like someone just opened a jar of butterflies in my stomach. The crisp white edge of the ultrasound picture sticks out. At the top right of the picture, there's info with my name and the number of weeks I am. I close my eyes as my thumbs tremble against the envelope. Deep breaths, I tell myself, before sliding the picture out. I can't help but tear up once I see the tiny image of my baby. Damn, this is for real. I'm really gonna be somebody's momma. I pull out my phone, so I can snap a picture to send to Miguel, but I hear the lock on the door twisting and the bathroom door flies open. I panic and toss the pic behind the shower curtain, before quickly sitting straight.

"Erykah, I was calling your name and you didn't say anything. I thought you passed out in here." Momma stands over me, pale-faced. I don't know if she's more in shock because she thought I was dead or because her bathroom looks like a school cafeteria food fight.

"I'm okay, Ma." I try to lift myself up, but she gestures for me to stay where I am.

"I don't want you going through this alone, you hear me?"

There's a twinkle in Momma's eye that makes me feel safe.

"Is throwing up a normal symptom? Maybe I should call that nurse and see what she says." Momma digs for her phone in her back pocket.

Shit. No. She can't call Jill. Even though Jill isn't allowed to tell her my decision, I don't want her telling Momma to take me to the ER, which will probably mean I'll have to tell her the truth.

"Momma, what happened in here?" Jayden peeks in the bathroom, making a stank face. "Ooh, Erykah messed up your towels! You're in trouble now," he teases.

"Shut up and get out!" I growl.

He's so lucky I don't have the strength to smack his butt out of those little dinosaur pajamas. If there was an award for the most annoying kid brother in the Heights, Jayden would take home the trophy every year.

"Hey now, yall knock it off," Momma warns us. "Your sister's just not feeling well." She looks over at me with a tight smile.

"Is she gonna die?" Jayden asks with a smirk.

"No, but you are if you don't get out," I say.

"Erykah!" Momma gives me a hard stare. "Jayden, go back to bed and stop nagging your sister." He makes sure to stick his tongue out behind Momma's back before darting off to his room.

Momma focuses back on me, expressionless. I start to feel a little uneasy, but maybe it's just all the millions of emotions that are rushing through my soul right now. She leans toward me, with her hands folded between her thighs.

"Erykah, you know you can tell me anything."

I feel my body tensing up. *Damn, she knows.*

"Anything like what?" I ask carefully.

She shakes her head. "Don't let that boy stress you out. You made the right choice. Everything's gonna be okay now." She smiles.

I give her a stiff smile back. If relief wasn't a thing, I don't know what is.

"Go on to your room and I'll clean all this up." She waves me off. "You don't need to be holed up in no bathroom."

"Okay. Can you just give me a minute?"

"A minute for what?" She looks around.

"I just need a minute, Ma." I look toward the toilet, trying to give her a signal. I threw up so hard, I already peed on myself. I know, TMI, but for all Momma knows, I gotta go again.

"Ohhhh." Momma scrunches her face. "Okay, just call me if you need me, baby."

Soon as Momma walks out, I reach into the tub and grab the pic, sliding it back in the bag. I take baby steps to my room, doing my best to show her I'm in some kind of pain. After carefully locking the door behind me, I change into an oversized long tee and curl up in my bed. I clutch the ultrasound photo to my chest, wondering how I'm going to keep the baby a secret from Momma long enough that abortion is no longer an option. I guess I didn't realize how hard keeping something like this from her could be, and now all I can think about is how I'm going to keep it a secret from the world, too.

CHAPTER SIX

Kelly

E: I'm home, safe. Call me.

Me: FaceTime?

E: K.

My hands tremble as I begin to FaceTime E. Since I've been back in the hotel room, I've been going insane, worrying that something went wrong. I know if it were a true emergency, Ms. Monica would've at least called my mom, but still. Effia and I are rooming together, but she decided to meet up with some other students from our trip to work out in the gym downstairs. My screen turns into a little square, and I see E, with her hand resting against her forehead. Her brown skin is glowing, even though her room is dim.

"Heey. How you feeling?" I ask.

I try to look calm as I hold the phone to my face with both hands. E pushes herself up, propping her phone on the stand beside her bed. She looks down, then back at me with tears filling her round eyes.

"I . . . couldn't do it," she chokes.

"You mean like, you couldn't get the abortion, or . . . keep the baby?"

She shakes her head, fighting back tears.

"E, you know I'm not here to judge."

"I know. You're like the only person." She looks up with a laugh, tears still flowing. "I decided to . . . not get the abortion." Her wet eyes stare into mine.

I fight to keep a smile on my face. I probably look like a damn mannequin, but I don't want E to know how blown away I am. I can't even wrap my head around the idea of being a mom at sixteen. Honestly, I didn't think she was going to keep the baby. Before I went on my trip, we talked about this a few times, and she seemed like she was more afraid to go through with the pregnancy than to go against her mom.

"Oh my God, how'd Ms. Monica take the news?"

Erykah pauses for a sec before answering. "Uh, she was fine."

"She was fine? But just last week, she was threatening to kick you out if you didn't have the abortion."

"Well, I told her what I wanted, and she understood."

"Just like that?" I love Ms. Monica, but I've never known her to change her opinion on a subject.

"Yeah." E shrugs, looking off to the side.

There's an awkward silence between us. Something is telling me that there's more going on. E is definitely not telling me the whole story. If this was any other situation, I probably would nag the hell out of her until she gave in, but maybe she doesn't want to tell me everything quite yet. I mean, it's kinda hard to believe that Ms. Monica is now cool with her keeping the baby, when she's the reason Erykah went to the abortion clinic in the first place. I don't want to make things seem more awkward, so I play along. E flicks her lamp on and flashes a small white envelope into the camera.

"The nurse gave me a copy of the ultrasound." She stares down at it, waiting for me to speak.

"For real? You better let me see."

"Okay . . . ," she laughs.

She holds the picture in front of the camera next to her plump cheek. There's a thin white arrow pointing to a little image that looks like a faded white gummy bear with a large head. I giggle a little with E, who's probably laughing at the same thing.

"Tell me why my niece got a big head like you?" I joke.

"Girl, go to hell. My baby is cute. And I don't know if it's a boy or girl yet. The nurse said it was too soon to tell, but . . ." Her smile fades a little as she places the picture into a small envelope. "Kelly, I'm nine weeks."

"What?" My mouth drops.

"Yup."

That's definitely more than what E thought she was. "So,

what about Miguel?" I ask. "Was he supportive or just agreeing with whatever, like always?"

"You and Momma swear he's just the worst thing." She rolls her eyes. "But he's cool with it. Told me he's gonna be here no matter what."

"Mm-hmm," I say.

"Why can't you just be happy for us?"

I look at Erykah with a side eye. What kind of best friend is happy that their best friend is having a baby by a deadbeat loser who already has a toddler?

She waits for me to continue.

"I low-key feel like he trapped you, but listen, I don't want to make this about him. I just want you to know that I'll be here for you, even if he changes his mind."

"He's not gonna change his mind. He's already working more hours so we can be straight. I know he's not up to yall standards because he doesn't go to East Prep or isn't a star athlete like Ray. But he loves me and our baby, which is worth more than all that shit that looks good for social media."

I peer into the phone. WTF does that mean? I mean, yeah, me and Ray post a lot and whatnot, but that's not what our relationship is based on. Who doesn't obsess over social media? At least Ray knows better than to knock me up because he's too lazy to wear a condom. For all Erykah knows, Miguel's ass probably has kids all over Vegas. I wish she never met him. I felt like I barely saw her when they first started dating, he had her so sprung. We'll see how much he'll be around now that he has more responsibilities.

There's another awkward silence, which never happens between us, and in the last five minutes, there have been two of them.

E leans closer to the phone, looking down again. "Listen, I'm just tired. It's been a long day, sis. My bad." Erykah pleads with her eyes.

"I get it, girl. That's your man and you gone stick beside him." I wave my finger. E bursts out laughing.

"It's been a long day for me too, and even longer tomorrow. It's our last day out here, and Ms. Naiter is trying to do everything but let us chill."

"Damn. I thought you were having fun. I've been looking at your posts. The picture yall took in front of the MLK statue was dope. Oh, and that friendship arch thing too. Gotta visit that together one day," E says.

"Girl, yesss. Can you believe we go back to school in like three days?" E looks even more stressed when I say this.

"I'm not ready. I need a whole do-over for my summer," she sighs.

"So, the baby's due around spring?" I ask.

E doesn't respond; she's staring down at her phone, typing aggressively. Her lips tighten as she finishes her text. She's probably texting stupid-ass Miguel, who usually makes her upset over everything. I wish I could just wave a magic wand and make his fuckboy ass disappear, but that's who she chose to love. I'm hoping the baby changes him for the better, but he's so damn triflin', I doubt it.

"Sorry." She looks up. "Yeah, but I don't know the exact date yet."

"E, please don't let him stress you out. It's probably not good for the baby."

"Huh? You know me, Kelly. I'm not gonna let no dude fuck me over. Miguel's just overwhelmed." E laughs a little. "I know you don't think Miguel is as loyal as Ray is to you, but I promise you he is. I'm more than just a baby momma to him," she says, more like she's trying to convince herself that Miguel isn't a whole clown.

Yo, I swear sometimes I don't even know this girl. She used to be super independent and headstrong before Miguel popped into the picture. And no offense, but it's not like Miguel is about to put a ring on it, so technically she *is* going to be a baby momma.

"What you thinking about?" E asks.

"Nothing. Just tired." I yawn.

"Well, I'm gonna let you get some rest. Promise to hit me up as soon as you wake."

"Promise. 143," I say.

"143."

I blow a kiss and end the call. I get into bed and try to process what just happened. My best friend is going to be a mom. By the time we finish our junior year, she'll be changing mad diapers and keeping hella bottles on deck. I don't know if that's something I could ever do at this age. I can barely decide which Js I want to wear each week. How does someone our age survive pregnancy and high school, anyways? I hope things don't get too hard for her once she's actually showing. If I was her, I'd be so scared. And I still can't believe Ms. Monica is cool with it, since it was her idea for Erykah not to have a baby right now in the first place. I can't even cap, being pregnant at this age is just way too much, but I'm not gonna leave her hanging. I plan on remaining loyal and sticking by her side no matter what. I mean, isn't that what a real best friend is supposed to do?

CHAPTER SEVEN

Erykah

12 Weeks

Last night, I had the worst nightmare ever. I was in a hospital room, about to give birth. But it wasn't like those perfect births women have in the movies. I was in so much pain and could barely breathe. There were panicked nurses and doctors surrounding me, and Momma and Miguel were forced to leave the room. I kept screaming, asking the doctor if my baby was okay, but it's like they couldn't hear me. No one could hear me. Then Nurse Jill appeared. She looked like she'd been crying or something and she says to me, "I'm sorry, Erykah, we did all we could do."

I woke up, drenched in sweat. It took me a minute to calm down. I Googled what it could mean, but all I could find was a bunch of websites that said nightmares are common during pregnancy. Something to do with hormones, but that dream seemed so real. Like a sign that something might happen to me or my baby.

My first real doctor's appointment is today. The office isn't open on the weekends, so I had to schedule it on a school day and pray that the school doesn't notify Momma to tell her I missed any classes. Miguel should've been here by now, but of course his ass is on CP time. I think about waiting for him outside, but then I smell the familiar scent of cocoa butter and freshly pressed hair, which means Momma is getting ready to step out too.

I really don't know if I can keep this lie going for too much longer. I did some research, and in Nevada, you can't have an abortion after twenty-four weeks, which means I gotta keep this pregnancy a secret for another three months. That's gonna be hard AF, because my momma is really good at detecting lies.

If I can get out of here soon enough, Momma won't think anything's up. I grab my stuff and head to the kitchen. No use in hiding in my room.

"Erykah, you still here?" Momma is sifting through a high cabinet.

"Yeah, bout to leave soon."

"Well, you hungry? I'm tryna cook up the last of this bacon before it goes bad."

Bacon sounds good, but I'm pretty sure it's gonna make me gag, and anyway, I don't have time to eat.

"No. I'm good, Ma."

"Okay," she says. "Kelly and Ray running late today?"

"Uhh . . . yeah. But she just texted me to say they're like five mins away. Ray had to pick up Marsaun, too."

Momma has her hair tied with a silk scarf, even though it's been laid and fried.

"You going to work today, Ma?" I ask.

"Yeah, I got work today," she says.

My phone buzzes in my pocket.

Miguel: About to walk up.

Shit. No. Momma can't know that Miguel is picking me up instead of Ray and Kelly. She'll definitely know something's up if she sees him. Besides, he's supposed to be at school today, but he had to ditch school too.

Me: Wait in the car. I'll be out.

Momma gives me a side eye as she slides pieces of greasy bacon onto a paper towel. She stirs a pan of potatoes with wizzled-up peppers. My mouth waters a little, but I'm too afraid of throwing up if I eat any of it.

"Jayden! Brush your teeth and come eat. Don't make me tell you twice," Momma yells before insisting that I eat something.

"Momma, I'm good," I tell her.

"Girl, if you don't eat this . . ."

"Okay," I mumble.

I give in and devour two crunchy pieces of bacon.

"I'm a go finish getting ready. If Jayden's not in here in the next minute, drag his ass out that bed." Momma rushes off to her room.

This bacon is so good, I sneak another piece before scooping some potatoes into a bowl and slathering them with hot sauce and ketchup. It's like I'm in breakfast heaven until I feel something bumping me from behind.

"Momma, Erykah's eating up all the food," Jayden whines, standing behind me with his shirt half tucked into his khaki pants.

Both our schools make us wear uniforms, but his isn't a prep school. Most of his friends' parents don't make a lot of money, so the school thought it would be smarter to only allow the kids to wear a polo shirt and either black pants or khakis. Kinda boring if you ask me, but I guess little kids don't care as much about fashion as kids my age.

"Shut up. You always whining about something. Get on my damn nerves," I snap.

Jayden plugs his ears with his thumbs while wagging his tongue at me.

Momma comes back in the kitchen wearing her work scrubs.

"You better watch your mouth, Erykah, and Jayden, there's plenty of food for you. Hurry and eat, so you can ride with your sister."

I turn my head so fast, my neck almost snaps. Jayden can't ride with me today. Sometimes, Ray'll give him a ride when Momma's in a hurry, or Ms. Benita, who lives in the building next door, will walk him. I cannot have Jayden tagging along with me today. That'll ruin everything.

"Momma, I'm already running late. We can't give Jayden no ride. Can't you just ask Ms. Benita?"

"I don't have time to run over there and bother her, Erykah—I can't be late today. I'm sure Ray and Kelly won't mind." She plasters a big kiss on mine and Jayden's cheeks before grabbing her keys. "Don't forget to take the pork chops out of the freezer when you get home today. Love yall. Have a good day at school."

She rushes out of the house, and all I can do is pray she doesn't see Miguel.

Miguel is leaning all the way back in the driver's seat, holding his phone above his head. Lucky for me, he didn't park in front of our building, but I'm still about to cuss his ass out for being late.

"Aww shit, that nigga dumb as fuck!" He laughs hysterically at some video on his phone.

I pull at the door handle, startling him. He does a double look before unlocking it. Jayden yanks his door wide open, before slinging his Spider-Man book bag in the back seat.

I throw myself into the seat, letting the door slam.

"You was supposed to be here like thirty minutes ago." I snatch the phone out of his hands.

"Damn. Chill. I had shit"—he notices Jayden sliding in the back seat—"I mean, stuff to do this morning. We still gone get there in time." He grabs the phone back.

Jayden leans forward, eyeing Miguel's phone.

"Can I play Roblox on your phone?" Jayden asks.

Miguel gives me a side eye, but I just turn my head off because I don't even want to look at him right now. He knows how important this appointment is, and he's acting like it's no big deal.

"We gotta drop him off on the way," I say, looking straight ahead.

It's like today was destined to go wrong or something. First I wake up terrified, then my boyfriend can't even be on time for the most important appointment of our lives, and now I've been tasked with taking my nosy little brother, who's probably gonna tell Momma all about how Miguel gave him a ride instead of Kelly and Ray, to school.

"He go to that school on D Street, right?"

I nod with my arms folded. Miguel attempts to start the car. It groans like it doesn't want to, but after a few presses on the gas, he's swerving out of the parking lot, making the car rattle even more with heavy bass from an NBA YoungBoy song. I'm so irritated, I don't even tell him to turn that shit down. Too much going through my mind to even initiate an argument. I glance at my phone, and we're officially late to the appointment. Hopefully they don't make us reschedule. The receptionist said that there's a forty-five-dollar fee for missed appointments, and I sure as hell don't have that kind of money just hanging around. We creep in front of Jayden's school, car still rattling. Jayden's hands are glued to both ears, like he's trying to keep his head on his shoulders. I reach for the volume knob and turn the music all the way down. Miguel's eyebrow rises, but the sharp look on my face causes it to fall back down. I turn to Jayden, softening my face.

"Jay, if Momma asks, you didn't get a ride from Miguel, okay?"

"But that would be a lie, and I'm not supposed to lie," he says confidently.

I can feel my lips tightening. Jayden is the best little liar I know, and *now* he can't lie?

"Well, it's not a lie if you just don't tell Momma anything. Either you keep it a secret or"—I reach over and snatch his book bag—"I'm a tell Momma that you've been sneaking snacks to school and selling 'em."

I hold up plastic bags full of various chips and candies, along with a few dollar bills and quarters. I actually don't blame Jayden's little hustle, but if Momma knew he was selling her food at school, she'd flip.

His eyes grow wide as he quickly snatches the bags from me.

"You can't do that," he complains.

Miguel covers his face, laughing hysterically. I slap his shoulder, because he has some nerve. If he would've gotten to me on time, I wouldn't even have to be negotiating with my annoying little brother.

"You snitch on me, and I'm a snitch on you," I say.

"Whatever. I won't tell," Jayden groans as he gets out of the car.

We're now twelve minutes late and Miguel is driving like molasses. The car is silent this time as he carefully stops at the next light.

"We'd be there by now if you wouldn't have taken so damn long," I say.

He looks at me from the corner of his eye, one hand on the wheel, before sucking his teeth. His cornrows lie neatly against the top of his shoulders. I try not to stare him down too long, because the more I look at his thick lips, the less angry I get. I pull my dress out of my bag and start to change.

"Man, chill out. We almost there. I had to make a few runs this morning," he says.

"Well, that could've waited. We almost got caught."

I look out the window, staring at the mountains. In the sunlight, they are a celebration of grays and purples, dusted with splatters of white. I feel like telling Miguel to just drive me to the highest mountain peak, where I can take in its beauty and peace. Just me and my baby that's inside of me. No one to hide with. No one to fight with. The road suddenly gets really bumpy, and I feel like I'm going to puke. Matter of fact, I know I'm going to.

"Pull over!" I reach for the door handle.

He gives me a look and realizes what's about to happen. He swerves to the side of the road, and I throw the door open just in time. I lean over a curb as chunks of bacon and potatoes spurt from my mouth. The bitterness of my spit makes me gag even more. Miguel scrunches his face like he's about to puke too. I reach in the car, searching for something to wipe my mouth with. Miguel sifts through his pockets and hands me a burgundy bandanna. It's his territory rag. In our hood, you're either burgundy or black. I grab the crisp rag and run it across my mouth, before sliding back into my seat.

"I'll get you a new one," I mutter.

"Nah, you good. Got plenty of 'em." He turns his music back on, but not as loud. "You gone be alright?" He pulls me closer to him.

"Yeah, sorry you had to see all that." I lower my head.

He shrugs, before pulling back into traffic.

Pretty soon, we're at the doctor's office, arriving late as hell. It looks like the doctor is running behind schedule too, because the waiting room is packed with women in all stages of pregnancy. One of the office assistants is shouting in Spanish to a woman next to me, who has two kids standing on either side of her. Her belly is huge, so she's gotta be like eight or nine months. I fill out the paperwork at the counter before handing it back; the reception-ist barely looks at it before telling me to wait for my name to be called. Since all the chairs are filled, some with toddlers squeezed next to each other, me and Miguel stand against the wall, eyeing the chaos. For some reason, I stop caring about everything that happened this morning. Because in a few minutes, I'll meet the doctor who's gonna be helping us to get through all of this and get to see my baby again. After what seems like forever, the assis-tant calls me to the front. I weave through a line of women and children before staring at the plexiglass.

"You got your insurance card and ID, Ms. Smith?"

She doesn't seem as friendly as the receptionist at the abortion clinic, but I figure she's just overwhelmed. I slide my insurance card and school ID across the counter. She gives my ID a frown before sliding it back.

"You don't have a state ID?" She starts to flip through a chart, waiting for me to respond.

"Just a school ID. I'm only sixteen," I say.

She breathes heavily, before checking something off on a form, then placing it in the chart that has my name on it.

"Next time, bring a state ID. Welfare requires it." She eyes me up and down.

"I'm not on no—" I fight back curse words. *What makes her ass think I'm on welfare?* Momma's got good insurance from her job. If this lady would take the time to actually do her job, she'd see that.

"You'll be seeing Dr. Palmer today," she says.

"Oh. I thought I was gonna see Dr. Richards."

"Dr. Richards doesn't take your type of insurance. You have an HMO." She says the three letters to me like I'm in kindergarten, then slides the card back to me.

"What's that mean?"

She lets out a heavy breath and rolls her eyes.

"It means you can only see doctors that your insurance authorizes, which is why you get Dr. Palmer or nothing at all, honey." She shrugs.

"Is Dr. Palmer a woman?" I ask.

The assistant gives me a flat look. "No, but he's what your insurance will cover, unless you'd like to cancel your appointment for the day."

"No. I don't want to cancel." I tighten my lips.

"You can go ahead and have a seat and Pauletta will call you back soon."

I go stand next to Miguel with my foot pinned against the dingy wall. How come the lady on the phone didn't tell me that I needed a special type of insurance to see Dr. Richards? Miguel looks over at me, taking an earbud out.

"What's wrong?" he asks.

"They switched my doctor because I don't have the *right* insurance." I bite my lip. I can feel my cheeks burning. "I don't understand why it even matters. This place is janky as hell!"

The noisy lobby goes quiet. Even the kids who have been fighting over a board game in the corner halt. A woman who looks like she's about to give birth shakes her head, like she can relate. I didn't mean for the entire office to hear me, but it pisses me off that my insurance isn't good enough.

"Damn. But at least they aint just turn you away. It's no big deal, babe." Miguel shrugs, making me even more upset.

I'm glad he feels so chill about it all, but having a doctor who's like Nurse Jill *is* a big deal to me. Kelly was telling me all this stuff about how Black women die during and right after childbirth at higher rates because we get treated like shit, and people don't believe us when we say we're in pain. From what I've just experienced and the looks of this office, I 100 percent believe it.

A little girl starts to scream at the top of her lungs, pulling me out of my thoughts. Her momma aint paying her no mind cause she's too busy arguing with the rude lady at the counter. I can feel my stomach growling. Right now, I'm craving seafood and a big salad with extra ranch. I sift through my purse, hoping to find something. At the bottom, there's a mini bag of Ritz crackers and a warm apple juice box. Not exactly Red Lobster, but it's better than nothing. As soon as I put a cracker in my mouth, a heavyset lady with an updo and a clipboard calls me back. I gather my things and head toward her and realize Miguel is so busy with his phone, it's like he doesn't even notice I walked away. I hurry back, popping him upside his head.

"C'mon, damn," I say.

Miguel drags behind me as we walk toward the medical assistant.

"Erykah? I'm Pauletta. C'mon back with me." Pauletta pauses. "We can only allow parents to go back." She looks Miguel up and down.

"He's the father," I say.

Miguel stands next to me, arms folded, awaiting her approval. Pauletta gives me a weak smile, then motions for us to follow her. She takes all my vitals and asks me a million and one questions. Most of them, I either don't know the answer to or can't answer. Like, she asked me when my last Pap smear was. I just shrug because I've never had one of those. I know that Momma gets them, and she says they're uncomfortable, but she's never taken me to get one.

I can tell Pauletta's trying to be patient, but the more I don't know, the more she huffs between questions. The room looks similar to the one at the abortion clinic, except it smells like bleach and it's tiny. She tells me to change into a paper gown, so that she can start the ultrasound. After a few minutes, she returns with a probe and gel. She slathers cold gel all over my pelvic area, and I squirm. I was expecting to not really feel anything like at Nurse Jill's office. Miguel is on the other side of the room, glued to his phone. Pauletta flashes a look at him, shaking her head. I should've just come to this appointment alone. Obviously, Miguel's phone is more important than this visit. She begins to move the probe around my stomach, pressing firmly.

"Let me know if it's too much pressure. You're still kinda early, and I don't want to do a transvaginal if I don't have to," she says while focusing on the monitor.

"It's fine," I say.

My heart is fluttering like a butterfly. I try to keep as still as possible, but my anxiety is making it almost impossible.

"Looks like the baby is measuring at twelve weeks and two days. Have you two heard the baby's heartbeat?" she asks.

I shake my head as my excitement builds. "Can we?" I pull up on my elbows, glancing at the screen.

Pauletta lifts the probe and slides the plastic cover from it, then begins to press a few more buttons. She adjusts the screen so that I can see better and turns the sound on. It doesn't sound like a normal heartbeat. Instead, it's a series of loud whooshes that grow louder and faster. The baby is floating on its back, flopping up every few seconds. The image looks the same as the pic I have at home, but a little bigger. I reach back and nudge Miguel. He looks up with the phone between his hands and gives a faint smile. She turns off the volume and begins to reorganize everything.

"Can I get a copy of the ultrasound to take home?" I ask eagerly.

Pauletta opens a drawer and then hands me a small slip with directions of how to download the ultrasound app. She explains that all my ultrasounds will be uploaded to an ultrasound app they use, I just have to make sure to download it on my phone. Before she leaves, she tells me to keep the gown on and wait for the doctor to arrive. It seems like we've been sitting in this freezer forever before Dr. Palmer comes rushing through the door, almost tripping over his dress pants. He kinda looks like he could be Mr. Morgan's older brother, except Dr. Palmer is taller, and his salt-and-pepper hair covers his entire head.

"Erykah Smith?" He glances at a clipboard, before heading to the ultrasound machine.

I pull myself up with my elbows, stabbing through the tissue paper, waiting for him to say something else, but he just grunts at the screen as he rattles the mouse. He slathers gel on the same scanner Pauletta used.

"Hmm," he says as he rolls it over my lower belly.

"Is everything okay?" I ask.

"Just lay still, please." He moves the scanner some more, then goes back to the screen.

"So, did Pauletta tell you two how far along you are and

everything?" What does he mean by everything? Aint that his job? He hands me a thin towel, while looking at Miguel through his thick glasses. Miguel sits up straight, then looks over at me to answer.

"Yes. She said I'm twelve weeks," I say shyly.

"Are you taking any prenatals?"

"Yeah. I started some about two weeks ago."

"It's best to take the kind with DHA, good for the baby's brain development. Any questions for me?"

He's talking so fast, I scramble to remember what I wanted to ask him. "Um . . . I've been having really bad nausea and I throw up everything. Sometimes I even throw up on an empty stomach. I can't even drink water without gagging. Is that normal?"

"It's very common early on in your pregnancy. Just eat the foods that don't make you as sick and maybe eat ice chips if you can't keep any water down. It'll subside around fourteen weeks. If not, we'll see what your insurance is willing to cover. Anything else?"

Is he for real? I'm damn near starving most days and can barely even stomach the thought of food. Homeboy is pissing me off, and Miguel is pissing me off even more. Instead of speaking up or defending me, his ass is back on that phone again, bobbing to something with his earbuds in.

"I'm just worried that my baby isn't getting enough nutrients. Isn't there something I can take for the symptoms?"

Dr. Palmer stands at the edge of the exam table with a straight face, like I'm annoying him or something.

"Ms. Smith, I wouldn't worry. You're not the first to experience morning sickness and won't be the last. What's most important is that you're taking those vitamins and don't miss any appointments." He waves his finger at me like I'm two years old. "If you start feeling cramping, notice any bleeding, or if your vomiting gets too severe, go to the ER." He moves toward the door, so I guess that means this appointment is done. "Anything else?" he asks again.

I feel so helpless at this moment. Like this doctor could offer me more but doesn't want to. I wonder if I wasn't a teenager or if I was a different race, would he be so quick to brush me off? I wonder if Miguel wasn't so dense, would that even make a difference? I shake my head, and Dr. Palmer rushes off to his next patient.

On the way out, I schedule my next appointment, which is a month from now. Luckily, I was able to make it on a day the teachers have professional development, so I don't have to worry about Momma finding out. But with the way Miguel acted today, I kinda wish she knew. I wish she could be here instead of him. She probably would've made that doctor give me something for the sickness and probably would've even told that receptionist a thing or two. I know Momma would make it all better. She would have my back, unlike Miguel, who's starting to make me wonder if I've been wrong about him all this time.

CHAPTER EIGHT

Erykah

14 Weeks

These symptoms are kicking my ass. I've already missed two days of school this week because Momma thinks that I have a stomach bug. I told her it's from the pizza I ate when I went out with Kelly and Ray on Saturday night. We didn't do much but chill at the arcade, along with every other teenager who goes to East Prep. I showed Kelly my latest ultrasound pics; she insists that I'm having a girl, but I won't know for sure until my next appointment. I can't even lie. I feel like shit this morning, and I would give anything to just lay in this bed all day. After managing to slide from the covers, I fight with the button on my pleated skirt, which is squeezing around my stomach. My school uniform polo is tight as hell too. The weather app on my phone said that it's gonna be in the high eighties all week, but the only thing I have to wear that won't show my bloat is an oversized

UNLV hoodie. College gear is the only thing my school lets us wear in place of our uniforms, so I slip it on before gelling my hair up in a messy bun.

I'm surprised Momma hasn't tried to take me to the doctor, but she's been pulling double shifts at work a lot, so maybe she just doesn't have the energy to interrogate me. I figure if I'm low-key most of the time, she won't notice how much my body's been changing. Lately, my morning sickness has been off the charts. And whoever named it that needs to get slapped, because I get sick all damn day. I usually run the shower while I'm puking my brains out so that Momma and Jayden don't hear me. I read online that if I eat a cracker before I get out of bed, it'll settle the icky feeling I get before I throw up, but that barely works for me. I've also been reading all these old wives' tales that tell you how to figure out if you're having a boy or girl. One post said that throwing up like crazy means you're having twins, and I know that aint the case. I really want a little girl so I can dress her like a doll baby and buy her a cute little pink Range Rover play car that she can cruise up and down the sidewalks in. She'll be a huge Nicki Minaj fan like her momz, so she'll definitely be rocking pink like crazy.

There was this gender reveal on Instagram of this girl who was so sad when she found out she was having a boy. It was low-key messed up how she stormed off when the confetti from the balloons were light blue. People were all in the comments talking about how she don't love her baby, but it probably was just her hormones making her feel some type of way. Kelly wants to throw me a big gender reveal party, but who is she gonna invite? I'm just not ready to tell everyone about my pregnancy yet, especially the kids at our school. I already know people are gonna talk shit, but the first person to say something smart is probably gonna get smacked. Besides, it wouldn't be right to have a gender reveal without Momma. I'm still trying to find the right time to tell her the truth, and I don't think surprising her with that news in front of our neighborhood would be the brightest idea.

It's bad enough she keeps sweatin' me about my grades. I got chewed out because Mr. Morgan called and said I'm on the verge of failing and how he had to wake me up a few times during class. His ass really do be on some hater shit. Momma gave me a whole lecture about how she don't got time to be worrying about me at school and how she don't got time to be talking to my teachers about petty stuff on the phone while she's at work. I'm usually really good at math. But I missed a quiz in Mr. Morgan's class the day of my first doctor's appointment. Momma said I'm on restriction until I can get my grades up and not to even think about asking her for anything. It's not as if she gets me the things that I ask for, no way. Momma knows I love me some McDonald's and that I will do anything for an Oreo McFlurry and a hot and spicy chicken sandwich (with sweet-and-sour sauce on the side). She's one of them mommas who lives by the phrase, *We got food at home.* The other day we passed by a Mickey D's, and I had a huge craving.

She hit me with the famous Black Momma response, *You got McDonald's money?*

I couldn't do nothing but take that L, heat a frozen chicken patty, slap it with hot sauce, and call it a day.

I stare in the fridge, wishing there was more to choose from. But there's only leftovers from yesterday's breakfast and a slug of ground beef that will probably be turned into a few meals for the week. Momma aint in the kitchen throwing down like usual, so I'm a have to whip me up something real quick.

I wait for the leftovers to finish heating while checking Miguel's Instagram profile. His last post was at 11:03 p.m. last night. There's a picture of him and his homeboy Dre posing in front of Dre's crib with their fingers curved in the air. Dre has a burgundy bandanna hanging from his jeans pocket. *My ride or die,* Miguel posts under the picture. Whatever that means. There's 102 likes. I guess spending time with Dre is more important than returning my calls. Since the doctor's visit, I've only seen Miguel a couple of times. He brought me food I was craving and stayed over for like an hour. The rest of our communication has just been dry-ass texts. He claims he's so busy grinding, but he has time to kick it with his homeboy. I stare at my plate of food: one burnt sausage link, a stale biscuit, and a heap of piping-hot grits with a few scrambled eggs at the edge of the plate. I push the eggs on top of the grits and sprinkle them with sugar, just like I like them. And that's not a pregnancy craving either. I've *been* eating my grits with eggs on top. And yes, sugar goes on grits.

* * * *

The ride to school is dead silent. It's like Momma is deep in thought, but then again, she's always deep in thought. Always worrying about bills and if she's gonna have enough hours to work for the week. I sure wish that I could help. I told her I want to start braiding hair again on the side, but she says I need to focus on school, because right now, that's my job. She swerves through the orange cones in the school parking lot and stops in front of the school doors. Momma looks over as if she has something to say, but she just lets out a heavy sigh. It's not like her to be hesitant when she's got something to say.

I furrow my eyebrows.

"What?" I ask.

"Girl, don't *what* me." She smiles.

I pull down the mirror above my head, trying to see if I still got food on my face or something.

"I'm just concerned about you eating me out of house and home," she says.

There's a beat.

"Not that I want you to starve, but Erykah, baby, you are getting a little . . . *heavy*." She forces the word out of her mouth.

Jayden bursts out laughing from the back seat. If I could turn red, I'd be the brightest hue, but I play it off like what she says doesn't faze me.

"I'm just bloated, Ma, cause I started my cycle." I roll my eyes, pretending to be annoyed and praying she falls for my lie.

Momma examines me, and I try not to look guilty.

"What, Momma? It's true!" I turn around to look at my brother. "And Jayden, you better shut up."

"Well, I know period bloat," Momma says. "Maybe try going for walks instead of cooping yourself up in that room all the time."

I press down on my seat belt and push the door open. I hear the first bell sounding off, so I jump out the car because the last thing I need is to be late. I wave at Momma before I walk through the tall navy double doors. She waves back as she begins to drive off, still looking at me like she can see right through my lies.

As soon as I slip through the classroom door, my friend KO motions for me to come sit with him. Most people call him KO because his real name is long as hell. It's dope AF, though. It's Kahikookeakua, which means *divine rain* in Hawaiian.

I put my bag under the table and pull out a seat, hoping Mr. Morgan doesn't notice that I'm late. As soon as I sit down, KO leans back and starts fanning himself all dramatically. He just wants to show off his nails, which are purple-and-pink stilettos.

"Bitch, you not hot?" he whispers a little too loud.

"No." I shrug, feeling a little self-conscious that I'm the only one with a sweatshirt on.

Mr. Morgan turns around, looking dead at me over his thick-ass glasses that are practically falling off his face.

"Okay, who's ready to solve some equations?" He smiles.

I fake a smile back. I aint forgot how he got me in trouble. I should've just signed up for regular Algebra II with Ms. Daily, instead of trying to be all fancy taking this honors Algebra II class instead.

"His ass knows he outta line for wearing them doo-doo brown polyester pants," KO mumbles. His arms are folded and he has a sneaky smirk on his face as he looks straight ahead. He is one of the cutest boys at this school. Too bad he doesn't see me as more than a homegirl.

"Bruh," I say, before laughing my ass off.

"Did you hear about Jamarion Davis and my sister?" KO scrolls through his phone with his lips pursed out. He shows me his sister's feed, which is filled with memes about breakups. I lean over to get the tea.

"No. What happened?"

"Girl, they broke up," he whispers with his hand cupping his mouth.

"Damn. Is your twin okay?"

"Yeah, she'll be aiight, but how much do you wanna bet they'll be back together before lunch?" He shakes his head, causing his wavy ponytail to sway.

"How much you wanna bet they'll be back together before second period?"

We both giggle, drawing Mr. Morgan's attention.

"Glad you two are in good spirits today. Ms. Smith, could you please solve the system of equations on page twenty-four?" Mr. Morgan projects the problem on the board.

KO is scrunching his face like he's thinking real hard. The entire class is focused on us, like this is a game show or something. I dig into my bag to pull out my notebook and pencil and start to work on the problem. It only takes me a hot minute to get the answer.

"X equals one, y equals two, and z equals negative five over three." I lay my pencil flat.

Mr. Morgan nods with a chin rub. "Well done, Ms. Smith. Would you like to come up to the board and show the class how you found the answers?"

Not really.

There's a burning in my chest, probably from the plate of grits I devoured, and now I'm feeling even more sick. I close my eyes, hoping the pain will go away, but the burning gets worse, and my stomach isn't letting up. KO looks over at me, with his pencil stabbing the middle of his notebook paper.

"Erykah, you good?" He drops his pencil, eyeing me up and down.

"I think I need to throw up," I whisper.

I'm doing everything in my power not to let this food explode all over the place. I hold a fist to my mouth, praying that I can at least make it till the bell rings. KO gently pats my back, his perfectly arched eyebrows furrowed.

KO's hand shoots up.

"Yes, Mr. Akino." Mr. Morgan moves closer; he smells like a sack of mothballs mixed with Old Spice.

"Erykah doesn't look so good. Can I take her to the nurse?" KO asks.

Mr. Morgan takes a few steps toward me. Shit. I can feel it coming up. He looks at me closely. I make a sour face as I cover my nose and mouth. *Mister, please back up.*

"Erykah, are you going to be okay?" Mr. Morgan leans in.

Big mistake. Before I know it, there are chunks of yellow and white and burnt pieces of hot link dripping down Mr. Morgan's shirt. What I think is a burp turns out to be a sludge of grits, and it sprays all over Mr. Morgan's shoes.

I feel like I'm an inner-city fire hydrant opened on a hot summer's day. The corner of my arm has specks of scrambled eggs and coarse grains nudged in the elbow. Everyone is staring at me. They're all disgusted. They all look like they want to help, but I wish I could tell them it's not that simple.

Mr. Morgan's entire fit is fucked up.

My bad, mister.

His chest is going up and down. He stands in front of me like a scarecrow in a cornfield, with a shocked mug on his face. I slowly lift myself up, making sure I don't step in the mess I just made.

"So . . . can I be excused now?"

CHAPTER NINE

Kelly

As soon as I finish my presentation in Dr. Holiday's AP Lit class, my phone chimes. Luckily for me, it's during my round of applause, so Dr. Holiday doesn't notice. Instead, she hands me a rubric, with all perfect scores and a 100 percent written in red ink at the top. I slip my phone out as soon as I sit down, just as Darrion Clemons starts his presentation about Langston Hughes.

> E: Kelz, can U meet me in the girls' bathroom?

> E: 200 Hallway

> E: Please. I'm freaking out.

When I get to the girls' bathroom, Erykah is sitting on top of the middle sink, with her head down. Once she notices me, she puts a finger to her lips and eyes a stall in front of her. I get the hint that we're not the only ones in here, so I make sure to whisper.

"Are you okay?" I stand next to her. She looks about two shades lighter, and her eyes are damn near bloodshot.

"I guess."

She hunches her shoulders, then sips a ginger soda she's clenching. I don't know how she can drink that stuff. It's hella bitter and just straight-up nasty.

"I threw up all over Mr. Morgan." She looks at me pitifully.

I can't help it, I burst out laughing, and Erykah immediately joins me. We're silenced by a loud flush from one of the stalls. It's just some freshman, who's acting like she's scared to wash her hands in front of us. After the girl scurries out, I sit on the sink that's next to E.

"I'm sorry, best friend. I guess my niece don't like breakfast," I joke, but E just takes another long sip and gives me half a smile.

"Nah, I think I just ate too much." She hops off the sink, staring in the mirror like she doesn't know who's on the other side. I almost say something about how full her face is or the way her hips have spread in the last two weeks, but I don't want to make her more self-conscious. She rolls up her sleeves and splashes water on her face. Before I can hop down, she looks up at me, pale faced, then darts to the nearest stall. I follow her, and as she throws up, I rub her back with my nose plugged as she continues to let it all out, just like always. Dr. Holiday is probably wondering where the hell I am. I can't just dip out on E right now, but I do need to get back to class so that I won't have to explain myself.

"Hey, E, you should probably go to the nurse," I say after the last flush. Erykah looks at me in defeat.

"And tell her what? That my morning sickness is outta control and I need to go home?"

Well, she has a point. I'm like the only person who knows about her pregnancy, but I don't know how much longer E thinks she can keep her secret from everyone here.

"I mean, it's not uncommon for someone to have an upset stomach," I say.

"Then she'll call my momma, and I can just hear her trippin' out on me because she had to miss work to come get me." She stares up at the tiled ceiling. "I just wanted you here because I dead-ass feel like shit. Miguel's not answering his phone, so . . ." She stands up and leans against the stall.

How many more signs does she need to realize that Miguel is a bum? Aint no way I'd let some low-life clown try to play me like that, but I guess love makes some people do the unusual.

"Listen, I know it isn't the best timing, but you probably should just call Ms. Monica and tell her that you've been throwing up like crazy," I say.

Erykah gives me an emotionless stare, then sits on the toilet with her chin in her hands. "Yeah, well, some things are better left unsaid." She looks back up to the ceiling, with her lips tight and her arms folded.

"E, your momma has had two babies before, so I'm sure she'll understand what you're going through. . . ." My words drift.

Erykah holds her hand up. "Kelly, chill. Please."

"My bad. I mean, I'm just trying to help. You seriously don't think Ms. Monica would understand?" I'm starting to get annoyed.

Erykah lets out a sigh, like she's thinking of a response. She rises from the toilet and calmly pushes the stall door open. I follow her, trying to figure out why she's being so damn defensive. She pauses, then turns to me with tears flowing from her eyes. My heart instantly sinks.

"Oh my gosh, don't cry! I can call and tell her if you don't want to, or maybe you should go to my mom's office, and she can—"

E shakes her head, wiping her tears with her sleeve. "No, Kelly. That's the thing. I haven't—" She starts to choke on her words, and the tears begin to flow like an open stream.

"E," I say slowly. "What's going on?"

She lets out a sigh, wiping her tears with her sleeve. "My momma doesn't know that I'm still pregnant."

"Wait . . . what do you mean?" I'm so confused I can barely get my words out. "You told me that she was cool with your decision."

E stares at her all-white Forces, then shrugs.

I feel a slight blow to my stomach, but it's not a physical one. I've been hit with a pain I can't explain, and it hurts deep inside because it's coming from this person I care about deeply. I can't believe all this time E has been playing me when she knows she can come to me about dead-ass anything.

I wait for her to explain herself.

Say something.

Make it make sense.

But she just rocks with her head down.

"But what about your first doctor's visit? You said she went with you. You told me she stood up for you at your appointment."

E just stares at the ground.

"And what about that cute onesie you said she bought for you?"

I think back over the last few weeks. "Wait, is this why you've been acting weird every time I ask to come over?"

The last few times I wanted to come over to her house, she would suggest she come to mine instead. I really didn't think much of it, just thought maybe my house was more of a vibe, but now I see it was because she didn't want Ms. Monica to find out that she never had the abortion. Why couldn't she just keep it real? We tell each other everything. But this whole time she's been playing her mom . . . and me too.

E just looks at me with watery eyes.

"Erykah! Say something!"

After what feels like an eternity, she finally decides to speak.

"I faked everything because I didn't know how to tell her the truth," she mutters.

I take a step back, almost as if something just pushed me.

Didn't know how to tell her the truth? It's been a while since the abortion clinic. Why would E not have told Ms. Monica?

"E, what were you thinking? She's going to find out eventually!"

"I know! I just need time. And according to Nevada law, you can't have an abortion after twenty-four weeks no way, so if I can just keep it a secret a little longer—"

"E, for real? That's like the worst idea ever."

Erykah leans back on a sink, shaking her head. Something hardens in her expression.

"See, this is why I didn't tell you. Matter of fact, I don't even know why I confided in you. You're supposed to be my best friend, but instead you act more like you the ops for my momma or something. My bad for not being all perfect like you."

CHAPTER TEN

Erykah

14 Weeks

I know I should have been straight with Kelly from the get-go. Still, this is not the reaction I need. All I need right now is for her to have my back and understand where I'm coming from. She knows my situation with Momma, and me being pregnant has been a problem from the start, so I don't get why she's acting so brand-new.

"All perfect? What's that supposed to mean?" Kelly clenches her hip with her lip curled.

"You know how you can be, Kelly."

"How I can be?" she repeats. "Umm, and how is that?"

"You know, like judgmental or whatever. And it's obvious how much you hate Miguel."

"Yeah, well, pretty much everyone does except for you. I'm supposed to be okay with some fuckboy treating my bestie like shit?"

"Oh, I forgot that Ray is perfect." I cross my arms, staring deep into Kelly's eyes. She stares at me like she wants to talk more shit, but she just shakes her head instead. Kelly's really going in on me, but she doesn't understand that there was no way I could've told Momma in that moment that I wasn't getting an abortion. It's not like I'm proud of lying, but who knows what would've happened if I had told Momma the truth?

"At least he's not stupid enough to forget how to wear a condom." She throws up her hands.

Kelly lost her virginity to Ray two months ago, but she's been on birth control for a while. Her mom got her on it because of Kelly's irregular period. I mean, part of that might be true, but Kelly's mom doesn't know she's having sex. It's crazy how she's pointing the finger at me for not telling my momma the real about my pregnancy, but her momma don't know the real about everything either. If I was as fucked up as Kelly is being to me right now, her mom would know the truth about Kelly not being a virgin. She's sweating me about keeping it real with my momma, but she's not even keeping it 100 with her own.

"See, stay judging. That's why I didn't tell you everything."

"Cap. When have I ever judged you?" she asks.

At first I think she's trying to be funny, but then I realize she's serious.

"Uh, just now, about Miguel, for one."

"Other than just now."

I rack my brain, trying to remember the many times Kelly

has made me feel judged, but I'm so worked up I can't think of anything specific. "I don't know, like you making me feel stupid because I didn't understand *Hamlet* right away. . . . And you telling me what I should and shouldn't eat." Kelly gives me a quizzical look, and I know I'm making no sense. "I mean, look how you're acting now. I thought coming clean to my momma would be hard, but you're not that easy to confide in either."

"So, it's my fault you lied to me?" Kelly pins her finger to her chest.

"No, stop twisting my words. It's just, like, you expect too much or whatever," I say.

"Oh, I'm really sorry I want what's best for my best friend and think she deserves a boyfriend who doesn't make her feel like shit and that maybe it would've made sense not to keep something like this from her mom, who deserves to know the truth."

"See, there you go, being all judgmental. . . ."

I had a very good reason for not telling Momma the truth. For one, I need a roof over my head, and two . . . I honestly don't know how to tell her. Kelly is making me feel guilty as hell for not telling Momma the truth. It's not like I wanted it to be this way, but not everyone respects your decisions, especially when you're still a minor. And Kelly knows that if she was in my shoes, she'd probably do the same. And it's crazy, cause even though me and Kelly wear the same shoe size, she probably doesn't even believe my shoe would ever fit.

"You know what? I gotta go." She waves a laminated purple pass. "I should've been back to class a long time ago."

I'm about ready to grab her by the shoulder and beg her to just hear me out, but I'm frozen in place by the sound of a flush behind one of the stalls. Kelly freezes too. Shit. *Was somebody eavesdropping on our convo this entire time?* The speckled black door swings open. Anxiety creeps over my body, twisting my stomach in knots.

Blaise steps out, tossing her hair with a little smirk on her face. Me and Kelly give her the dirtiest mean mug as she pushes past us, smelling like some expensive-ass perfume that she probably doesn't even own. Bitches is known for getting samples from Neiman Marcus and acting like they can afford to wear Chanel. She stops at the middle sink to wash her hands and flashes us a look like she's annoyed.

"What?" She pulls her AirPods out of her ears. "Is there a problem?"

Her high-pitched annoying-ass voice bounces off the bathroom walls. She's playing dumb, but I know she heard every word that was just said. *Fuck.* Yeah, there's a big problem. The most popular girl at my school, who has diarrhea of the mouth, just learned that I'm pregnant.

Which means it's only a matter of time before everyone else knows too.

CHAPTER ELEVEN

Kelly

It's been three days since my fight with Erykah. We didn't talk for two of them, which sucked, because I'm used to talking to her all day every day. Big TJ, who deejays for everybody and their momma when there's a big event in the Heights, is hosting his annual fall fling, right off the Vegas Strip, and it just wouldn't be a party without my best friend by my side, so I asked her to roll with me and Ray. Me and E aren't even allowed to go into the city without one of our parents, but Ms. Monica thinks E's at my house and my parents think I'm at hers. Ray was cool with picking her up, as long as annoying-ass Marsaun could tag along too. Marsaun has been on IG live since he's gotten in the back seat, and I'm tempted to snatch his phone and throw it out the window. While we cruise down Las Vegas Boulevard, I scroll through my Instagram feed and notice that Blaise is posted up with Jayla Dillard and her crew, who are making duck faces with peace signs, #BigTJsparty2night.

Surprisingly, since the bathroom incident, Blaise has kept her mouth shut. Still, E and I have been on high alert. I'm not gonna lie, the fact that Blaise hasn't said something is a bit suspect, but I keep telling Erykah that maybe Blaise *didn't* hear anything.

Ray pulls up to the two-story mansion, which looks like the ones that are in those rapper videos. People are crowded along the sidewalk. I think every high school kid from Vegas is here. East Prep kids, gangbangers, ratchets, the smooth-ass Latinx crew and the rich white kids that go to the prep school that's not too far away. Everyone admires Ray's silver Challenger as the trunk rattles like an old washing machine. The smell of weed almost knocks me out as soon as we get out of the car. Before I can even close the door, I see Blaise and her little uppity crew looking thirsty as hell in outfits that barely cover their nipples and butt cheeks.

"Daaamn, I'm a fasho get me some tonight." Marsaun rubs his hands together. He lights a blunt and walks up to Blaise and her crew, looking just as thirsty.

"We shoulda camped out here last night," E says as she surveys the line that's now wrapped around the block.

I felt bad about our falling-out, but I also felt like it was on E to make things right. After waiting for two days, I caved and called her. There was a lot of tension at first, but by the end of the call, we were getting back cool. We both felt like shit about the things we said to each other, and I told E that I would try to be more supportive of her, even though I still don't think it's a good idea for her to keep this lie going on. She said that she's planning on telling Ms. Monica about her pregnancy as soon as she finds out the gender, but that's a while from now and honestly, I don't get why she just won't tell her now. I highly doubt Ms. Monica would kick E out at this point, but E just keeps saying that she's got this.

I notice a carload of kids pouring out of some beat-up Toyota. I'm praying no fights or shoot-outs break out tonight, since that's always a common theme with Heights hangouts.

"Eww, is that Junie and them over there?" E peers at this swarm of dudes loading out of the Toyota. She used to date Junie back in the day, and I never thought I'd say this, but I'd rather she be with Junie than Miguel. She broke up with him to be with Miguel because she claimed that Junie wasn't mature enough. Junie was always nice to me, plus he's funny as hell, but I guess E just lost feelings.

"Yeah, that's him and his crew." I scrunch my face at the line that's not getting any shorter. "Yall sure yall wanna wait in that long-ass line?"

I'm in a black strapless dress. There's a cool breeze, so I wrap my arms around myself. At least my feet are comfortable. Me and Ray decided to wear our Concord Js tonight. Ray pulls out his phone and starts texting rapidly, like he's negotiating a deal. I can hear the ratchetness brewing as people sing along to Megan Thee Stallion's latest bop.

"Berto says he can get us in." Ray looks between us.

"The dread-head dude that works in the cafeteria?" I ask.

"Yeah, he cool peoples and he always got the hookup," Ray says.

"Well, how much is that gonna cost us?" E asks with her arms folded.

"Fifteen dollars"—he double-checks his phone—"apiece."

E turns around and stands at the car with her hand on the door handle.

"Yeah, I'll just be chillin' in here until yall ready to go," E says.

I turn to Ray, telling him to see if he can get a better deal so that everyone can get in. He rolls his eyes and begins to type again, then says that Berto says that TJ will let us in for ten apiece, nothing less. I reach in my pocket and pull out a crumpled twenty-dollar bill and hand it to Ray.

"C'mon, bestie. We in." I wave to E.

At first she's hesitant, but she walks toward us, burying herself in her jacket. I feel a tug on my shoulder and turn to E, whose eyes are as bright as the moon gleaming above us.

"You think anyone will notice? Is this jacket too much?" She opens her jacket a little, to show me her small bump.

If I didn't know E was pregnant, I wouldn't think twice. She could still get by with saying she's bloated. Her denim jacket overpowers the dark blue dress she's rocking, but I get why she's wearing one. Anyways, it's probably so dark inside that house, no one will even know who we are.

"Nah. Just stay close to me. And no twerking, E." I point at her with my eyebrows raised.

If E weren't pregnant, I'd still be telling her not to. I'm praying City Girls doesn't come on and tempt her.

"I aint, dang." She pops some gum in her mouth with a laugh.

Even though this crowd is a bit much, I feel like we deserve to turn up tonight. It's been a while since me and E have hung out and had some fun. A few guys from Ray's basketball team notice him and call him over. He jogs toward them, engaging in some small talk. There's some people up the block, just parking-lot pimpin'. They basically are having their own party in the street, playing music from their cars and clouding it up with that good-good.

"Kelly, Erykah, heeey!" A familiar voice causes me to whip my head around.

KO is waving his pink sparkling nails all in my face with a tank top on that says, BI AND PROBABLY HI in rainbow colors. We've been down with KO since elementary, but I never knew a thing about his sexuality until he told us one day in the eighth grade that he's bisexual. Coming out was especially hard when it came to his conservative-ass parents, but they've grown to accept KO for who he is.

"Okay. I see you. Your shirt is cute." I reach over to give him a hug.

E does the same and also reaches over to hug a light-skinned girl with thick baby hairs, who's posted next to KO.

"Kelz, you know Kammy? She was in our PE class in eighth grade," E says before turning her head off to the side like she's had a whiff of something strong.

I smell it too—Kammy's Love Spell body spray is strong as hell. It's like she poured the whole bottle all over herself. I nod and smile like I remember this chick. Kammy waves at me with a wide smile, showing off her multicolored braces.

"Yall ready for homecoming next week? My dress is gonna be fire," KO brags.

"It better not be more lit than mine," I laugh.

E looks the other way like she's trying to avoid the conversation. She already told me that she's not sure about the dance because every dress hugs her stomach, and Ms. Monica's been struggling with getting hours at her job, so right now money is real tight.

"We better go find Ray so that we can get inside," E says.

"Yeah, we should. We'll see yall inside," I say quickly as I interlock my arm with E's.

KO throws us a fake smile. "Right. Well, we gone catch up with our crew over there." He points to two girls who look like they don't even live in the Heights. One is heavyset with scalp braids going back and the other looks like she's barely in high school.

Me and E wave bye as KO and Kammy bounce off.

We finally make it inside the cramped house and squeeze through sweaty bodies, as I let E take the lead to find us a spot where maybe we can breathe. The thick stench of weed fills the air, and it feels like the floor is about to crumble from people stomping while doing the latest TikTok trend. I'm tempted to join in and show them how it's really done. E's thick wand curls bounce off her shoulders as she leads me to a table that's lined with red cups and a big punch bowl. There's a few bottles of dark liquor behind the bowl, so I'm pretty sure this punch aint the kind people serve at kids' parties. A girl with a hoop nose ring and lime and pink braids is behind the table tapping away on her phone. I guess she's supposed to be the bartender. I've seen her around, but she doesn't go to school with me and E.

"The punch is two dollars." She holds up two fingers with nails almost as long as KO's.

"You got any regular punch?" E asks.

"I got bottled water." The girl holds up a sweaty bottle of generic water.

I get the punch, and E gets bottled water, asking the girl to pour it in a cup, I guess so no one can tell that she's not drinking. We continue to float around, looking for a spot to dance at. E holds her cup up high, swinging her hips through the crowd. I spot Marsaun in the corner, back against the wall, while some girl is grinding on him. Yeah, that just made my stomach turn even more. I can feel my head starting to throb, but I'm tryna get lit, so I take a swig of my strong-ass drink and continue to snake through the crowd like it's nothing. The DJ starts to play a hype mix that gives snippets of Chris Brown and Lil Baby. Me and E start getting low, like we're at a Jamaican dance hall. Guys are gripping girls' hips while they twerk and grind. I'd be surprised if half of the girls at this party aren't lined up at Walgreens tomorrow to buy some Plan B. I feel my phone pulsating in my pocket.

Ray: Where yall at?

Me: Over here by some ratchets that's doing the Toosie Slide

"I'm glad you still wanted me to come out with you tonight," E says into my ear.

"Of course. Just cause we don't always see eye to eye don't mean I'm a just turn my back on you," I say.

E is a whole vibe. She's moving from side to side and twisting around like she owns this party. For a minute, I forget that she's pregnant. Then it dawns on me that this could be the last time we'll ever be this carefree together at a party. The DJ announces he wants to see everybody do their thang and switches it up to the "Cupid Shuffle." *Hey*s and *aah*s spread around the room as everyone kicks from side to side. Me and E are vibing to the beat as we walk it out for the third time. The DJ switches it up with some old-school nineties songs. "Poison" comes on, and me and E start shouting out the lyrics. I kill my drink. A minute later I'm ready to move with the music, hands in the air, body moving like a snake, eyes on fire. The joy is like a shot of dopamine and all at once I'm vibing, one with the music, one with my bestie, who's stunting in the crowd. Everyone starts moving in to cheer us on, phones waving in the air with bright lights surrounding us like fireflies. I notice Darrion squeezing through the crowd. He looks like a celebrity with his vintage-style Gucci belt (probably not the real thing) and bucket hat to match.

"Yall killin' it on this dance floor." He waves his red cup. "What up, E, haven't seen you in a while." He smiles at her.

E barely smiles back, but I know she's feeling his vibe by the way she's eyeing him up and down.

"That belt is fire." She nods at him.

The song switches up to "Crank That" by Soulja Boy. Everyone starts doing the Superman dance, bouncing left to right.

"Thanks. You wanna dance?" he asks.

E and I exchange a look. She's blushing hella hard. I widen my eyes as I take a step back and let Darrion take my place.

I hear a few gasps behind us, but I assume it's just because E and Darrion are dominating the floor. I take a step back as Darrion and E do their thing.

They really are a vibe. Out of the corner of my eye, I catch a glimpse of Blaise; she's whispering something to KO and his crew while pointing our way. Their expressions go from bored to shocked. KO starts scanning the crowd, and I get this awful feeling like he's trying to find Erykah. My throat tightens as I swallow a big lump. I turn back to E and see a group of girls looking at us with their eyes bucked. *Oh no.* Pretty soon, more and more people are looking at us like we've been spotted from *America's Most Wanted.*

They know. Blaise is telling everyone that E is pregnant.

E slows down her moves to chug her water. Darrion starts to notice all the whispers too. He slows down his moves, giving me a *what's going on* look.

"What's wrong, Kelz?" E looks around the room, wondering why nobody is dancing.

The DJ lowers the music, like he's in on the secret too. I damn near want to go up to the booth and slap his ass, but that would probably just validate what everyone already knows.

"I thought drinking was off-limits when you're pregnant," I hear someone say.

"E, we should go," I whisper to her.

"What? We just got here. And this might be the last party I ever go to for a minute."

I feel a headache coming on. Ray joins us, with a look on his face that's giving, *we need to talk.*

Fuck.

He's probably wondering why I didn't tell him first. But how do I explain to someone I promised to never keep any secrets from that I promised my best friend I wouldn't tell hers? The room feels like it's getting smaller. I feel like MJ and his girl when they were surrounded by those zombies in the "Thriller" video. KO's voice brings me back to reality.

"E, why didn't you tell me you were pregnant? You could have trusted me." KO holds both of E's hands with a devastated look.

E looks at me, pale-faced, then back at KO as if she's at a loss for words.

"What? I'm not pregnant." E sounds so convincing, she almost makes me believe her too.

"Damn, she triflin' as hell, partying like she aint bout to be somebody momma any day now. It's *giving* irresponsible," a voice says behind us.

A bunch of cackles burst out.

It's definitely time to get the hell outta here.

"Wonder who's the BD?" I hear another voice say.

"Babe, you wanna tell me what the hell is going on?" Ray leans over, trying to maintain a whisper.

"Ray, we gotta go." My voice trembles.

I clench E's hand and zip through the crowd, tuning everything out.

We got to get the hell out of here.

And we almost make it out, but E pauses right before we bust through the double doors. Her phone is chiming like crazy. People are staring at us, still talking shit, but I don't pay them any mind. I watch her sift through the wide pocket on the side of her jacket for her phone. She taps on the screen, and her eyes immediately begin to water. She tosses her phone at me, then runs out the doors.

There's a bunch of texts from Ms. Monica, but only one stands out: Erykah, I can't believe this whole time you've been lying to me.

This is all bad. I don't want to be the one to tell her I told you so, but E keeping this a secret was bound to cause more harm than good. People in the Heights gossip like old church ladies, and I already know her mom is not taking this easy. I push through the double doors and through a crowd of kids. E is kneeling near Ray's car, bawling with her arms locked tight. I jog to her, lifting her up, telling her that it's all going to be okay, even though I know it's not.

CHAPTER TWELVE

Erykah

15 Weeks

Right now, I'm trying to think of how I'm gone survive when I walk through that door to face Momma. Kelly is turned around in her seat with her chin pinned to the edge of it. I brace myself as Ray speeds through the streets like we just hit a lick. Marsaun stayed at the party with some friends, so it's just us three, riding in silence. The cool air from the sunroof of his car hits my face as I stare into the navy sky. There aint a star in sight. Rare, since there's no clouds, but it kinda makes sense being that this aint no average night.

I can tell Ray's not too happy with Kelly, but he's still cool toward me. He held the door open for me while I slid in the back seat, his eyes droopy like someone just set his favorite pair of Js on fire. I feel like I'm causing more problems than I should. The last thing I want is for my best friend's relationship to be fucked up because I asked her to keep a secret. A secret that I never meant to hurt so many people. I just needed more time. And by then, I was hoping Momma'd be less likely to freak out, maybe even happy about the whole thing.

"I can't believe that bitch Blaise just telling your business to everyone. I feel like going back and handling her," Kelly seethes.

"For what? That aint gone solve nothing. People was bound to find out eventually," I mumble.

If I weren't pregnant, I'd handle Blaise myself. I don't need anyone defending me, but for some reason, I'm not even focused on what Blaise just did. I'm more focused on what's gonna happen when I'm confronted by Momma and if I'll have a roof over my head after tonight.

"Let me go inside with you. That way you don't have to face Ms. Monica alone," Kelly says.

I stare out the window, stomach turning the closer we get to my place. Ray starts a playlist from his phone. There's a soft beat bumpin' from the car's speakers of a neo-soul R & B song. I can barely hear the words against Ray's engine, but it's like they're fighting to be heard. *"Thank you for hearing me, always believed in me. Never let me fall even when I wanted to let go."* It makes me think of Momma and all the times she's lifted me up, even when she was at her lowest point. I hate to admit, but Kelly was right. I should've kept it real with Momma. Should've known that me lying was just gonna make things worse.

"Or I can just be there for moral support. I won't say anything if you don't want me to." Kelly's voice snaps me back into reality.

"It's alright. Momma's probably just gone tell you to leave anyways." I shrug.

"I still don't understand how she found out that fast," Kelly whispers to herself. "Maybe she still doesn't know. Maybe somebody just told her they saw us at the party?"

I look at her with my chin deep into my chest. *And maybe Momma is just ecstatic that I'm still having a baby and wants to shower me with gifts and a comfy-ass bed to sleep in from now on.* That's what I wanna say, but I know Kelly is only trying to help. It's possible that Momma doesn't know, but it's also very much possible that she does.

I'm pretty sure somebody at the party made a post or something and Momma was tagged in it. Either way, she knows something, and I'll be lucky if it's just about me being at Big TJ's party.

"Just let her go off and don't be too defensive. Sometimes when my mom gets all mad at me for things, I just let her go off and eventually she calms down," Kelly suggests.

Yeah, I'm sure Mrs. Lancaster does, but we're talking about Monica Smith. Her temp gets higher than Vegas's in July when she's mad, and she hates to be lied to. Kelly should know that as many times as she's seen my momma go off.

"I mean, if you just tell her that you couldn't go through with it, she has to understand, E. She might be mad for a minute, but she can't stay mad forever."

"Yeah, but it's more than that, Kelly. I lied to her about hella shit, not just faking an abortion."

Up until yesterday, Momma thought:

I got the abortion almost a month ago.

I stopped talking to Miguel.

I was finally starting to be the daughter she's fought so hard to raise right.

I put my head down and send Miguel a text, while Kelly continues to think of ways I can win Momma over.

> Me: Momma knows

A minute later, three dots appear, disappear, appear, then disappear.

Ray parks with his headlights shining like the police against the front windows of the apartment.

"You sure you don't want me to go in with you, E?" Kelly pleads. "Ray can come in too, and then she for sure can't turn up." Kelly looks over at Ray.

"Girl, you must not know my momma." I lift my head.

His eyes buck at Kelly like he rather not be involved. He turns to me with a forced smile.

"I don't mind having your back, E. Not sure if that will make it better or worse, but if you need us to—"

I stop him there. I'm not dragging nobody else into this. If anybody should be here with me, it should be Miguel, but I see that I can't depend on him anymore.

"Nah, I really need to do this by myself," I sigh. "But thank yall."

My phone rattles, along with my heart. It's probably Momma threatening to come drag me out the car if I don't hurry up.

> Miguel: Knows what?

Damn, he can be so clueless. Maybe if he was around more, he'd know.

> Me: Someone told her I'm preg still.
> Everyone knows . . .

I don't wait for a reply, because who knows when that'll happen. Kelly reaches her arms out for a hug. She squeezes me like I'm about to get on a plane and never return. Actually, that's exactly what I feel like doing right now, but what will that even solve? I let the door close on its own as I drag my feet across the damp grass that leads to my apartment building. Ray and Kelly wait for me to wave before driving off. I already know what I'm about to face on the other side of the door, and even though I told Kelly I can handle it, I'm starting to feel like I can't. My pocket vibrates.

> Momma: U better be in that house
> when I get back.

Where the hell is she at?

Just like my momma to rush me home, only to make me wait. I was hoping it was Miguel to say he's on his way, but he aint said shit else. I slide my key in the lock and turn the knob halfway, before feeling the instinct to just run. But to where? With who? I should've just listened to Nurse Jill and told Momma the truth in the beginning. I should've listened to Kelly. I should've known better than to keep this from Momma. I really thought I could fool everyone, when all the while, I've just been fooling myself.

CHAPTER THIRTEEN

Erykah

15 Weeks

I've only been scared two times in my life. Well, maybe three.

When Daddy left us.

When I found out that I was pregnant.

And . . .

Right now.

After I change out of that tight-ass dress, I curl up on the couch in my oversized East Prep Spirit Day T-shirt and await my fate. I can't stop thinking about how stupid it was for me not to tell Momma sooner, but she would've kicked me out, and where was I gonna go? I'm sure Miguel's sister wouldn't have minded, but that house is already crowded as hell, and Lita's housing projects are always on the news. They call them the BGs, aka the baby ghettos, for a reason.

I'm about to get my head chopped off, and all I can think

about is eating. I'm convinced that this baby's mission is to get me fat. Right now, I'm craving something salty and sweet. I scan every cabinet for something to snack on, but nothing is appealing. There's a rolled-up bag of stale tortilla chips and a box of generic Fruity O's on the top of the fridge. Guess that'll be my salty-and-sweet treat. I look inside the fridge to check the expiration date on the milk. It shoulda been thrown out a week ago, but I take my chances. I'm probably gonna throw all this up anyways, so might as well enjoy it while I can.

I flick the TV on, since it's so damn quiet in here. Silence makes fear ten times worse. Reminds me of how I feel when I'm watching a scary movie. Seems like the scariest shit always pops off right when it gets nice and quiet. There's a message scrolling across the bottom of the screen that says the cable bill is five days past due. I wish Momma would just let me help out. When I was braiding hair in the neighborhood, I was bringing in bank. Not enough to pay all of Momma's bills, but enough to keep the cable on at least. The longer Momma takes to get home, the more my insides tighten. I can't even sit still, I'm so damn nervous.

As I finish the last of my soggy cereal, I surf through the channels and pause when I see a headline flashing across the screen.

"Good evening. I'm Leslie O'Neal and thank you for joining us for the ten o'clock news. We come to you now with a breaking story. Bryant Hall is live at the scene of a shoot-out that took place between MLK and Lake Mead Boulevard, on Englestead Lane."

Yo, that's where Big TJ's party was.

"Let me help you," I say, scurrying toward her.

She puts her hand up, like a crossing guard.

"Uh-uh. You, go sit your ass over there." She nods toward the kitchen table.

I feel a lump in my throat. She aint playin' no games. Instead of trying to fight her, I just comply. I start to ask her where Jayden is, but I remember he's spending the night with his friend Corey in the next building. Momma carries a few grocery bags over and drops them on the counter. She begins to stuff the cabinets with generic boxes of mac 'n' cheese and cans of ravioli.

"I should've known better than to have believed you was gone tell the truth." She slams a cabinet door.

"I wasn't trying to—" I start.

Momma turns to me, giving me a look that makes me slide down into my seat. After filling the shelves and stuffing the freezer with packs of meat, she pulls out the chair that's across from me and sits with her hands folded, silent for a minute.

"You thought I wasn't gone find out, huh?" She cocks her head to the side.

I don't know what to say first.

I'm sorry?

I just needed more time?

I was scared out of my mind that you wouldn't understand?

I sit with my ankles crossed, speechless.

"Erykah!" Momma slaps her hand on the table.

I snap out of my trance, staring back at her. Looking at her is

The scene changes to a Black newscaster, who i
the camera and firmly gripping a microphone.

"Thank you, Leslie." He hesitates, plugging his
finger like he's getting some important info. "I'm he
702 Englestead Lane, where a violent shooting has
As you can see, the area has been taped off and inv
still on the scene."

There's yellow tape and hella police cars everywh

"What was supposed to be a festive gathering en
violent shooting between two rival gangs," Bryant co

The camera pans around, showing a clip of kids r
and right, speeding off in their cars and on foot. I
must've happened right after we left.

"Police say that fortunately, no one was injured,
vehicles did get hit. The suspects are still on the loos
ities are asking that anyone who has information call
hotline. All reports will remain anonymous. Back to yo

The crime hotline number flashes across the scre
minute, I start thinking about how Kelly, Ray, or mysel
been shot. A chill runs down my spine as I bundle into
blanket beside me. I hear the door click, and I instantly s
Momma is struggling to get through the door with a sh
grocery bags. She kicks the door shut with the bottom of
and places the bags down, panting. I'm tempted to ask
the hell she was able to afford all of this food, but by th
mug on her face, I don't even breathe it.

like looking at myself, because the tears rolling down her cheeks match mine. The shakiness in her voice sounds just like how I would sound. She presses a fist to her lips as she fights to keep words in, probably some she'd regret.

"I'm sorry, okay? But you didn't really give me much of a choice!" I say.

Momma scoots back, like she's been blown away. I don't apologize this time. I look at her trembling lips. She slowly lowers her hands, laying them flat on the table.

"Little girl, have you lost your mind talking to me like you payin' some bills up in here? I bust my ass to make sure you and your brother have a somewhat decent life and you repay me by sneaking and sliding behind my back? And then wanna talk smart?"

"If I woulda told you the truth, you was just gone kick me out." I look up at her.

"Kick you out?" Momma winces at me. "Erykah, stop playing with me. Is that what you going round here telling everybody?"

"You literally said that with your own mouth," I snap back.

"Little girl, that's strike two." She holds up two fingers. "I don't care if I told you that I was gonna send you to the moon, aint no excuse for you to be lying to me," she says in between claps.

I think twice before clapping back. Momma's never been this angry before, and even though she's never physically put her hands on me, I'm not about to find out what strike three looks like.

"I . . . was gonna tell you," I stutter.

"Oh, you was?" She folds her arms, leaning back. "Erykah,

do you know how hard it is to be a single mom, raising two kids alone, in a fucked-up neighborhood, making pennies on the hour?" She counts each obstacle on her fingers. "It *never* gets easy, but I do all I can so you and Jayden can do better than me. Last thing I need is to be—"

"I was going tell you soon, okay? I was gonna tell you." I start to choke on my words. I feel like all the air around me is being sucked out of nowhere. "I just needed more time. . . . I just couldn't kill my baby. I couldn't do what you and everybody else wanted me to do!"

I can't control the tears or the heavy breaths or the anxiety that's making my heart beat like a drum. Momma sits across from me with a puzzled look on her face.

"Erykah, what are you saying? I was talking about you going to that party behind my back," she says slowly.

My body freezes. She doesn't even know. This whole time I thought word got back to her that I'm still pregnant and she doesn't even know shit.

"You're still pregnant?" She looks at me like she can't comprehend what she just said.

I nod uncontrollably, bawling.

"I . . . swear I was gonna tell you. Please, don't kick me out. I need you, Momma," I cry.

It's dead silent again.

Momma is frozen. She can't even look at me. Her shoulders drop and her hands form into a ball under her round chin.

"Lord, you've been pregnant this entire time, and I didn't even know," she mutters.

I nod carefully, swallowing salty liquid that seeps through the corners of my mouth. Momma reaches for my hand and grips it tightly.

"Why didn't you just tell me you couldn't go through with the abortion?"

Because you were going to freak out.

Because I thought I had more time.

Because I didn't want you to convince me to change my mind.

I slip my hand from Momma's and bury my face in both, sobbing. I hear Momma shifting out of her seat as she comes around the table, gently squeezing me, her wet cheek pressed against mine. She strokes my hair, then pulls my face toward hers, rocking me as we cry together.

"Don't cry, baby."

"I let you down," I sob. "I'm so sorry that I lied, I'm so—"

"Uh-uh." Momma grips my chin, looking at me with watery eyes. "This aint all on you. I shouldn't've pressured you into doing something you didn't want to do. I wasn't really gonna kick you out, baby. You know sometimes we say things we don't mean when we're . . . caught in the moment." Momma says this like she's ashamed.

At first I didn't understand why she would threaten to kick me out, but I kinda get it now. Maybe the thought of seeing me like this or bringing on another responsibility freaked her out.

Deep down inside, I don't think Momma would just throw me out, but I did put her in a weird situation, so it's probably all she knew to say. I once read something at school that said people use fear as a tactic to get what they want. I wonder if that's what Momma was tryna do with me. She gathers a few napkins to give to me while patting her cheeks.

"When you first told me that you was pregnant, it felt like I was living one of my worst nightmares. It's not that I don't want to see you have a child of your own one day, but all I can think of is you losing every opportunity because you're forced to do things that girls your age shouldn't have to think about. Not yet. Look, I'm gone love you and that baby regardless, but I just don't want you to miss out on all the things we've fought so hard for." Momma balls up a napkin, patting her eyes.

"I'm not gone let that happen, Momma. I'm working on seeing about graduating early and maybe even switching to doing school online, so that I don't fall behind. And me and Miguel are gonna take turns watching the baby, so you don't never have to worry about babysitting."

She raises her eyebrow, shaking her head.

"I don't know about online school, but you think you got this all figured out, huh?"

"Not all figured out, but I'm not just gone drop everything and be on welfare all my life. I'm still going to graduate with honors, and as soon as I graduate, me and Miguel will get our own spot."

At least that's what Miguel promised at first. It's a little hard to believe these days because he's been so wishy-washy, but I know he's not all cap. He told me that by the time our baby is born, he should have an apartment for us. I think it only makes sense that me and the baby move out, so that Momma can see that we really are responsible and can handle parenthood even though everyone is doubting us. Momma looks off to the side like she's not impressed.

"Erykah, you need to just focus on you and the baby's future for now," she sighs. "I'm not saying people can't change, but I don't want you getting your hopes up, thinking this boy is gone be Mr. Stand-Up Man and ends up crushing your heart. Now that I know you're having a baby in a few months, I'm a be here as much as I can to get you through this, okay?"

I just wish Momma would have a little faith that Miguel will change once the baby is here. I mean, he's never abandoned Mitzi, so why would he leave me to raise our baby alone? Mitzi is with him every weekend, and sometimes he keeps her longer if his other BM doesn't mind. I'm tempted to just gone ahead and tell her that this aint gone be his first child, but I really don't want to open up that can of worms right now.

"Yeah," I whisper.

"How far along are you?" She squints at my belly.

"Almost sixteen weeks."

"Uh-huh, and just as tiny as you wanna be. Just like I was with you. You gone blow up once you're six months. Watch." She waves her finger. "I guess we should go shopping tomorrow so you don't have to keep wearing those baggy clothes."

"Shopping? Ma, we can't afford that. I'm still tryna figure out how you made groceries."

Momma digs in her back pocket and slides a card toward me that says Nevada EBT.

"You went to the welfare office?" I look at her, puzzled.

"Didn't have no choice. My hours been so low, they told me I qualified for $550 a month in food stamps. Ms. Benita bought a hundred dollars' worth from me, and I went shopping with the rest."

The words drag out of her mouth like each one is a heavy load. I know Momma aint proud about being on welfare. She always makes a song about how she'll work twenty jobs before she asks the government for a dime, so I know her going to the welfare office must've been hard for her.

"I can start back braiding hair on the weekends, like I was before . . . all of this." I look down at my belly.

"Erykah, no. You got enough on your plate, and you don't need to be straining and stressing tryna help me out."

"But, Momma, I can at least start a savings for when the baby gets here."

Momma sighs, shifting her mouth side to side. Deep down, I can tell she doesn't want to agree, but she doesn't try to fight me.

"Only if you keep your grades up and it doesn't put no strain on you. Right now, you experiencing the light work, but I'm telling you once you get in that third trimester, you aint gone wanna do nothing but eat and sleep."

Hell, that's all I want to do now. That sleep be hittin'. Sometimes I just want to sleep in for the day.

"Did you find a good doctor yet?" she asks.

"I did, but she didn't take our insurance, so I had to be seen by Dr. Palmer, who was acting like he didn't even wanna talk to me and Miguel."

"Oh, homeboy actually was there too?" Momma leans back.

"Momma," I huff. I was hoping she'd just keep her little smart comments to herself, but between her and Kelly, I don't know who's worse.

"I mean, I'm just surprised, that's all, but if he's been helping you, I guess that's a good thing." She looks off to the side. "So does this doctor that you've been seeing specialize in high-risk pregnancies?"

"I don't know. That's a thing?" I ask.

"Erykah, when you're under eighteen, you're supposed to be seeing a specialist, not just a pregnancy and delivery doctor. Kids your age have higher risks of things like high blood pressure. Especially if you're not getting good prenatal care. We're going to be on top of that. Remember when your cousin Kiara was pregnant with the twins? She had to go to a high-risk doctor. Same with cousin Toya when she was pregnant with Julian."

I shift in my seat. No one's even mentioned any specialty doctor to me. Thank God me and Momma are having this conversation, because without her I probably wouldn't even know anything about this. I'm starting to think that Momma should be at my next visit.

"I don't think he's a high-risk doctor. He didn't say he was, but the woman behind the desk said that he was the only doctor I could see, so I just rolled with that." I shrug.

"Well, I might not be a doctor, but I know you aint supposed to be under any ol' body. I'm a try real hard to see if I can take you to your next appointment. Maybe I can even talk to somebody up there about getting you the right doctor, cause I don't like the sound of this."

I get up and come around to where Momma is sitting and give her a real tight hug. I squeeze her so hard, she's probably gonna pop. Momma plants a big kiss on my cheek, telling me again that everything's gonna be straight. I wanna believe that she's right.

"Thank you, Momma," I say, tearing up again. "For understanding me and not giving up on me. I love you."

Damn these hormones got me crying over *everything*. Last week I cried like fifty times over the most random shit. I kinda feel like I'm going crazy, but I read online that pregnancy hormones will have you moody as hell.

"And I love you." Momma holds up my chin. "I'm just glad everything is out on the table—no more secrets, Erykah. I don't care how scared you're feeling. You hear me?" Her eyes narrow in on mine.

"I hear you," I say softly. "And I promise Momma, no more secrets."

CHAPTER FOURTEEN

Kelly

My dress is fitting my body like it's purposely trying to make me look like I grabbed the wrong size. I swear it's like I should've gotten a size six instead of a four. I twist and turn in the mirror, smoothing down the silvery satin over my stomach, but deep inside I just want to throw on a hoodie and b-ball shorts and go in on some Oreo ice cream while binge-watching *Insecure*. Dressing up is not my thing, but I do look forward to it for nights like this. I don't know. This homecoming night feels so incomplete without E getting ready by my side. I always thought we'd share every high school memory together, and even though I've been looking forward to this night for the last few weeks, I know it won't be the same. Lately, I've only seen E at school—her mom is not playing. Even though E promised that she'd only go to the dance and back, Ms. Monica was still not giving in. I wish she did, though, because this is a night that we'll never get to redo.

As I scroll through Snapchat, I notice how everyone from East

Prep is turnt. The theme this year is *Casino Royale*, and everyone is looking flawless. I take a few selfies in front of my door mirror, trying to get all the best angles, but it's hard without a selfie stick. My long silver dress hugs my body as it shimmers under the light. I practice some poses in the mirror for when me and Ray take our pictures.

There's a gentle tap on my door before it slowly swings open. My mom is leaning against the doorframe, with a huge smile.

"You look beautiful, Kelaya."

When she starts using my government name, that means she's being for real. Mom wraps a black feather boa around me, still grinning.

"Mom, seriously?" I make a sour face.

If she thinks I'm wearing this tonight, she's tripping.

"What? It goes with the theme." She waves me off before pulling out her phone, aiming the three lenses my way.

I cross my arms in front of me, forcing a smile. She instructs a few more poses, before draining me with this cringy photo shoot.

"Mom, let me see those so I can delete the ugly ones before you start going crazy on social media." I reach for her phone.

My mom is already creating a Facebook post to brag about how her baby aint a baby no more. I swipe through the pics and delete at least three before handing the phone back.

"Now why would you do that? Those were cute!" She frowns, selecting more pictures.

"Not the ones you were about to post."

I shuffle through my closet and pull out the rhinestone heels that cost me almost half of my savings to get. Tryna put these bad boys on while standing is way too hard, so I plop down on the cushioned chair in front of my vanity.

"Well, when Ray gets here, I'll be taking even more, so you should probably practice some more cute poses."

"I feel like I'm a need extra practice, then," I mumble, while strapping my heels on.

"Kelly, what are you talking about now?" Mom raises her brow.

"I just don't feel . . . pretty. I wish E could've done my hair, and this shade of foundation makes me look like I have sunscreen on my face."

Mom stares at me like she's confused. Her honey-brown eyes peer into mine.

"Girl, have you lost your mind? You are damn gorgeous, and I'm not just saying that because you look like me."

She makes me smile, even though I'm trying to hold it in. People always mistake us for sisters, even though my mom is twenty-eight years older than me. She's always being told that she looks like Mary J. Blige. Mom does resemble her, except she's taller and her nose isn't pierced.

"There's nothing wrong with your makeup, and there's nothing wrong with *you*." She stands behind me with her warm hands on my shoulders, before leaning in to kiss my cheek.

"Thank you, Mom." I look up at her.

"I wish I could be there with you tonight, but I get to do that in a few months at the prom." She shrugs with a fake pout, then we both start laughing.

Yeah, I don't feel bad for my mom at all. I'm kinda glad that the other administrators are chaperoning instead. Who wants their mom at their school dance, watching them like a hawk the whole time? I mean, it's bad enough she's at school with me all day. We both need this break.

"Did you talk with your dad? I need to send him these photos." Mom starts back tapping on her phone.

"Yeah, FaceTimed him. He's not gonna be home until after the dance is over. He said he has to do inventory with the soldiers tonight, so I'm just gonna send him some pics too."

Before I can ask Mom to take a few pics with me, her phone starts ringing as usual and she's scurrying down the hall, talking administrator stuff with one of the other assistant principals.

Ray: Be there in about 15 minutes babe.

He sends a pic of himself in a pin-striped suit, his hand gripping his chin.

Me: Sex-C!

I scroll through the selfies I just took and send him the best one.

> Ray: Damn! I'm so lucky I swear.

> Me: TY babe. C U soon. Oh and be prepared for lots of pics LOL

> Ray: Bet!

After Ray learned with everyone else about E's pregnancy, he was pretty hurt that I didn't tell him, but when I explained to him why, he understood. He knows that I would never intentionally keep anything from him, especially if it's going to jeopardize our relationship.

> E: Did yall leave yet? And how come you haven't posted no pics or sent me N E?

> E: I got some good news :) :) <3

I immediately FaceTime E. She picks up on the first ring. Her rose-colored bonnet is pulled down low as she holds her phone in the air, looking comfortable as hell in her bed.

"OMG, you look bomb. Let me see your whole dress!" E sits up, holding her phone with both hands.

I reverse my camera and stand in front of the mirror, tugging at the stomach part.

"Thanks, bestie. Okay, what's the tea?"

"You were right." She sucks her teeth with a smirk.

I have no idea what she's talking about. Most of the time I'm right about everything when it comes to E. I sit back down, looking into the camera with my lips pursed.

"About?" I grin.

"I'm having a girl!"

"What? Yessss! I can't wait to start training her on the court," I tease.

E just shakes her head with a laugh.

"You gone have my baby doing layups on that little Fisher-Price hoop?" she jokes.

"You already know. But damn, E, I'm so happy for you. What did Ms. Monica say?"

"Oh my God, she's already buying way too much pink," she laughs.

"Aww. She's just excited."

"Your dress is everything," E says.

Her eyes water up a little, but I don't ask why. I know she wishes she were here with me and that she was dressed up also, as we wait to flex on everybody on campus. I wish she were here too. I wish things between us could be like they used to be.

"I'm not feelin' it. I should've got that black dress instead," I say.

"Girl." E stares at the camera. "Shut the hell up, you killin' it. You look like you could be on the cover of a magazine." She gazes into the phone with her chin in her palm.

"Really? Thanks, E. Okay, but like, be honest. Does my makeup look crazy?" I hold the phone in front of my face. E looks at the screen closer, then holds her mouth to the side like she's thinking of the right way to respond.

"I mean, it don't look cray cray. You just probably shouldn't have put so much foundation on." She nods.

"I knew it," I sigh.

"Okay, but it's an easy fix. You got concealer that's like a shade darker?" she asks.

I lift the top of my vanity and pull out a foundation stick that says DEEP MOCHA.

"Like this?" I ask.

"Yeah. Now mix that with the stuff you put on your face. Just a little bit, though, and blend it in," she instructs.

I do like she says and instantly start to see the glow in my skin returning.

"Okay, and you need some lipstick. Do the Ruby Woo color. That always goes good with silver," she says.

"Wait, how you know I got that?"

"Cause I'm always borrowing your shit, duh?"

E is always in my closet or in my makeup. Not lately because she hasn't been out much, but she probably knows my room better than I do. I slide the red lipstick over my lips and pat a few times to make it pop. It's like an instant makeover in five minutes.

"This looks so much better. Girl, I should've called you at first." I admire myself in the camera.

"Yeah, you should've."

We both laugh.

"Where are yall going after the dance?" E rests her head to the side.

She looks like she hasn't slept in days, but I know better than to mention it.

"Probably gonna go eat at Red Lobster and then chill at Ray's house, since his dad is out of town." I hold in a grin.

"Eww. Yall so nasty," E teases.

"See, you're thinking all nasty and that's not even what I'm talking about," I laugh.

"Yeah, because everyone knows that sex after a dance hits different," E says.

"E!" I cover my mouth, even though she's right. I turn my volume down a little, praying my mom didn't hear any of that.

"What? I'm just keepin' it real. At least you and your man will be together tonight. I haven't seen Miguel in like a week," she sighs.

"Damn, really? Why?"

"Work . . . his daughter . . . pretty much any excuse he can think of." She lays back down.

I'm surprised he's still communicating with her. I really wish I could just convince E to move on and stop sweating Miguel, but it's useless.

"I've been wanting to talk to you about how I've been feeling, but you've been so busy with school stuff," E says.

"I know, but I'm all ears now. What's been up?"

"I just feel overwhelmed. I wish I had more energy and help. Momma's been working more so that our insurance doesn't lapse, and I've been braiding hair on the weekends, but it's starting to affect school and I keep begging her to let me do school online but—"

Ray sends me a group pic of everyone that's in the limo. I gasp when I see KO's dress—it looks almost identical to mine. Marsaun and his date are all cuddled up in matching red fits, and Darrion has his arm wrapped around a pretty Latina girl who he met at Big TJ's party.

"Kelly, are you even listening?" E asks.

"Yeah . . . Ray just sent me this pic."

I forward it to her. She gives it a half smile.

"Everyone looks cute," she says dryly.

"And can you believe KO has on *my* dress?" I shake my head at the pic.

"Umm . . . his actually looks better," she laughs.

"Okay, so now you're team KO?" I snap, holding in my laugh. "No, but for real, I was listening and you need to stop worrying about Miguel. I read somewhere that the baby can feel everything you feel."

"For real? Damn," she says to herself. "It's just—"

Ray: I'm walking up babe.

Me: K. Be right there.

I turn my eyes back to the screen.

"Hey, E, I gotta go. Ray's here. We can talk more tomorrow. I'll try to see if my mom can drop me off at your place."

E gives me a little stank face, then forces a smile.

"Aiight. Have fun," she says.

Three
Months Later

CHAPTER FIFTEEN

Erykah

28 Weeks

Last night, I had another bad dream. I was laying in the hospital bed, having an emergency delivery, but this time Daddy was there. He was begging for the nurses to let him be with me in the room, but they kept telling him he wasn't on the emergency contact list. In the dream, I kept going in and out of consciousness, and this time I even heard the baby crying, but the nurses and the doctors were huddled around and were in a panic. I was screaming, but no one could hear me, just like in the last few dreams. But something else happened that was different. Nurse Jill was there and when the staff saw her, they let her take over. Next thing I knew, she was walking toward me, smiling, with the baby all bundled up. She rested the baby on my chest, but just when I got ready to lay eyes on the baby, someone let out a spine-chilling scream.

"Good morning, Erykah. Did you sleep okay?"

Kelly's momma is standing in the crack of the door with a large coffee mug in one hand and a bowl of something in the other. She walks over and carefully places the bowl on the nightstand. I feel like I'm getting the royal treatment with breakfast in bed. I look over, and it's a bowl of fresh grits with fluffy scrambled eggs sitting on top.

"Oh my God, thank you, Auntie."

That's what I call her when we're not at school. Since me and Kelly are practically like sisters, it only makes sense. I stir the eggs into my grits and dig in. They're lightly seasoned with pepper and sugar, and I'm surprised she remembered that I like them this way. It's been so long since I've spent the night at Kelly's, but lately me and Momma haven't been seeing eye to eye. Momma has been tripping on me about everything. She still won't let me do school online, even though I hate the way everybody looks at me and even though the school counselor said it would be the best option. She banned Miguel from coming over because he made me miss my last appointment and Momma had to pay a twenty-five-dollar fee. And even though I'm no longer on restriction, she don't ever let me go nowhere. Always talkin' about how I gotta be careful because I'm so far along with my pregnancy. I'll be seven months—twenty-eight weeks, to be exact—tomorrow, and she acts like I have some rare medical condition that forbids me from socializing. Last night our argument was so bad, I walked half a mile and took the bus to get here.

Kelly's mom sits at my feet, giving me a warm smile. I realize Kelly's nowhere to be found. We shared the bed last night. I remember Kelly waking me a few times, telling me that I was being loud, but I don't know what that was all about. Momma says I been snoring really bad, but I'm always exhausted, so how am I supposed to help that?

"How are you and the baby feeling this morning?" Mrs. Lancaster asks.

"Good. She kept kicking me last night, but I'm starting to get used to it."

"I remember those days. Surprised you got any sleep. Kelly used to be doing somersaults," she laughs. "Makes perfect sense why she still can't sit still."

I continue eating my breakfast. Before I know it, I'm scraping the bowl.

"Mom, have you seen my East Prep sweat top?" Kelly rushes into the room.

She looks over at me like she's surprised I'm still in bed and shakes her head.

"Check the dryer. I think I washed it last night," her mom says. She gives Kelly a kiss on the forehead. "I'll see you at school." She pats my foot before swishing out the room in her long sunflower-print dress.

"E, you gotta hurry up. Ray's on his way. Coach'll bench me if I'm tardy to any of my classes. You know Coach Steph don't play when it comes to her athletes setting the standard, and tonight is a big deal for me." Kelly shuffles through her closet and pulls out her favorite pair of black-and-red Jordan1s.

I'm tempted to just lay here, but I lift myself off the bed. I reach down and grab one of the outfits that's stuffed in my duffel bag. Then it hits me. I run to the bathroom, almost knocking Kelly over, and chunks of grits shoot out of my mouth. Thank God I don't miss the toilet. Yup. I'm still throwing up like hell, even though I'm way past my second trimester. Momma was able to help me find a high-risk doctor, but I still gotta go to that other doctor every month as well.

Dr. Taheri is way nicer, though. He prescribed an anti-nausea medicine for me and diagnosed me with something called hyperemesis. It's when pregnant women suffer from extreme vomiting and dehydration. More than just usual morning sickness. I've had to go to the hospital twice for emergency IV fluids because sometimes I can't even sip water. The meds have been helping, but they make me super constipated. His only other recommendation was to make a journal of the foods that trigger me the most, which aint really helping. I asked him if throwing up affects the baby, but he said that by the time I'm praying to the porcelain god, the baby has already gotten her nutrition.

"Hey, you okay?" Kelly stands at the bathroom door with her eyebrows furrowed. She looks more grossed out than concerned.

"Yeah, I'm okay." I flush everything down. "You got some bathroom cleaner?"

"Pine-Sol, under the sink." She points.

I wipe down the seat real good, then wash my hands.

"Ray's not that far," Kelly says while looking at her phone.

"Oh, okay, well, I just need to brush my teeth and do something with my hair, and I'll be ready," I say.

I squeeze through the door and head back to the room to grab my toothbrush. I brush my teeth in quick strokes, but my toothbrush hits the back of my throat and I'm throwing up all over again. I manage to gel my hair into a neat ponytail, looking somewhat decent. Kelly anxiously waits for me to wrap it up so she can finish getting ready. I sit on the cold toilet seat, watching her quickly put on a layer of foundation.

"I don't think I can do this too much longer," I mumble, rubbing my stomach.

Kelly looks at me out of the corner of her eye with the makeup sponge pressed to her cheek.

"Kelly . . . do you think I'll have to drop out?" I stare at her Paris-themed shower curtain, wishing I could take a trip there just to get some peace of mind.

Kelly pats her entire face with more makeup, opens her eyes, and stares at her reflection in the mirror.

"Drop out of what?"

"Of school."

Damn, is Kelly even listening to me?

"You mean to do online learning? You already told me about that." She waves me off.

"No, like really dropping out. What if it comes to that? All my hard work gone down the drain."

After word got out that I was pregnant, school's low-key been like hell for me. I couldn't even walk the hallways sometimes without people staring and pointing. And it's only gotten worse since returning from winter break, now that I look like I've swallowed a watermelon. Bitches is back to being ignorant, and keeping my composure aint been so easy.

It's bad enough that I can't clap back, but what's worse is what it does to me emotionally, mentally. I try to tell Momma about these things, but she just says that when people stop talking about me is when I should worry. That doesn't really help. She has no idea what it's like to be the main gossip of the day. I sometimes feel like anytime I complain about something, in the back of everyone's mind they're saying, *You shouldn't have gotten pregnant.* And right now, I'm getting the feeling that Kelly feels like I shouldn't have gotten pregnant either.

"What did the school counselor say?" Kelly continues her makeup routine.

"I mean, she said they could probably modify my schedule if I need them to, like a hybrid-type thing. Some classes online, some in person, but I don't know. I really want to finish strong, but these symptoms lately have not been coming to play." I rub my belly again.

Kelly doesn't say anything. Just continues to apply mascara to her already full lashes. I lean against the cold toilet, feeling like my words just don't matter. Why did I even say anything to begin with? Everyone is so wrapped up in their stuff and then there's me, all wrapped up in mine. Still trying to figure out how to prep for my ACTs while trying to figure out how to sleep through the night without being kicked in the ribs fifty million times. Still trying to convince myself that my situation will get better and still trying to believe that everyone hasn't given up on me.

CHAPTER SIXTEEN

Kelly

Here we go. This is like the third time Erykah has hinted about this dropping-out thing. I don't know how many times I have to convince her that she needs to just chill, but I'm getting really tired of preaching to her. I pat my face, open my eyes, and stare at my reflection in the mirror.

"E, seriously? Why are you even thinking about becoming a dropout, when you can just finish your classes online if you want? Now, can you please swoop my edges, like you do yours?"

I spray my body spray from head to toe, forgetting that Erykah's nose is probably sensitive as hell right now. She fans the scent of Moonlight Mist and sucks her teeth. She's feeling some type of way since I'm not entertaining her ridiculous idea, I guess. I heard exactly what she said, but I'm tired of hearing it. Maybe if I ignore her, she'll chill out with all this high-school dropout mess. She reaches over me and pulls a toothbrush and a small black jar from the drawer. The bristles are stained brown from being dipped in Pro Styl gel a million times. The goop inside the jar looks like gelled coffee, but it slays my edges.

"E, we've talked about this before, and you know there's options. You've come too far to not graduate. Besides, I'm not walking across that stage without you." I look over at her.

She switches places with me, smiling to herself, then dips the toothbrush into the jar, covering the bristles with a small blob of brown goo. I sit extra still because I don't want to get stabbed in the eye like last time.

"I mean, I guess you're right. Miguel told me if I stayed at home, he'd take care of me so I wouldn't have to do as much. I can just braid from home and then when I turn eighteen, I can get my braiding license so that I can open up a little shop."

I tilt my head to the side, pausing. "Girl, Miguel can't even get you to a doctor's appointment on time."

Erykah stops gelling my edges with the brush flat on my temple. "Wow. That's how you feel?"

She takes a step back, holding the toothbrush in her hand. I don't say anything, hoping she'll finish up so we're ready by the time Ray gets here.

"I didn't mean it like that. Can you please finish?" I plead.

She's a little aggressive with my edges as if she really doesn't want to do them. The silence between us is making me uncomfortable.

"All done." She looks at me with her lips poked out.

Maybe I shouldn't have said that about her BD, but like, damn girl, Miguel *is* straight-up a piece of shit. Ray even said that he wouldn't trust Miguel after he sold Ray some fake Js last year, but let Erykah tell it, Miguel copped them from the Nike store on release day. I reach for my phone on the counter and text Ray that we're ready. I can only imagine how Erykah is feeling right now, and I'm trying to be patient with her, but she acts like being pregnant is the worst thing on earth. Last week, she said the same thing about dropping out. After she went through an entire box of Kleenex, I convinced her that lots of girls our age go through worse. Having this baby might be her biggest blessing. My mom always reminds me that God works in mysterious ways.

"Beyoncé's sister got pregnant at your age," I throw out there.

One thing about E, she loves her some Beyoncé, even though her mom named her after Erykah Badu. She grins, standing with the toothbrush in her hand, and places one butt cheek against the counter, looking down at me.

"And? Solange is rich," E adds.

"*And* rich people have dreams too. Solange didn't stop hers because she got pregnant, E."

E turns around with a hard sigh. She presses her thumb in the center of her baby hairs and strokes the teeth of the comb gently against them, making a beautiful swirl pattern.

"So, if I'm Solange, does that make you Beyoncé or something?" She folds her full lips, trying to hold in a laugh while moving her head side to side in the mirror.

"Umm . . . I wish." I grin.

"What? I can see you and Ray as Bey and Jay," she teases. I give her a serious stank eye, even though Ray and I are a dope-ass couple.

"Seriously, E, I want you to know that you got this. You're one of the strongest people I know. I'm not letting you drop out."

I can see her eyes watering as she puts all the hair supplies back. She shoves my makeup pouch in the drawer and stares down at the porcelain sink.

"You really think I'm gonna make it to the end of the school year? The counselor said there's an alternative high school in Henderson that's for girls like me." Her voice drifts.

Girls like who? E's making it sound like she has some rare disease that requires her to be quarantined. I raise up and plant my hands on my hips. Her tight brown eyes stare back at me with resentment.

"Girl, don't listen to that old white lady. If you transfer to an alternative school, your momma will have to drive like forty-five minutes every day just to get you there."

Her head drops to one side as her bamboo earrings dangle.

My phone buzzes in my pocket.

> Coach Steph: Just a reminder, Lady Eagles, if you get any demerits on your progress report, you will be benched for the first half of the game!

Damn. We gotta get our asses out of here because being tardy will definitely get me a demerit with Dr. Holiday's mean ass. If I'm benched for the first half of this game, I can throw *my* hoop dreams in the garbage. Tonight is probably the only shot I'll have to impress the recruiter who's coming from Howard.

Ray: Outside

"Ray's here." I bounce while stuffing my phone back into my pocket.

We head down the hall, but E makes a sudden pause in front of me, causing me to almost crash into her.

"I gotta take my prenatal." She rushes back to my room.

It seems like she's taking forever. If we don't leave like right now, I'm gonna be warming up that bench tonight.

"E, did you find them yet? The bell rings in like"—I glance at my phone again—"seventeen minutes."

All I hear is her scrambling through her bag, and I'm getting pretty impatient.

"E, c'mon." I open the front door. "I'm leaving."

Just as I rush down the driveway, E is behind me asking for the house keys so that she can lock the door. I toss them to her, then slip into Ray's car. It'll probably take Ray ten minutes to get us to school. That's *if* he's doing at least forty-five and *if* there's no crazy-ass construction going on in the streets. Ray hops out of the car so that Erykah can slide in the back seat.

He looks finer each time I see him. His short dreads are sprouted out on top of his head with a thin band holding them in place, and we have on our matching Js. We didn't even plan to match our sneakers, but that's how I know we're soul mates. I want to kiss his soft lips, but that can just wait till later. As we pull into the school's parking lot, the first bell is sounding off.

"Shit!" I say as I push open the car door.

I lean in to grab my heavy-ass gym bag. I cannot be late today. I cannot be late. Dr. Holiday could give two shits that my mom works here. She always says that she can't get in trouble for following the rules.

"Coach Steph aint gone bench you for being one minute late," E says, peeling out the back seat.

I bite my lip from saying what I want to say. I should've just left without her. E doesn't understand how important tonight is for me. The only thing she seems to care about is her life and her stupid-ass boyfriend.

"If I get a demerit, I can't start," I say, walking as fast as I can.

We make it to the inside of the school, squeezing through crowds who are acting like the bell never rang. Ray gives me a quick kiss, then heads the opposite way to his gym class. E straggles behind, barely able to keep up, but I can't wait. Her class is a few doors down from mine.

"Kelly, wait up." She waves, but I just keep power walking. I usually take the elevator with her, but today I gotta take the stairs. Just as I begin to climb them, E taps me on the shoulder.

"You're not gonna ride up with me? It's probably faster," she says, panting.

The warning bell rings.

I squeeze my eyes shut. This can't be happening. I jog up a flight of stairs, leaving E behind. She stands there, occasionally getting bumped. I can see her fist tightening like she's about to sock the next person who doesn't say excuse me. She looks at me with a pained expression, but I gotta put me first.

"E, I'm sorry. I really gotta go," I say superfast. Then I dart off toward my first-period class like my ass is on fire.

CHAPTER SEVENTEEN

Kelly

Today has been the absolute worst. Dr. Holiday marked me as late even though I barely missed the tardy bell. I'm glad she didn't make me get a late pass. Instead, she gave me a warning and said that she still has to mark it on the attendance tracker. In stats class, I could barely keep my eyes open. Effia had to bump my shoulder a few times just so Mr. Morgan didn't catch me dozing. Maybe if Erykah wasn't snoring so damn loud and waking me up all night to use the bathroom, I wouldn't be so damn tired.

I have no idea how I'm going to keep up in basketball today, but I know Coach Steph is not going to go for any excuses, especially since we're playing against a team that's undefeated tonight. Warm-ups started fifteen minutes ago, and I barely have any energy to dribble. I sneak off to the locker room to recoup for a bit. When I return, the team is practicing layups on the court. I try to blend in, but Coach Steph is no dummy.

"Lancaster. Over here. Now!"

I fall out of the line and jog over to her.

"What's up, Coach?" I breathe heavily while bent over.

Her tall figure overshadows me. She doesn't even blink. Coach used to play for the Los Angeles Sparks before she became a high school basketball coach. I would give anything to be in the WNBA one day.

"Why were you late to first period today?" She doesn't take her green eyes off me.

Damn.

"About that. See, what had happened was, my mom couldn't give us a ride this morning and—"

She holds her palm up.

"I don't wanna hear your excuses, Lancaster. I don't care about *we*. I want to know why *you*, my star player, were late. Did you not see my text this morning?"

She crosses her arms, waiting for a response. Her face is tight. A few curls are spiraled outside of her high bushy ponytail. Some of the girls call her Coach Keys for giggles, cause everyone swears she looks like Alicia Keys. She usually doesn't trip about it, but I know now would not be a good time to basically call her anything but Coach.

"Listen, Lancaster, I don't have time for this nonsense. Do you want to play tonight?"

I blink a few times, like she's asking me a trick question.

"What? Yeah, Coach, of course I do. I'm really sorry about

today. Please don't bench me. I'll do extra suicides on the court. I'll even do Rosemarie's job."

Rosemarie is our manager, aka the girl who washes all of our sweaty towels and makes sure the Gatorade container is full every game, and let me just say that she does make the best orange Gatorade. Tastes better than the bottle.

Coach takes a step forward. She stares at me for a moment, then lets out a sigh. "I've been letting you slide all week. You were late to practice three times this week. What kinda message does that send to the team? You're the freakin' captain and the girls look up to you."

Coach is right. On Monday, I had to stay late after biology to get an extension on my science project. On Tuesday, Erykah asked me to ride the bus home with her since it was raining and Miguel was a no-show. Today, I was exhausted because Erykah was making so much noise last night. I had to sleep with my headphones, just to get some rest. I know I've been slacking, but I just feel so tired all the time and my brain is all foggy.

"I'm benching you for the first quarter."

What? No. I need game time. I can't be sitting on no bench while the recruiter from my dream school is here. Coach Steph turns to walk away after she's just shattered my world to pieces.

"But, Coach—"

She turns around sharply, like she's hella annoyed.

"You wanna be benched the entire game, Lancaster?" The bass

in her tone is telling me to shake my head and get back on the court. So, that's exactly what I do.

Damn, this sucks. I want to scream, curse, and flatten this damn ball. What if the recruiter sees me riding the bench instead of killin' it on the court? If I'm gonna go to Howard, I'm gonna need some type of scholarship. My parents have made that very clear. I don't qualify for financial aid because they make "too much," and even though I can use my dad's GI Bill, it still wouldn't be enough to cover tuition, books, and my dorm.

After warm-ups, I hang out in the locker room to lace up for a game I'm not even starting in. All because I was marked tardy and wasn't even tardy. I wish I could call Ray right now, but he's probably about to start his game soon. And E is out of the question, because she's the reason I'm in this situation. I wish I could call Mom or Dad, but they're so tied up with work, I'd probably only get an answer if I text 911 first. I say a little prayer instead, praying that since my day sucked, my night will be the opposite.

The good news is, it's five minutes before the second quarter and I don't see a recruiter in sight. I mean, I could be wrong, but I know just about everybody's parents, and the rest of the people in the bleachers are kids from school and some of the players from JV. The bad news is, we're down by twelve points, and Coach Steph keeps mean-muggin' me like I'm the cause. I'm not even on the court, and whose fault is that? The girls from Desert Valley High look like giants compared to our team, and number 23 plays like she doesn't even need a team. I guess that's why she's rockin MJ's number. Not gonna lie, he was the GOAT, but once Kobe got swooped up, Michael Jordan's greatest-of-all-time status got snatched. That's why I rock the number 24. I don't think there'll ever be another player as great as the Black Mamba.

Everyone is basically just passing the ball to number 23, like she's the only one who can shoot. TBH, she probably is. I gotta give it to her, she's smooth with the ball, but not better than me. Alondra Martin lets some girl who's built like a refrigerator dribble the ball right out of her hands.

"Martin! Next time, why don't you just hand it to her?" Coach throws her hands up, then calls a time-out.

Even though I'm keeping this seat warm, I hustle over to the huddle anyways, just in case Coach comes to her senses and decides to put me in the game.

"Listen up, Lady Eagles, you need to get your freakin' heads in the game. Why are you letting them take the ball? You're practically giving them points," she says with her lips tight.

"Coach, them girls is big as hell," DeAsia Brown mutters with her hand on her hips. Rosemarie passes out cups of Gatorade, while Coach continues to go in on them.

"Then the harder they fall," Coach snaps. "Stop worrying about how big they are and remember the plays we've been practicing. Put your guard up. Number 23 is their star player, and she is aggressive. Now, quit being scared and let her catch some fouls."

Everyone gives each other side eyes. Coach is trying to send our team to the ER.

"Man, when is Kelly getting some game time?" Shakeema Reynolds asks.

"When I say so," Coach huffs, making everyone's necks jerk back.

She orders everyone except for me and Alondra to get back on the court. Coach replaces Alondra with Jessica Novack, who's okay on the court, but I think she only made the team cause she's like six-three. The clock starts, with four minutes and thirty-six seconds left until the end of the quarter. I want to play so bad. I look over to my left and see the coach chatting with a woman who has to be the recruiter from Howard—her navy-and-crimson top with the Howard logo on the front kind of gives it away. Coach points my way, making it obvious that I'm benched. The woman nods, then writes something on a clipboard before focusing on the players who are on the court. It's really dope to see another young, successful Black woman doing her thing.

I sink in my chair, embarrassed that my team is now losing by fourteen points. A minute before the end of the quarter, Coach Steph stands in front of me with her hands pinned on her hips.

"I'm putting you in, Lancaster."

When I touch the court, it's like magic. It's like something mystical happens and my entire world changes. The adrenaline and anxiousness I feel on the court is not like the kind I have on the sidelines—this feeling gives me a natural euphoria that I live to experience every time my hands meet with Spalding. I call a play, and the girls take their positions. It's like our team got its mojo back, cause we damn sure need it. We're not in the lead yet, but we've scored a few points, so we're no longer sinking like the *Titanic*.

With two minutes on the clock and four points needed to win, I'm praying to the hoop gods that we bag this one. As I dribble up the court, I quickly pass the ball to Jessica, who is wide open. She takes a shot, but the ball barely hits the rim before bouncing back on the squeaky floor. Luckily, Shakeema rebounds it, passes it to me, and I go for a three. It's like we're in slow motion the way the ball rolls in the air toward the hoop. It slowly spins around the rim, before dropping through—we're tied. The crowd roars as the scoreboard changes. We got a minute and fifteen seconds to win this game. Offense starts to head toward the other side of the court, and of course, one of their players tries to shoot a three like me, but it's a straight miss. As soon as the ball tips over, it lands into my hands. Forty-five seconds. Coach calls a time-out. Basically, she wants us to win this game, or we'll be running so many laps next week, people will think we're auditioning for NASCAR. That was her exact words too. After we yell "Lady Eagles," I scan the gym for the recruiter. She's posted right next to Coach Steph, analyzing my every move.

I weave the ball through two girls, who do their best to block me. I've got two options. Go for another three or pass the ball to Jessica, who's more open than the Pacific Ocean. *C'mon, Kelly. Make a choice. Don't let your team down.*

"Let's go, Lancaster! Take it home for the win!" Coach Steph yells.

I seriously feel like my heart is pounding harder than I'm pounding this ball on the court, and my stomach is starting to get hecka queasy, but I can't stop now.

Ten seconds left on the clock.

I take a chance.

Maybe one that I'll regret. Maybe not.

I let the ball fly over number 23's head. Jessica catches it and goes for a layup. The ball circles around the rim like it's scared to fall through the hoop. I could've gone for the win myself, but homegirl was wide open.

Buzzzzzzzzzzz!

Game over.

Lady Panthers: 55.

Lady Eagles: 57.

The locker room is lit, and all praises are going to *moi*, of course. Coach Steph stands in the doorway of her office, looking directly at me.

"I got somebody who wants to meet you, Lancaster." She waves me over.

I shoot up and go straight to her office. All eyes are on me as I weave around the lockers with Coach. A few of my teammates give me smiles, with hopeful looks in their eyes. The recruiter is standing next to Coach's desk with her hand extended.

"Nice to meet you, Kelly. I'm Coach Mya Van Ness. I heard

your heart is set on being a Bison. Coach Stephanie has said some good things about you, and that means a lot coming from this grouch," she says with a laugh.

Coach Steph's cheeks blush.

Her voice isn't as deep as Coach's, but I can tell by her crisp tone that she means business. I laugh to myself, looking down, and notice she has on some fresh red-and-black Jordan 1s. Ayeee! Okay, she's got swag *and* coaches my favorite college team? This must be destiny.

"Nice to meet you. Coach Steph has been a true mentor, so thank you and yes, I'm hoping to play for Howard. It's my first choice."

My nervousness is creeping all through my veins and inside my stomach. I feel like I need to go to the bathroom, but I don't want to be rude. I probably should sit my ass down since I'm feeling exhausted as hell, but I don't want Coach Van Ness to think I don't have stamina.

"What's your second choice?" she asks.

"Oh . . . umm . . . I've kinda always had my heart set on Howard, but I also plan to apply to a few other colleges," I say, while rubbing my sweaty palms against the sides of my shorts. I'm starting to feel a little dizzy.

Coach Steph furrows her eyebrows at me. "Lancaster, are you okay? You look a little flushed." She tosses me a water bottle from behind her desk. I take a few gulps, then brush things off with a smile.

"I'm good. Just leftover adrenaline from the win tonight." I try to laugh it off.

Coach Van Ness exchanges a look with Coach, then leans against her desk with one shoe crossed in front of the other.

"I've watched a few YouTube videos of your past games, and you're pretty nice on the court. I could tell you were nervous tonight, but still quite impressive. I admire your leadership on the court," Coach Van Ness says.

Coach Steph nods in agreement.

I fix my mouth to say *thank you*, but I feel a wave of nausea come over me suddenly. Beads of sweat start forming on my forehead, and I feel like I can't control whatever it is inside of me that's determined to ruin this moment.

I brace myself, flattening my palm against the cold brick wall.

Coach Steph rises from her chair, walking toward me.

"Kelly, are you okay?" Coach Van Ness asks.

The room starts spinning and before I know it, I'm blowing chunks all over my Js. I'm throwing up worse than E when she was lighting up my bathroom this morning.

I've been feeling fine all day, and I barely finished my leftover ramen before the game, so why am I throwing it up? It has to be nerves. Just all the emotions of winning tonight's game and meeting the head coach from Howard.

A few of my teammates rush in to make sure I'm okay. Shakeema hands me a bottle of water.

"Here, girl. You gone be okay?" Shakeema tilts her head.

I grab the water and take a sip, mentally doing the math. The only other thing I can think of is . . . but that can't be possible. The last time I had my period was right before winter break, which was more than five weeks ago . . . which means I'm a week late. And I am never late. But I'm on the pill, so it *has* to be something else.

Another one of the girls hands me a towel, and I wipe vomit from the edges of my mouth as tears start flowing down my cheeks. The more I think about it, the more I'm starting to think that my biggest fear might be coming true. I honestly couldn't imagine today getting any worse, but this just put the icing on the cake.

"I think she's just played a little too hard tonight. You remember how burned out we'd be from intense games back in the day," I hear Coach Steph say to Coach Van Ness.

But I don't hear Coach Van Ness's response. I hear Shakeema telling the other girls to give me some space. I hear my stomach growling at me. I hear my heart pounding. I hear my subconscious telling me that this wasn't supposed to happen.

Coach Van Ness tells me she hopes I feel better and that I should get some rest tonight. She's looking at me like how I looked at E, when she was kneeling against the toilet gripping the bowl this morning: disgusted and confused. I run out of Coach's office and lock myself in a stall in the nearby bathroom, bawling uncontrollably into my jersey.

twenty-eight-week appointment, Dr. Taheri said that I should be counting her kicks each day; he said I should feel at least ten per hour. Sometimes I feel way more. By the end of the school day, I've usually counted around sixty-five kicks, but today baby girl has been real chill. It's probably no big deal since I haven't had a big meal, but I'm gonna mention it to Dr. Taheri when I see him.

The school's parking lot is almost empty, and I'm starting to get cold. This thin-ass jacket aint giving, plus these heavy clouds are blocking any chance of sunlight. I'm just praying it doesn't start to rain. I got thirty-three minutes to get to my appointment, and I'm praying Miguel don't make me late for yet another one. He should've been here five minutes ago, and he's not responding to any of my texts. I try not to get too anxious and decide to scroll through Pinterest to look at baby shower themes. Kelly put me on game with this app. It has ideas for everything. I even use it to look for hair-braiding tips sometimes. Momma's been on my head about throwing a baby shower, since I've only got two months before the baby arrives. There's a nice banquet hall on Lynwood Boulevard that would be perfect, but the owner says I have to put down a three-hundred-dollar deposit and only get half back if everything is cleaned and there's no damage. Kelly's mom said we could just use their church's banquet hall, but I really don't want to be around bougie church folks who are just gonna whisper behind my back. I get enough of that on a daily basis. Like at lunch, the cafeteria lady tried to tell me that I shouldn't eat the ham sandwich because it's not safe for pregnancy. I don't remember asking her opinion, and I'm tired of hearing about all these things I can't do. We'll probably end up having the shower in the park. I know Momma'll be down because parks are free.

Ten minutes have gone by, and I'm still being left on read by Miguel. I button my jean jacket and wrap my arms around my body to keep warm. I can't call Momma, because she's at work and there's no way she can make it to me in time. The only other person I could ask is Kelly, but she's been mad distant lately. To be honest, we haven't really talked or hung out much. First of all, I don't even know what her deal is. And she's been hanging with that Effia girl a lot too. I'm not being a hater or anything, but still. I was gonna try and sit with Kelly at lunch today, but her, Effia, and Ray were laughing with their phones, having a good ol' time, reminding me of how *we* used to be. It's not like Kelly has completely turned her back on me, but things feel . . . different. Every now and again, she'll send me funny videos from Pregnancy TikTok. She sent me one last week that was a video of a social media influencer who's a single mom. She was giving a tour of this brand-new house she just bought. It was so dope. I aint even gone front, watching her story low-key inspired me, but I know it'll be a miracle if I can just make it out of the Heights. I miss talking late at night with Kelly, spending the night at each other's spots on the weekends, and sneaking off to parties. I hella miss my best friend. It really feels like she's fading away. Lately, I've been seeing her drive her parents' other car to school, but as I scan this dead-ass parking lot, all I see is two school vans, a few cars that look like they belong to teachers . . . and Blaise Hamilton, who is headed straight toward me.

What the fuck does she want?

"Hey . . . umm, can we talk?" Blaise asks.

She waits for me to answer. I don't get up from the bench; I just stare at her dumb ass, while I debate whether I want to slap her or hear her out.

"Talk." I suck my teeth.

"I just wanted to tell you that I'm sorry for telling everyone that you're preggo." She plays with a few long braids that are hanging from her shoulder. "I thought they all knew."

Oh, now you wanna say sorry? Girl, get the fuck out of my face. For real. If I didn't have friends who care about me, her messy ass could've really caused some damage to my reputation. I press my eyes shut, fighting back the urge to smack the shimmery highlight off her cheek, but then I remember that me being mad at Blaise is really not worth it. People were bound to find out.

"Well, nobody knew until you went running your mouth. I aint the one to be holding grudges, so it is what it is, but I hope you don't think I'm finna be cool with you now or something."

She shakes her head with her palm up.

"No, I wasn't even thinking all of that," she says. "I know it was so messed up the way it happened, and I shouldn't have said shit."

There's a beat.

"KO's been on my ass about apologizing. I was waiting for the right time to do it. I know you might be all hormonal and stuff. When my sister was pregnant, she was bitchy all the time," she says with a shrug.

I knew her ass wasn't being sincere. Makes sense now why she decided to be "the bigger person." KO *is* a really good friend. I know he was hurt to find out the way he did, but to be fair, my own momma didn't even know the truth. Once I explained everything to him, he wasn't trippin', but he truly is a real one. He probably told Blaise that he wasn't gone be cool with her until she said sorry. Receiving an apology from her is the last thing I would've expected, but I honestly don't care about her or her stupid apology.

"I'm not upset. I've got bigger things to worry about than to be keeping up with all the rumors people are spreading about me."

Instead of watching her swing from side to side in her extra-short pleated skirt, I pull out my phone again to see if Miguel has texted back.

"So, was that all you wanted?" I ask with my phone in the air.

Blaise opens her mouth to say something else, but a shiny Mercedes SUV slowly pulls up like we're in a rap video. That's definitely not Miguel, even though I wish it was. That would be something for Blaise to run back and tell everybody, that Erykah's boyfriend is a baller and makes sure she don't walk home, but Blaise is a hater, so if that were true, she'd probably keep it to herself. Blaise swings her MCM backpack over her shoulder, then jogs toward the car. The tinted passenger window rolls down and a woman who looks like an older version of Blaise is waving at her from the driver's seat with a rock so big on her finger, it's blinding me. Blaise slides in, and I notice the woman is asking something while nodding in my direction. Probably wants to know if I'm the pregnant girl on campus and if the rumors are true. East Prep is not a school for girls like me. I doubt I'm the first to ever get pregnant, or maybe I'm the first to openly be pregnant. People send their kids to this school because it's the "crème de la crème," as my French teacher would say. But lately, it's like I'm the school's latest attraction. Lynwood Heights' latest attraction. Blaise looks at me like she wants to say bye, but instead she leans back in her comfy seat, and I watch as the window slowly slides back up.

It's almost three p.m. and Miguel still aint here. I try to call him one more time, but again, it just goes to voicemail. My only other option is to take the bus. All I have on me is five dollars, which is exactly how much I'll need for a round trip. The nearest stop is across the street, so I slip my book bag on and join the people waiting. The bench is filled, so I stand against a lightpost. I can't help but feel like shit right now. I pull out my phone and send Miguel a long-ass text to tell him how fuckin' sorry he is. As the words come to my mind, tears start to fall. I don't want nobody to see me crying, cause I don't feel like explaining. It'll just make me feel ten times worse. I lean against the ice-cold pole, wiping my tears with my sleeve. How could someone be like this to the mother of their child? I just want to rip my heart out, but it no longer belongs only to me, and as much as I want to just let my eyes drain all the hurt I have inside of me, I've got to bear the pain with the hope that our child will never have to.

"You bout ready to have that baby?" a husky voice asks.

It's a woman sitting on the bench.

"Yeah, but I still got two more months," I sniffle.

She squints at me. "What you having, twins?" Her laugh sounds like she smokes ten packs of Newports a day.

I shake my head with a faint smile, trying to see if the bus is almost here.

"Here, chile, come sit down. I need to get my blood circulating anyways." She stands up from the metal bench and trades me places. I whisper a thank-you as I wait patiently with everyone else. A few minutes later the bus arrives. Everyone lets me get on first, and there's even a seat in front with my name on it. It would be nice if people at school were this nice, hell, if my best friend was too. It's crazy how a bunch of strangers seem to care, but the people who I thought would never turn their backs on me don't seem to care at all.

I get to Dr. Taheri's office just in time. The receptionist calls me back, then asks me to step on the scale. I've gained a few pounds since my last visit. I've been trying to ignore the fact that my ankles look like cans of busted biscuits or that I sometimes can't fit in my shoes. I know you gain weight while pregnant, but I didn't think I'd be gaining this much. I've already gained twenty-five pounds and I still have two more months to go.

"Have you been experiencing any unusual symptoms?" the nurse asks while helping me climb onto the reclining chair. Badges dangle from the Golden Knights lanyard she's wearing. One of them says CAITLYNN LEFEUR, RN.

"I've been getting these headaches . . . and my ankles are swelling." I lift my feet to show her.

She lowers her clipboard, then thinks for a second.

"Any pain besides the headaches, like in your belly?"

"Umm, sometimes." I shrug.

"Hmm. Well, I'll let Dr. Taheri know. We don't want it to be a more serious condition."

She asks me to lift my top and then puts some jelly on my stomach.

"Do you know what you're having?" She focuses on the computer in front of her, typing rapidly.

"Yes, a girl," I say.

The staff asks me this all the time. Momma says it's so they don't accidentally share the gender with someone who doesn't want to know yet. I watch everything on the flat screen in front of me. The baby is rolled up like a little bug. She looks so comfortable inside of me.

"Is she sleeping?" I ask.

"She sure is. Babies are sometimes less bouncy during the third trimester. Do you find her to be more active in the day or night?" She motions the probe across my pelvis.

"More so in the night, but she hasn't been as active lately, so I'd say a bit of both?"

She pauses for a second. "Erykah, have you noticed any other changes, like extreme nausea and vomiting or peeing excessively?"

I thought these were all normal symptoms that women have at this stage of pregnancy, but the nurse is making me nervous with these random questions.

"I still throw up sometimes, and like I said, I get headaches, but that's about it. Why? Do you see something wrong?"

"Just want to make sure you and the baby are not at risk for anything severe, sweetie. I'm gonna have you do a urine sample, so when I'm done here, you can just try to fill one of the cups in the bathroom. There should be some on the tray as soon as you walk inside." She pats my shoulder.

She finishes up, then helps me to slide off the table. I follow her to the bathroom, feeling a little nervous, but maybe that's just routine when you're pushing thirty weeks. After I fill the cup and place it inside the metal box on the bathroom wall, I check my phone again, with hopes that Miguel has at least reached out, but nothing. There's a text from Momma, asking me if I got to my appointment okay. I text her yes, since technically I did. If she knew Miguel stood me up, she'd be pissed.

I settle back into the recliner just as Dr. Taheri taps on the door lightly, before rushing in. The nurse follows behind him, taking a seat next to the sink.

"Erykah, hello. How are you and baby?"

He goes straight to the ultrasound machine, spreads a little gel on the probe, and places it back on my stomach. His thick black eyebrows complement his tanned skin.

"We're good." I force a smile.

"Great." He starts moving the probe around, focusing carefully on the big screen. "Baby is measuring well, fluid looks good," he says to himself. He detaches the probe, then hands me a fresh towel to wipe off the gunk.

"From looking at your scans, the baby looks perfect, but I am concerned about your vitals."

He grabs his rolling chair and glides toward me with a chart in his hands.

"Is everything okay?" I ask nervously.

"Well, your blood pressure is 156 over 93, which is high, Erykah. At first I was leaning toward something called gestational hypertension, which solely means that you are experiencing high blood pressure, but there are some other factors from the labs from your last appointment with Dr. Palmer that are concerning," he says. "Plus, you have an abnormal level of protein, according to the urine sample you just provided. These are all symptoms of a condition called preeclampsia."

"I've never heard of that," I say slowly.

"It's when the mom's blood pressure and protein levels are high, which can cause damage to your organs and can be harmful to the baby. It can lead to a condition called eclampsia, which is more critical. Unfortunately, this condition is more common with adolescent mothers, so we're going to have to monitor you and baby very closely.

"I'm sending you home with this blood pressure cuff—we'll show you how to use it. You'll need to measure your blood pressure sitting and calm three times every day. Call if you have two readings in a row that are over 140/90 or if you have severe headaches, bad swelling, or any spots in your vision."

It's like I heard everything Dr. Taheri just said, but I can't make sense of it. Did I do this to my baby? I can feel tears forming again in my eyes. I try to blink them away, but they fall down my cheeks.

"Is my baby going to be okay?" I ask.

The nurse hands me a tissue, patting my back.

"I think so. Erykah, I'm not telling you this to scare you. It's best that we start a preventive plan now, so that you and your baby will both remain healthy. Sound good?" He hands me another tissue.

I pat my cheeks, but I can't look into his eyes. I'm devastated at what he's telling me. How did this even happen? I thought people get high blood pressure because they eat too much salt or because they're old, not because they're having a baby.

"Am I gonna have to be on medication?" I ask.

"For now, I think we can avoid meds and focus more on your nutrition and activity throughout the day. We'll have to take more precautions, and you'll have to come in more often."

"So, what kinds of foods am I allowed to eat?" I ask.

"You can still enjoy a lot of your favorite foods. You just might have to learn to make them at home."

"My mom's a pretty good cook. We don't go out to eat that much."

"That's good. My suggestion is that you avoid eating food high in sodium or adding salt to your meals. Burgers, tacos, and even chicken nuggets are okay, but instead of eating fried foods, try baking them and season your food with a salt substitute. I would also avoid sodas, though you can have flavored sparkling water. You also want to avoid anything high in caffeine, because it spikes the heart rate."

So, basically I have to eat like I don't have taste buds. I guess I don't have much of a choice, but this is gonna be so hard, when I'm craving junk food all the time.

"Now, let's talk about school," Dr. Taheri says.

"What about school?" My voice shakes.

The doctor sets his clipboard down and scoots a little closer.

"Erykah, I know school's *really* important right now, and I know you don't want anything to interfere with your education. But I need to put you on bed rest until we can get your blood pressure under control. That means you have to rest a lot, though you should still walk around and move at home so that you don't get a blood clot. At least a few weeks."

Damn, this is more serious than I thought. I press my body into the soft leather recliner and stretch my legs, trying to loosen the stiff muscles. I can feel my anxiety rising. This can't be happening. Maybe I'm just having another bad dream, but I know that all Dr. Taheri is saying is very real.

"Do you think you can take a couple weeks off from school without getting too far behind?" he asks.

"I can try. It's just, my mom's not gonna like this," I mumble.

"Understandable, but I don't think she'd like to see you and the baby at risk. If we don't start treating this now, it can turn into something very serious. Eclampsia can lead to a premature birth or death." He folds his lips. The nurse nods her head, agreeing.

"How is this happening? Is it something I've been doing wrong?" I lift myself up.

"No, no," he says. "There are things that put you at risk, but those aren't things that you can help. Do you know anyone in your family who has high blood pressure?"

"Not that I can think of," I say.

I honestly don't know, because Momma and Jayden are the only family I have. If my dad has high blood pressure, there'd be no way for me to know.

"Well, that's okay. There are other factors too."

"Like what?" I ask.

"Well, these types of conditions are more likely to affect African American women, patients under eighteen, or patients whose families have a history of hypertension."

Dang. I never knew all these things could happen to me. I thought being pregnant was just that, like the girls in the magazines who have beautiful round stomachs and no stretch marks, or the actresses on TV who don't even crave weird shit like I do. Now I'm being told that if things don't get better, me and my baby could die?

"So what do I gotta do? Stay in bed 24/7?" I ask shyly.

"No, not quite," he chuckles. "You will have to take it easy, though. Light activities, not too much time on your feet, and most importantly, watch your diet. I know cravings are hard to fight, but no more junk food, especially foods that are high in salt," he warns. "I'm going to give you a handbook that will give you more info about preeclampsia. It has some great recipes and tips that may help. I can even refer you to a dietician if you'd like. Let's start with two weeks of bed rest to see if things improve. If you start to feel dizzy, have any unusual pain, or don't feel the baby moving as much as you normally do, especially when you're resting, I want you to go to the ER, okay?"

"I will," I say.

"Don't worry, Erykah. I believe that you will be able to overcome this. You're a smart, strong-minded young lady. You've got this." He smiles.

"Thank you." My voice cracks.

Dr. Taheri and the nurse leave the room so that I can clean the rest of the gel from my stomach and get dressed. When Nurse Caitlynn returns, she helps me to get down, then tells me to wait in the front for the papers about my new condition. A few minutes later, she brings me a thick packet and tells me to remember to have Momma give the school my doctor's note. She reminds me again that I need to take it very easy and not to eat anything that may raise my blood pressure. I zip up my coat and roll the papers up, struggling to fit them in my book bag. The fact that me and my baby are at risk isn't sitting well with me. I feel so scared right now, but the best thing for me to do is hurry home so at least Momma can calm me down.

As soon as I push the heavy glass door open, a disrespectful gust of coldness whips my face. It'll take two buses for me to get home, and if the bus is delayed at all, Momma might beat me getting there. But I have to get home before her, so she won't know that Miguel didn't show. Just as I start walking toward the stop, I see a bus approaching. I try to walk faster, but there's no way in hell I'm going to catch it. I definitely can't wait for the next one, and calling an Uber is out of the question. I've pretty much given up on reaching out to Miguel, and I don't know anyone else with a car who'd be willing to take me home, except for one person. I struggle to catch my breath from my little power walk, so I take a pause, then dig in my pocket for my phone. I stare at my screensaver for a minute. It's a pic of me and Miguel, hugged up at the fair from last year. I would've never imagined he'd ever leave me hanging. I brush a tear from my cheek, then swipe up to unlock my phone screen. My gut is telling me to call my best friend, tell her that I need her more than anything right now. More tears fall from my eyes. I take a deep breath, inhaling the harsh, cold air. *Stop being stubborn and call her, E.* I don't know why I'm so apprehensive about calling Kelly, but I swallow my pride and do it anyway.

CHAPTER NINETEEN

Kelly

I stare at the two examples on the wrinkled paper that's sprawled on top of my bed, analyzing the difference between a negative and a positive pregnancy test. Of all the tests I've studied for in my life, I've never wanted to fail one this badly. I run my finger across the results section of the pamphlet: *The control line is designed to validate the test and should be crisp and clear in intensity against the white background.* I take a deep breath before flipping over the white stick that is lying flat on the edge of my vanity. My hand trembles the closer it gets to the stick. Before I flip it over, I pause to glance at the pictures of me and Ray that surround the edges of my vanity's mirror. My favorite is the one of him and me at the county fair. We rode every single ride without getting sick, and Ray even won me this huge Hello Kitty at the water-gun-race booth. Right below that pic is one of me and E. A selfie of us, the first day of sophomore year. She braided our hair in two thick French braids with zigzag parts, so we could look like twins. In the picture, she's squeezing me so tight around my shoulders, with her bright grin.

I never thought we'd ever drift apart.

I never thought this day would come.

I never thought I'd be doing this alone.

I flip the pregnancy test over. I can feel a warmth rushing through my veins that causes my heart to beat rapidly.

Weird.

I can't tell if the test says positive or not. The results control line is hella faint, not a bold line like the instructions say it should be. Maybe that's a negative? Maybe I'm in the clear. I reach for the manual and read it one more time just to be sure. I look at the picture of the positive pregnancy test on it and back at my test. There's a section in the manual that says, *Invalid Result: If there is no visible control line, discard the test. Repeat test with a new device.*

Except I don't have another device to take. I crumple the manual, gather the pregnancy test, and wrap it in the black plastic bag the man from the mini-mart gave me. This damn test was fifteen dollars and I had to drive hella far just to get one. I couldn't buy it at a local store in the Heights because word would've gotten back to my parents for sure that I was in the store buying a pregnancy test. I grab the car keys that are at the edge of my dresser. I've got to retest. I can't keep letting this anxiety eat me up inside, wondering if I'm pregnant or not.

Before I can reach for my knob, my door slowly swings open. I quickly hide the bag behind me.

"Kelly, you hungry? I'm gonna run to Pop's and grab a cheesesteak sandwich. Mom will be home a bit late, so I figured I'd get us something for dinner." Dad is standing in my doorway with his Air Force uniform on.

Cheesesteak sounds so good right about now.

"Sure, Dad. Get me one with extra peppers and an extra side of cheddar cheese for the fries."

I can't stop rocking from side to side. Dad arches his brow.

"Are you okay, baby girl?"

"Yeah, I'm fine." I shrug.

He steps inside my room and softly closes the door behind him. My heart starts racing. *Please do not ask to look inside this bag.*

"Kelly, are you sure? What's that you're hiding?" He cranes his neck.

I can't fix my mouth to move, not even the slightest. I feel my hands starting to sweat as they shake.

Quick, Kelly. Think of something. Do not let him look inside of the bag.

"I'm . . . it's a tampon. I was just gonna throw it away," I say quickly.

Dad takes a step back with his palms up.

"Oh, TMI," he laughs. "I'm sorry for putting you on the spot." He walks toward me and reaches for a hug.

"It's okay, Dad," I say as I drop the bag on my thick comforter.

I squeeze him tight, longing for some form of compassion. It seems like I barely get to see Dad unless he's on his way to work or to bed. I haven't really made myself available either. In fact, I've been purposely ghosting him and Mom. Not like locking myself in the room, but spending more time in the gym and studying more than I probably need to. If I stay on routine, no one will know that something's up. Then soon, this will all be over, and my life will be back to normal.

"I know I've been working a lot, but I promise we'll spend more time together soon. I heard there's a new laser tag place in the mall. Maybe we can try it out."

"Yeah, that sounds cool," I say.

"Well, I'll let you take care of that, and I'm gonna go grab us some grub." He pats his stomach.

"K, Dad. I'm gonna run to the store and get some more tampons, but I'll be right back."

"Sure you don't want me to grab you some? It's not my favorite thing to do, but I've done it for your momma so many times, I'm immune," he laughs.

"Umm . . . no, Dad. I've got this." I make a face.

Cringe moment for sure.

Soon as he shuts the door, I plop onto my mattress, letting out the biggest sigh of relief. That could've gone bad really fast, but luckily for me, Dad's not as nosy as my mom can be. From now on I need to be super careful.

* * * *

The cashier scans the few items I picked up: a pack of gel pens, edge control, and another pregnancy test. I decided to risk going to a CVS that's right outside of the Heights, with the hope that I don't get caught.

"Sorry. We're outta the small ones," the cashier says, holding up a large bag.

I give a quick smile, while I shove my card into the chip reader. There's only one person behind me, a man in a city worker uniform with a pack of wipes and formula in his hands. *Universe, I do not need this sign right now.* I tap repeatedly on the card reader screen, which is asking me a million questions just to approve my purchase.

No, I don't want to donate to the Lynwood Heights basketball league.

I don't want cash back.

I don't want to receive a paper receipt.

I just want to get the hell out of here, take this test, and be relieved of my anxiety.

"Here ya go, hon. Have a good day." She hands me my bag.

I quickly grab it, readjust my hoodie, then power walk through the double doors. It's overcast, and I hate driving in the rain, so I hurry and take everything out of the bag. I stuff the test and the rest of the things into my purse and toss the bag into a nearby trash can. As soon as I start the ignition, my phone chimes.

E: Hey, Kelz, R U busy?

E hasn't texted me in a few days. I arch my eyebrow, rereading the text. As a matter of fact, I am, but I can't text that.

> Me: Just omw home from the store. Everything str8?

> E: I just finished my appointment and I'm scared. Was wondering if U can pick me up? Momma's not off for another hour. Miguel's not answering. I'm really freaking out.

I want to scream into the phone so bad and tell E to just drop his ass, but I don't have the energy to even go there. I really need to get home and take this test, but I can't just leave my best friend stranded.

> Me: Scared about what? Are yall okay?

> E: IDK ;/

> Me: I just gotta hurry back home but I can come. Send me your location.

> E: Ok, sending now.

Me: Got it. OMW.

E: Thanks. 143.

Me: 143

My heart melts a little after I read E's last text. Those three numbers symbolize so much. Love. Loyalty. Trust. Friendship. Makes me grateful that I have a true friend who loves me no matter what. I wish I could tell her that I'm scared too.

CHAPTER TWENTY

Kelly

As soon as I find a place to park, I pull out my phone to let E know that I'm outside. There's a text from Dad saying for me not to get back too late. Once I step into the building, there's E, sunken in a chair with her head down. She sees me come in, and instantly, she starts to cry, her shoulders heaving.

"E, what's wrong?" I kneel in front of her.

She lifts her head, streams of tears running down her face.

"I just wish this wasn't happening. I wish I could just go back in time, Kelly. This is all my fault. It's all my fault," she chokes.

"Wha-what's all your fault, E? What happened? Is the baby okay?"

She looks at me, lips trembling. Her face is so dull, it's almost unrecognizable.

"They talking bout I can't go back to school and that I gotta take it easy and if I start bleeding to call 9-1-1," she says between sobs.

"Who said that? Why would you need to call 9-1-1?"

I sit beside E and place my arm around her shaking body. She's bawling her eyes out, and it's starting to freak me out. I hope there's nothing wrong with the baby, but if there was, she would've said something by now, right?

"Kelly, what if me and the baby die?"

Whoa. This is serious. I just wish E would tell me what she means, but she's so distraught, all she can do is choke on her tears.

"Is the doctor's office still open?" I ask.

"I think so," she says, wiping her nose with her sleeve.

"Wait right here."

I take the elevator to the high-risk center, making it through the door just before the nurse locks up.

"Can I help you?" she asks.

"Umm . . . my best friend is downstairs having a breakdown. Is there any way I can talk to her doctor, please?" I lace my fingers together.

"Oh, you just missed him, dear. Is your friend Erykah Smith?" She tilts her head.

"Yes. She said something about having to quit school and dying?"

The nurse furrows her brows.

"Oh my, do you want me to speak with her?"

"I just need to know that she's okay. She won't tell me what's wrong."

"I understand, but per HIPAA guidelines, I can't discuss her medical history with you unless she gives permission."

Shit. I was hoping she wouldn't hit me with no regulation bullshit. I'm pretty sure E put me on her emergency contact list, so that should at least count for something, but the nurse says that it's not the same thing.

"Well, she's downstairs. Can I just call her? I'm sure she'll agree. We've been best friends since third grade," I say.

The nurse gives a warm smile and nods. "Have her come up so that she can give her consent in person."

I walk to a corner of the office to text E.

> Me: Hey, can you come up here so that I can talk to the nurse? She says she needs your permission.

> E: K

A couple of minutes later, E slides through the door, eyes heavy and red. She carefully takes a seat beside me, then tells the nurse that it's okay to discuss her complications with me. Turns out E and the baby are fine for now, but her condition is not to be taken lightly. To be honest, I've never even heard of preeclampsia or eclampsia, and if I were E, I'd be scared too. The nurse said that if she shows some improvement in the next couple of weeks, she'll be able to go back to school and can still have a vaginal birth. I ask a bunch of questions for clarity, and as E listens to the nurse's answers, she starts to seem calmer. The nurse gives her a pamphlet with more information, as well as her cell phone number in case she can't reach Dr. Taheri.

No one ever talks about the ups and downs of pregnancy much. Especially not in school. When we took sex education, Mr. Mosher basically just told us to use condoms and showed us a diagram of what happens to the female body during the first through third trimesters. I mean, I guess it doesn't make sense to teach about pregnancy complications in school, but the way it's portrayed in society, you'd think that it's easy breezy.

I rise up from the plush chair so that we can head home, but I'm hit with a wave of nausea. In the last couple of weeks, it seems like I'm always queasy. "Are you okay, dear? I know that was a lot of info, but as long as Erykah takes it easy and watches her diet, she and the baby should be fine," the nurse says.

"You good, Kelz?" E lifts herself.

"Yeah. Fine. Just tired, that's all." I wave them off. "Miss, can I use your restroom?"

"Of course," the nurse says.

I hand E the car keys and tell her I'll be down in a few.

The nurse walks me to the back where the bathroom is. I hurry to the sink and splash water on my face. I stare at my reflection and take a deep breath. It has been two weeks since the recruiter came to visit and I vomited all over Coach's office. I still feel off. My body's been changing, like something's up, but I've just been pushing all of those thoughts out of my mind. *Please don't be pregnant. Please don't be pregnant.* There's such a thing as feeling pregnancy symptoms even though you aren't. It's like a trick your mind plays on you when you've missed a period. I did some research online and found out that a lot of pregnancy symptoms are similar to PMS, which is what I'm probably experiencing, and once I stop stressing and this whole pregnancy scare thing is behind me, I'll probably start my period the next day.

The nurse calls from outside the door, "Are you okay in there?"

"Yeah. I'll be right out," I say, my voice echoing.

I scramble through my purse and pull the test out of the box. The wrapper is almost impossible to tear, but I manage to get the stick out in one piece. I don't think twice before I begin taking the test again. I go through the steps and put the stick back into the box. I want to wait for the results, but I'd rather look at them at home. I snap the purse flap back into place, wash my hands, then head out.

The nurse and I enter the elevator together. There's an awkward silence between us. I wish I could just pull out the test now, but it would be weird to find out that I'm pregnant in front of a random person on an elevator.

Wait, no. I'm not pregnant.

I'm not putting that into the universe. I'm just late with my period. After this is all said and done, me and E will be laughing about how I really had a whole meltdown because I thought I slipped up. When I get to the car, I find E asleep, her seat fully reclined with her body curved. She's probably exhausted from all that she had to deal with at her appointment, plus going to school today. I don't bother to wake her. Instead, I just start the car and head toward her apartment. I drive fast, knowing that I need to look at my pregnancy test soon. I listen to the sound of the rain and E's light snoring. My mind is a wreck right now. I'm tempted to peek into my purse while the light is red, but we're almost to E's, so I don't bother. Soon as I put the car in park, her eyes pop open.

"Dang, I was asleep this whole time." She looks around like she's lost.

"Knocked out," I laugh.

She pulls her seat up, then turns to me.

"Thanks for giving me a ride and being by my side," she says. I notice that her face is more plump than usual, but it looks good on her. She reaches for her book bag that's nestled next to her foot.

"It's okay. I'm always here for you." I pause. "I know I've been distant lately, but I promise I'm gonna try to be better."

"Thanks, Kelz." She reaches across the seat and hugs me. Tears fill my eyes, and when she breaks the hug, I can see that her eyes are wet too.

"Oh my God, why am I always so emotional?" she says with a laugh.

I give E a faint smile. Lately, I've been asking myself the same thing.

"Text me if you need anything, E, and tell Ms. Monica and Jayden I said hi."

"I will."

I wave at E as she makes her way inside of her place. I would give anything to just have her by my side right now, but I feel like I need to do this on my own.

My hands are shaking as I reach for the test.

Deep breaths.

It's gonna be okay.

You're not pregnant. There's no way.

I slowly pull the test from my purse. My vision is blurry from the tears that are filling my eyes, but the result is standing out as if it's in neon letters.

Positive.

I stare at the two lines in the tiny clear window, blinking my tears away, but nothing changes.

My test is positive.

As soon as I get home, I rush to my room and lock the door behind me. A vibration from my purse startles me. It's Ray, asking if I want to go to some kickback this weekend. My heart feels like it's going to explode in my chest and my stomach is turning like a wheel right now. This can't be real. This has to be a mistake. I'm shaking so hard, the phone slips out of my hand and clanks against the floor. I hear footsteps coming toward my door, but I'm too shocked to move.

"Baby girl, you okay in there? I put your sandwich on the stove." Dad's so loud, it sounds like he's in the room with me.

"I'm fine. Just dropped my phone. Be out in a sec," I stutter.

"Okay, honey. I'm going to watch some TV." I listen as his heavy steps grow more faint. Then I hear his door close.

I start to text E, but what am I gonna say? I can't tell her like this, so I shove the phone in my pocket and pace around for a little bit.

I try to calm myself down. *Think, Kelly. What is your next move?* I pull my phone back out and do a search: *Abortion clinics near me.* Tiny red dots with stethoscopes appear all over a map of Las Vegas. I know a bunch of them are "crisis pregnancy centers" just waiting to get me in so that they can try to convince me not to have an abortion by telling me a bunch of lies. I know what they're up to; I wasn't born yesterday. I notice one in central Las Vegas, the one I'm pretty sure E told me she went to. There's no way I can call and ask her the name of that place, so I just take my chances, hoping someone will pick up.

I quickly dial while trying to hold back tears. It seems like the phone rings forever before someone finally answers. I understand why they're so busy, since some people can no longer get abortions in their state.

"Good evening, Compassionate Care Medical Office. How can I help you?"

My throat closes up. I almost hang up, but I can't.

"Hello?" the woman says.

"Yes, uhh, I've just found out that I'm pregnant and . . . I'd like to schedule an abortion."

CHAPTER TWENTY-ONE

Kelly

My appointment at the abortion clinic is three weeks from today. Thankfully, I can wait that long. I know exactly when my last period was, as well as the times Ray and I had sex, so I know I'm still in the window for getting an abortion. Still, I called other places to see if I could get in sooner, but with all the abortion bans and restrictions across the nation, women have been coming to Vegas to schedule their procedures, which is making most places not have availability for hella weeks. The receptionist said they'd contact me if there's any cancellations, but her skepticism over the phone didn't give me much hope.

I haven't told E about my pregnancy, but I can't keep it a secret anymore. I've thought about telling Ray. I *think* he'd support my decision, but what if he didn't? What if he wanted me to keep the baby? No, it's better if he doesn't know. He can tell something's up, and I've just been telling him that it's the stress of homework and basketball. I hate lying to him, but what choice do I have? I've also thought about telling my parents. I've seen the way my mom is with E, all kind and gentle and supportive. But I have no idea how she'd feel about her daughter being pregnant and having an abortion.

I feel so isolated not being able to talk to anyone, and three more weeks seems like a long time. To keep sane, I've been spending more time with E, helping her with her schoolwork and keeping her up to date with the latest tea that's been going on at East Prep. I miss having her around at school. I miss us hanging out with our friends. I miss the life we both once had. And I need to talk to my bestie about what I'm going through.

"Thanks for hangin' with me today," E says, bringing me out of my thoughts. "I know you'd rather be with Ray and them at the skating rink." E shakes some ice chips into her mouth. I munch on my ice chips too.

"It's cool. I'm not really into roller skating no way, and I heard Blaise is going to be there." I stick out my tongue. "I still can't believe she tried to give you that sorry-ass apology."

"Trick shoulda known I wasn't gone fall for that," she says, crunching more ice.

"Right?"

"It's good that you and Ray give each other space. I think it's good for couples to not be glued to each other all the time," she says while flipping through the top ten movies on Netflix.

I don't know if Ray feels that way. Lately, I've been giving him so much space, it's like we're not even together. He was really bummed about me not going out with him today, but he knows that E needs me, and for now, using that excuse gets me by. E selects the latest season of *Stranger Things*, which I've already binge-watched with Ray, but I don't tell her that.

"E?"

"Huh?" She keeps her eyes glued to the TV.

I turn to her with my legs folded like a pretzel.

Just tell her, Kelly.

She's your best friend.

She's not gonna judge you.

Damn. This is harder than I thought. Now I understand why E had a hard time being open with everyone when she first found out.

I lock my fingers together, heart beating so loud, I swear it's overpowering the TV.

"Are you okay?" E's words are in slow motion, or at least it seems that way.

I swallow the thick lump in my throat that's blocking the words I've been trying to build the courage to say.

E arches her eyebrow.

"Kelly?" E pauses the show, turning to me with the remote in her hand.

I open my mouth to speak, but it's so dry I can barely get the words to come out.

"You got any more ice?" I squint.

E gives me an odd look, like she knows that's not what I wanted to say, but she just goes along with it.

"*Yeah*, there's more ice." She slowly rises from the couch while balancing herself. "Let's go to the kitchen. I need to find something to eat anyways."

I follow behind her, invisibly kicking myself in the ass because why didn't I just tell her?

"Gimme your cup." She turns to me before opening the freezer door, letting the cold air soothe our faces a little before scooping ice into my cup.

"Thank you, ma'am." I smile while pulling out a seat at the kitchen table.

"Since when did you become an ice fanatic? You anemic?" She laughs.

I feel like there's a frog in my throat. E knows I'm not anemic, and she knows that me eating just as much ice as her *is* strange, but I just play it cool.

"Nope, just craving it, I guess."

"Craving it," she repeats with a nod, then turns back toward the fridge as she scans the inside. "Damn, there's barely anything good to eat." She rubs her belly; it's so big it's blocking my view of the inside of the fridge. She pulls out a bag of lettuce, some ranch dressing, leftover baked chicken, white bread, bologna, and a block of cheese.

All of it looks gross to me. I don't know what she plans on making with all of those ingredients. I don't want nothing slimy or anything that I have to put between bread. For some reason, bread has been giving me mad indigestion, and sometimes it just feels like it's stuck in my throat. I wish I could share this feeling with E. Maybe she could give me some tips, since she's more of the expert, but that doesn't strike me as the best way to let her know the news.

"A spicy chicken sandwich from McDonald's sounds so bomb right now," I say.

"Ooh, with some cheese and barbecue sauce, yessss! But you know I can't. Momma's been on my ass about not eating any fast food," she says with a pout.

"Hey, E, there's something—"

Jayden almost knocks me out of my chair as he zooms into the kitchen.

"Erykah, I'm hungry," he whines. "Fix me a grilled cheese sandwich."

"Umm, I'm a need for you to add 'please' to that, dude." E reaches for the cheese, mayo, and bread.

"*Please* can you fix me a grilled cheese?" he mumbles.

"Jayden, be nice. You should never piss off the person who's making your food," I say with a grin.

He gives me a toothless smile. Jayden's front teeth still haven't grown back in. I've been teasing him, telling him that if he doesn't use his manners, they'll never grow back. E says I shouldn't tell him stories, but hey, it helps him to not be so bratty.

"Kelz, you want a sandwich?"

"Nah." I frown.

"Oh, okay, guess you too good for some hood food. You can gone and get your little McDonald's." She waves her fingers.

Jayden's eyes get wide.

"I want some McDonald's." Jayden turns to me.

"Boy, no, we got food here," E snaps.

Damn, she's already sounding like somebody's momma.

"You know what? I'll take a grilled cheese," I say. Maybe since the bread will be toasty, it won't be so hard to digest.

"Me too!" Jayden yells.

"Okay, okay. I got yall," E says with a spatula in her hand.

She pulls a tub of butter from the fridge and slathers a large pan with some, then adds a chunk of mayonnaise to a few slices of bread. She carefully places thick yellow slices of cheese on the bread. The sandwiches sizzle in the frying pan, making my stomach growl. E makes a little salad for herself and heats up some chicken in the microwave. We all sit at the table because Ms. Monica don't play about eating in her living room, and even though she's not here, we still know better. Jayden scarfs down his sandwich, then turns to E, while scratching the top of his head.

"Momma said you gonna braid my hair."

"After you clean your plate and wash your hands, go get the comb, grease, and brush so I can hook you up," she says.

Jayden rinses his plate and rushes out of the kitchen. I try to finish my sandwich, but I can feel the bread sitting in my esophagus. I pick around at the crust while E cleans the chicken bones on her plate. I can feel a wave of nausea building up as I pray for this food to stay down. I push my plate away, clenching my stomach.

"You okay?" E asks in between chews. "I put too much butter, huh?"

I push my plate away. "E, I'm about to tell you something, but you gotta promise me that you won't tell a soul."

CHAPTER TWENTY-TWO

Kelly

How do I tell my best friend the truth about why I really came here in the first place? How do I tell her that all this time I've been riding her about keeping it real, but my ass can't even do the same?

"OMG!" Erykah covers her mouth with both hands. "Did you and Ray break up? That's why you've been over here so much?"

"Does that mean that Ray won't come over no more in that cool car?" Jayden says, returning with the hair supplies.

E shushes him, then turns back to me.

I ball my hand into a fist, swaying my thumb over my knuckles, trying to keep calm. Trying to keep my leg from shaking. Tears start to fill my eyes.

"Me and Ray didn't break up," I say, my voice cracking.

"Well then, what's wrong?" E pushes her plate to the side and scoots closer.

What's wrong is that I'm about to make one of the biggest

decisions of my life and I don't know how to tell the people I love. I wish this wasn't so hard to confess, but it's harder than I expected. Even though E gets me, I'm scared she won't understand why I don't want to have a baby.

"I rather not tell you in front of Jay," I say.

The pieces of my sandwich are slowly creeping back up my throat. I look between her and Jayden, but I can't hold it in anymore. I rush to the kitchen sink and cough up soggy bread and bits of cheese.

"Is Kelly sick like you?" I hear Jayden ask E.

"Go wait for us in the living room, K?" she whispers.

"Can I watch *Manga Madness* while I wait?" Jayden pleads.

"Manga what?" she asks.

"It's a new anime cartoon," I say as I clean the sink.

Manga and anime have been my thing since middle school. That's another thing that made me instantly fall in love with Ray. Sometimes we just binge-watch episodes of *Avatar: The Last Airbender* on weekends. I even went through my emo phase with him in eighth grade. E could never get into it herself, but she never judged me for it. She never judges me for anything, yet all the while I've been judging her, believing that pregnancy only happens to people who are irresponsible or who aren't at the top of their class. I actually believed that it would *never* happen to me, yet here I am, staring at my best friend, which is just like staring in the mirror. Once again, I feel like shit, but I don't want to make this seem like it's the Kelly show. Jayden leaves us in the kitchen. I pour myself a cup of water before heading back to the table.

E is trying to figure me out. She looks at me like the people on that *Wheel of Fortune* game who are trying to solve the last piece of the puzzle. When I was a kid, my granny used to make me watch it with her on the days she babysat. That and like every episode of *The Young and the Restless*.

My foot is tapping like crazy under the table as I try to find the right words to say.

"Yo, what's going on?" She reaches for my hands.

I close my eyes.

Breathe.

Then let it out.

"E, I'm pregnant."

CHAPTER TWENTY-THREE

Erykah

Whoa.

Did I just hear her correctly? I think Kelly just said that she's pregnant. *No, that's not what she just said. Yo, I'm hearing things.*

"You're what?"

"I'm . . . pregnant. I took a test last week." Kelly lowers her head. "And I need you to go somewhere with me."

Okay, I definitely heard her right, but I still can't believe what she just said. I try to process it all. Maybe Kelly is trying to pull one on me, but she hasn't cracked a smile. She just sits there, trembling a little, biting her lip. She slips her hand from mine and folds hers together instead.

"C'mon. Let's go to my room so we can talk in private."

Jayden doesn't pay us any mind as we walk past him into my room. I carefully close the door, then flop on my flimsy mattress. Kelly just stands near my dresser, hugging herself. I have so many questions going through my mind right now. I'm still having trouble believing her, but I don't think Kelly would play around with something like this.

"I thought you were on the pill?" I ask.

"I am. And I've been using the fertility tracker app. I really don't understand how I got pregnant. I was so good about tracking everything. At least, I thought I was."

Kelly is not stupid. Far from it, but the answer she just gave me was stupid as hell. I told her that no app can save you from getting pregnant. Technology is not foolproof, but let her tell it, it is.

"Kelly, it's not the app that let you down. It's a lot of work to keep track every single day and enter your info. I know you're organized, but if you're not tracking like you're supposed to, it's pretty much useless," I say.

"Well, it was working every other time."

"So, what was Ray's vibe? Is he cool with it?"

She looks away.

"I haven't told him. And I'm not going to." She sits on the bed with me and rests her chin in her hands. I'm hella surprised by this. Kelly and Ray are madly in love. They tell each other everything. I would've thought he'd be the first person she told. I mean, I didn't hesitate to tell Miguel when I found out, but maybe Kelly is telling me first cause she needs advice on how to tell Ray. I can't lie. I'm a little excited inside. I want to squeeze her and yell congrats, but I'm getting the feeling that this isn't good news for her.

"What about your parents? You gonna tell them soon?"

"Eventually." She leans back on her palms. "I'm not telling anybody right now but you. I just don't want anyone trying to convince me to do something I don't want to do."

Again, I'm thrown by this news. The reason why I didn't tell my momma was because I was scared as hell that she was gonna flip. But Kelly doesn't have those worries. I don't even think her parents could stay mad at her. Hell, they even have an extra room for the baby to sleep in, so there's no way they'd threaten to boot her out like my momma told me.

"Kelly, you know how that played out with me. You gotta tell them at some point."

"I just don't want to drop that on them right now." She raises all the way up and turns to me. "I made an appointment at that Compassionate Care place. It's three weeks from today at ten a.m. Can you come with me?"

It makes me feel good to know that Kelly is trusting in me. She could've just kept it between her and Ray. Hell, she could've told her mom at least, but she's confiding in me. I nod real fast.

"Umm, yeah. I mean, that's the day of the baby shower, but we'll just start it a little later. And make sure you get a referral to see a high-risk doctor. Momma had to put me up on game. You're gonna like Nurse Jill. She was really nice when I met her. She'll explain everything to you, and she even gives you your prenatals so you don't have to wait. I know it seems scary at first, but at least we can get through it together. Plus, our babies can grow up together."

I reach over to hug Kelly, but she's stiff as hell.

"Wait, what?" Kelly scoots back a little.

"I'm saying, I'll be here for you like you've been for me." I look at her, puzzled.

"E, I'm having an abortion."

CHAPTER TWENTY-FOUR

Kelly

"An abortion?" E says. It's like the word is new to her.

I nod.

"So, you're gonna come with me for sure to my appointment?"

"Wait. Do you even know how far along you are? Kelly, if you're scared—"

"Yeah, I am scared. Scared of my life turning upside down if I have this baby. I know this is the best decision for me. I can't have a baby right now. Later, maybe. But not right now. It'll ruin everything."

I reach for E's hand.

"Listen, I know it seems hard, but it's not as bad as you think." She stares at her feet that I notice she can't keep still. "I was hella scared at first, not gonna lie, but it feels like just yesterday I found out I was pregnant, and pretty soon I'll be holding my baby."

This is not going how I thought it would.

"I don't know, E. I just can't see myself being someone's mom right now when I'm still trying to figure out who I am. I get that you made the best decision for you—and I supported it. And now I'm asking you to support my decision and to be there for me." I cringe a little because I know I haven't really been there for her the last month.

Finally, Erykah turns to face me, and there's fight in her eyes. "So, why even tell me you're pregnant?"

"Because you're my best friend. . . ."

"I just don't think you should make this decision without Ray knowing too. That's kinda foul."

"Foul?" I laugh. "E! Did you tell Miguel first before you decided not to have an abortion?"

"Girl, that's diff—"

I hold up my palm to E. She gives me a serious eye roll.

"You wanted to keep your baby; I don't. I have a future. I got colleges looking to recruit me. I have a 4.0 GPA and parents who have high expectations. Being a baby mama in high school was never the plan for me."

Shit. I shouldn't have said that last part, but it's true. E always says that part of the reason she couldn't go through with the abortion was because this is like a second chance for her to get her family back. But that's not the case for me. If I were to have this baby, I feel like it would tear my family apart.

Erykah shifts to the side. Opens her mouth, closes it, then opens it again.

"Kelly, I have dreams too, and I work just as hard as you do in school. Just because I'm not a basketball star or in the running to be valedictorian doesn't mean that I've lowered my standards. I just couldn't come to terms with an abortion and I don't think you should either. You'd be a great mom."

"Look, I've made up my mind. I just need you to come with me to get the abortion. Can you please do that for me?"

E is looking at me like she can't understand what I'm saying.

"Nah, I can't do that." She shakes her head.

I'd rather she just slap me in the face, because those words just stung like she already did. I've been by her side this whole time, even more than her sorry-ass baby daddy, and now that I need her to support me, she doesn't want to?

"E, I've let you stay over, given you rides, helped you with school, researched things about pregnancy, and I've even lied for you. And you won't do this for me?"

"Okay, Kelly, but you're not the only one who's been by my side. You did leave me hanging for a min," she scoffs. "And you've even replaced me. If I didn't know any better, I'd think Effia was your new best friend."

"Girl, seriously? So now I'm not allowed to have friends? I'm literally at your crib almost every day."

E's head is low, like she's fighting the urge to even look at me right now.

I force myself to calm down. "I could never replace you," I say. "And I didn't leave you on purpose. . . . I . . . I was just scared. I was trying to figure out what was going on with *me*."

"Yeah, well, you were supposed to be by my side for the long run, not just a few months," she mumbles.

I can't believe how ungrateful she's being.

"That's way more than that sorry-ass clown you think is gonna be in your baby's life."

"He missed *one* appointment, Kelly." She holds up a finger. "Boo, try again."

"Yeah, and what was his reasoning for leaving you out in the freezing cold? And what about all the times he was late or didn't take your calls or left you on read? I was there for you." I'm so angry, hot tears are starting to run down my face. "If it wasn't for me, you would've had to catch the nasty-ass bus back, all alone."

"At least I know no one on that nasty-ass bus would've been betraying me." Erykah rolls her neck.

"Oh, you feel betrayed?" I clutch invisible pearls. "I was the one who rubbed your back when you were heaving over the toilet. I'm the one who stands to your defense every time somebody at school tries to talk shit. I'm asking you to be here for me, E. I can't have a baby right now. You know that. We are not the same!"

There's a beat.

"We show in the hell not." Her face is expressionless.

My chest heaving, I stand up and face her, fighting back more tears. Erykah just stares at me like she has no soul. Like she didn't hear a word I just said. Like I'm not even her best friend. I don't wait a minute longer for her to respond. I let myself out of her room, out of her crib, and out of her life.

CHAPTER TWENTY-FIVE

Kelly

It's been three weeks, and I haven't talked to or heard from E. I guess it's easier to avoid your so-called best friend when you don't have to look at them every day. I've been waiting to get a text or something from E, saying she wants to talk, but nada. Breaking up with your best friend is hard, but there's another type of breakup that's even harder: the one with your boyfriend of two years. I didn't want to do it, but I felt like I had to. Yesterday, Ray showed up with a single red rose and was looking good as ever to take me to the movies. We planned it a few days ago, but with all that's been on my mind, I completely forgot about our date. I hadn't even showered or changed from my baggy sweats from the night before. I told him I wasn't feeling good and that I thought we needed a break. The words *I just can't be in a relationship right now* stung worse than if a bee were digging its stinger into my tongue. I thought breaking it off would ease all the pressure that was on me, but I didn't think about how bad that would hurt the both of us.

"Listen, babe, if you need me to just give you some space, I can, but I aint tryna lose you," Ray pleaded with me, but I couldn't bear to keep looking into his puppy-dog eyes.

I told him I couldn't be in a relationship anymore because I really needed to focus on basketball and school. It was the only excuse I could think of. I told him that I still wanted to be friends, which almost broke me because all I want is to be with him. The hardest part was watching him drag to his car, not understanding the real reason I ended things.

I normally can eat an entire pizza on my own, but I can't even finish this slice. My abortion is scheduled for tomorrow morning, and that's really all that I can think about. I flick at the pepperonis, thinking of how everything will go when it's all said and done. I was reading one blog, and it said that the procedure is super quick, and as long as I take my meds afterwards, the bleeding shouldn't be too bad. The earlier you are in your pregnancy, the quicker the procedure can be. Since E turned on me, KO said he'd go to my appointment with me, but I didn't tell him that I was getting an abortion. I told him that I was getting an IUD and that I wasn't sure how I'd be feeling, so I needed someone to be there with me. To be honest, you don't even need a driver to take you home for something like that, but KO didn't question me or anything. My phone starts buzzing like crazy. My parents have this rule where phones aren't allowed at the dinner table, but I sneak and take a peek while Mom and Dad are in a deep conversation. Damn, five new texts. One is from Effia. One is from KO. The others are from Ray. None are from E.

> Effia: Hey. Thanks for the bio notes. If you're not busy this weekend, wanna hang?

> KO: So, do U want me to pick U up at 8:30 or 9?

> Ray: Can U please just talk to me?

> Ray: If I did something wrong, just tell me.

> Ray: I'm not tryna lose U.

I want to text Ray back so badly, but I just lay the phone flat on the table, then take a tiny bite of my pizza. Once everything is over, I'll feel so much better. Not telling Ray is not the end of the world. It's not like I need him to pay for the abortion or anything. I have enough money in my savings to pay for it. Every year, Mom and Dad give me what they call faux paychecks. Basically, it's money for making straight As and excelling in basketball.

Mom is taking sips from her wineglass as Dad goes on

about an unexpected shipment he had to help his soldiers with this week.

"They're just as lazy as they want to be. When I was an airman, I worked sixteen-hour shifts and never complained. You ask these young people to do one thing, and they're ready to get a medical discharge." He takes a huge bite of his pizza.

"The kids are like that at my job too. It seems like all they want to do is socialize. Everything is all about their phones," Mom says.

"Baby girl, you're not hungry?" Dad looks at me.

"Not really." I force a smile.

Him and Mom exchange a look, like they're not buying my excuse, but neither one of them presses the issue.

"I told you to order from the *real* pizza parlor up the street instead of this franchised mess." Dad nods at the box that's in the center of the table.

"Oh, so now it's my fault?" Mom laughs.

"Yall, the pizza is fine, okay? I'm just not hungry," I snap. My parents are both looking at me like I've lost my mind, which I have. I've never used that tone with them, and I'm ready for Dad to check me about it, but instead he just clears his throat and forces a smile.

"Well, hopefully tomorrow after I beat you in laser tag, you'll get your appetite back," Dad says.

Fuck. I forgot all about our dad-daughter thing.

"Isn't Erykah's baby shower tomorrow?" Mom dips her pizza into some ranch sauce.

I was hoping she wouldn't bring that up. Since E's not talking to me, I wasn't even planning on going. I was just going to make an excuse that I was cramping or something, which wouldn't be a lie. I'm pretty sure after the procedure, I'm not gonna feel like doing much of anything.

"Yeah, but I'm not gonna be able to go," I say.

"We can do laser tag another day, baby girl. I don't want you to miss Erykah's big moment," Dad says.

What about *my* big moment? She didn't care about being here for me when I'm about to go through the scariest time ever, so why should I break my neck to be there for her? I can feel myself getting angry. My skin feels like it's on fire.

"She'll be aiight," I mumble.

"Kelly, is something wrong?" Mom pushes her thick coils behind her ears.

I look between her and Dad.

"Actually, Dad, I can't do laser tag tomorrow either. I have practice in the morning. Coach just told us a few minutes ago," I look into his slanted brown eyes, the ones I pretty much inherited from him. He looks a bit disappointed, and now I feel hecka mad for lying to him. I know he's been looking forward to spending time together, and so have I.

"Practice?" Mom jerks her head back. "Umm, no. All the coaches were told in last week's meeting that practice on the weekends is no longer allowed, unless families are told a week in advance."

She rises from the table, irritated.

"Mom, what's the big deal? It's just for a couple of hours," I scoff.

Mom begins to walk back toward the table, tapping away on her phone.

"Well, I'm shutting that down. Coach Steph knows better." She looks at me with the phone between her hands.

Shit. She's about to text Coach Steph, and then they'll know that I'm lying about everything. I shoot up from the table, feeling my heart racing faster than ever.

"Don't text Coach Steph." I hold up my palms.

Her and Dad look at me strangely.

"Kelaya, are you being honest with us?" Dad focuses on me.

I take a deep breath. I don't want to tell them the truth, but I can't think of another lie.

"Mom, it's not that serious. You don't need to text Coach Steph," I say, my voice trembling.

She slips the phone into her jeans pocket.

"Kelaya." Mom walks closer to me. "Whatever is going on, you can tell us."

I start to blink uncontrollably, fighting the tears that are rolling down my face.

"I can't do any of those things tomorrow because . . ."

Mom kneels beside me with one hand on my thigh. She rubs softly, trying to calm me.

"Let it out, baby," she whispers to me, pulling me closer.

My tears are almost choking me, but I can't hold this in any longer.

"Because . . . I'm getting an abortion."

Mom's hand goes to her heart.

"I need to take a seat," she whispers, then slowly pulls away from me and sits back down.

Dad just sits with his hands folded under his chin. It's like my parents are paralyzed.

"How long have you known?" Mom's voice shakes. She stares straight ahead through the dining room window at the night sky that's as dark as my current mood.

"About the pregnancy? For like a month," I say.

She bites her bottom lip like she is thinking of the right words to say. The legs from her chair make a loud sound as she turns toward me. I've never seen my mom this angry. I've never gotten this much silence from my dad. I wish I didn't say anything.

"Kelaya, when I took you to get on birth control, it was made clear that it was to help regulate your periods, not for you to be sexually active. You remember when we had that conversation?" she asks.

"Yes, ma'am," I mutter.

I remember it loud and clear. I really did get on the pill for my period. But then, with Ray, I was all, why not enjoy some of the other perks? At first, in addition to me being on the pill, Ray and I always used condoms. But over time, we got more relaxed about the condoms. And if I'm being honest, I wasn't consistent about taking the pill like I should. With school, sports, and my social life combined, my mind is constantly in a million places.

But I knew better; I should have known better. I just got cocky.

"Are you sure you're not just late?" Mom asks.

"I took a test," I say.

"Do Ray's parents know about this yet?" Dad's voice cracks.

"Nobody knows, except for . . . Erykah," I say.

Mom and Dad look at each other again.

"How far along are you?" Mom asks.

"I don't know. Maybe like six or seven weeks." I shrug.

"Kelaya, this is serious. You can't just go behind our backs and get an abortion from some random place by yourself. You should've told us first," Dad says.

"I didn't want you guys to find out because I didn't want to make you mad, and I knew you'd be disappointed in me." I pick at the edge of the cream-colored tablecloth.

"We're definitely not proud," Mom says. "But, Kelly, we're not gonna let you go through something like this by yourself, baby."

I wasn't expecting Mom to say that. I was sure that my parents would be way more upset, but they seem more concerned than anything. I honestly thought my mom would be quoting scriptures right now, but I think she's just way too stunned to even go there with me.

"So, yall aren't mad?"

"Mad that you want to get an abortion? No, but we're definitely not okay with you lying and sneaking behind our backs," Dad says.

"Even if you want to keep the baby, we can work something out. I know you and Ray are young, but you don't have to get an abortion just because you're afraid of disappointing us," Mom adds.

"No, I still want an abortion. It's not about any of that. I just am not ready to have a baby," I say.

Mom sighs. Right now, they seem so mellow, it's almost scary. I was expecting for this to go way different, but I'm glad it didn't.

"What time is your appointment?" Dad asks.

"Ten a.m.," I say.

"How about me and your momma take you instead? We wouldn't feel comfortable with you going alone," Dad says.

"Really?" I say, looking up at them.

"Mm-hmm." Mom bobs her head up and down.

Mom reaches for me, and she and Dad wrap me in a big hug. I feel such a sense of relief, like all the knots in my shoulders and neck and stomach start to relax.

When I pull away from the hug, I decide to take a gamble. "Does this mean that I'm not in trouble?" I weave my fingers together.

"Oh, you're certainly not off the hook, but we'll talk about that later." Mom folds her arms.

Why'd I even ask? I should've known that was coming. After we discuss the plan for tomorrow, Mom and Dad go to get ready for bed, and I stay back to clear the table. I feel a little renewed and even manage to stomach the slice of pizza that was left on my plate. I text KO to tell him never mind about tomorrow, and as I'm doing so, a memory pops up on my phone. It's a video of me and E at the NHS field trip at Santa Monica Beach. E splashes waves on me, purposely getting my hair that I had just flat-ironed wet. Ray is in the background, cracking up as he encourages her. I watch myself snorting from laughter. For a minute, I forget I'm alone at my kitchen table and have to catch myself from responding to them. I save the video to my favorites, before slipping my phone back into my pocket. I really hope my decision doesn't prevent future memories with them, especially with E. But she has to understand that I can't do every little thing that people want me to do. Never have. I'm walking in that clinic tomorrow to do exactly what I've planned to do, for me, for sure.

CHAPTER TWENTY-SIX

Kelly

"Before we proceed, I have to ask you a series of questions. Is that okay?"

"Okay," I say.

Nurse Jill reaches for a pen that's latched to the pocket of her olive-green scrub top.

"Are you having this procedure done of your own free will?" She waits to mark the paper that's on top of the clipboard.

"Yes."

"Did anyone threaten you or the baby's life recently?"

"No."

"Did you have consensual sex prior to getting pregnant?"

"Yes."

"Do you understand that this is a permanent procedure and once it is complete you will no longer be pregnant?"

"Uh-huh." I nod.

She raises her eyebrow with a smile.

"I mean, yes."

"Do you prefer Kelly or Kelaya?" She smiles at me. I can still see the brightness of her light brown eyes.

"Kelly's fine."

"Okay, Miss Kelly, what form of birth control will you be using after the procedure?"

I look at her, dumbfounded. I don't even want to think about sex after this. I never want to be in this position again, not until I'm at least independent and done with college.

"I'll be on the pill."

She scribbles on the paper. "Just so you know, we do offer several forms of birth control. Dr. Thompson can perform an IUD procedure today, if you're interested. He's the one who will be performing your surgery. IUDs are very effective and can last from five to twelve years, though you can take it out any time you want. It can be easier than remembering to take a pill every day. You still need condoms to protect against STIs, but IUDs are very good at preventing pregnancy."

"I'm gonna try to practice celibacy for a while."

"That's okay. If you happen to change your mind, just give us a call. You may be able to get free birth control or at least receive it at a lower cost. Do you have a pretty good support system?"

"Yeah. I have my mom, dad, and . . ."

I used to have my best friend.

"That's about it," I say.

Jill comforts me with a warm smile. "The important thing

is that you're doing what's best for you. Walking through those doors isn't easy."

She stands in front of me with her hands crossed in front of the folder.

"It's just not in my plan to have a baby right now," I say.

"You don't have to provide any justification for why you want an abortion, Kelly. We're here to support you, even if you change your mind at the last minute, okay? Since you've chosen the surgical abortion instead of the medication abortion, we will have to put you under mild anesthesia. Is that okay?"

I nod. "How long will the procedure take?" I ask.

"You're just shy of eleven weeks, so the procedure itself will be about ten minutes, but you'll have to be monitored in the recovery room before you can leave. You should probably let whoever is giving you a ride home know that you may be here for at least another two hours." She flips her hand from side to side, causing her bracelets to dangle.

"Okay. Thanks," I say.

"Go ahead and change into the gown that's folded next to you. You can put your clothes in the green bag that's on the side of the exam table," she says, pointing. "I'll be back to give you your sedatives."

I put on the gown and fold my clothes neatly before stuffing them in the bag, then wait for her to return. My stomach feels like it can't handle any more anxiety. Just when I hop back on the table, my phone begins to vibrate.

Mom: Everything okay?

Me: Yes, starting soon. Just changing.

Mom: Okay. We love you.

Me: Love yall too.

I'm glad my parents understood my decision and didn't try to force me to change my mind. Having them here with me really was the best thing. Ray's probably been texting me like crazy, but I have him on DND. I just can't face him right now until everything is said and done. E was right, Nurse Jill is mad cool. At first I thought this place was gonna make me feel like a criminal, but I feel like I'm at a regular doctor's appointment. A few minutes later, Nurse Jill comes back with two pills and a cup of water.

"One is to relax you during the procedure, and the other is for the pain. You will receive mild anesthesia right before the procedure."

I take the pills, and Jill helps me off the table. I follow her to what looks like a surgery room. Two other nurses are preparing for my procedure. The one with the short brown hair helps me to relax on the bed as I stare into a bright light above my head. I can feel my pelvis tensing up. It almost feels as if I'm about to start my period.

Just then, the doctor comes in. "Kelly, I'm Dr. Thompson,

and I'll be performing your procedure today. Are you aware that you are getting an abortion?"

"Yes."

"Okay, you might be feeling some slight cramping because your cervix is dilating, but in a few minutes, Jen over there is gonna give you a mild anesthesia. Then I will perform the procedure, and you'll be able to rest in the recovery room."

I heard everything he said, but I'm so woozy all I can do is nod. My cervix feels like it's being stabbed with sharp needles. I can feel my heart racing as I slowly start to hyperventilate. *Everything is going to be okay,* I tell myself. Even though Nurse Jill said the process wouldn't be long, I feel like I've been laying here forever, and all I can think about is how I ended up here. I never thought that I'd be in a situation like this, especially not alone. A heaviness washes over me. No matter how many times I tell myself that it will be okay . . . I feel like it's not. I press my eyes shut, trying to prevent the tears from falling.

"Kelly, do you need more time to think about this?" I open my eyes to see Nurse Jill standing at my left side with a pained expression on her face.

I push myself up a little, sniffling.

"I'm just nervous about the anesthesia, that's all."

The thought of me being put to sleep does kinda freak me out.

"That's understandable. Jen is really good with the anesthesia. She'll explain everything to you about how it works. That might make you feel better."

"Okay." I nod.

Nurse Jill pauses. "Are you sure this is what you want to do, Kelly?"

When she says my first name, it lets me know how serious she is. Compassionate, yet straightforward. I take a deep breath and nod, before saying yes, too. Nurse Jill lightly pats my shoulder, and then Jen steps forward and explains to me that I'll only be asleep for about ten minutes and that she'll wake me up as soon as it's over. I look up at the smooth white ceiling, telling myself that I can do this. Dr. Jen begins the sedation process as I keep telling myself,

I'm doing the right thing.

It's going to be okay.

I know that I'm doing the right thing because my heart is telling me so. I kinda feel like I should be somewhat emotional, because I am about to lose something that has been growing inside of me. But all I feel in this moment is a sense of relief. Jill gently grabs my hand, as if she can hear my thoughts. I never thought I'd be in this position, a thought that has gone through my head like a million times since I took those pregnancy tests. Most girls my age don't either, but I know what I have to do. Maybe one day I'll reflect on the choice that I made, maybe not. What's important is that I'm 100 percent confident with my decision and I am doing what's best for my body.

CHAPTER TWENTY-SEVEN

Erykah

34 Weeks

"Erykah, baby, stand a little closer to your momma so I can get both of yall in this picture."

Ms. Benita motions for me to scoot, while she aims her phone at us. She has about twenty pink clothespins clipped all over her. She must be a baby shower OG. Every time someone says the word "baby" or crosses their arms or legs, she's been snatching their clothespin.

Momma puts her hand on my belly while leaning in with a smile. It's been cold as ever this month, so Ms. Benita helped us to reserve the clubhouse in our apartments for the baby shower. My preeclampsia has been under control for the most part. Momma's been making sure I don't eat anything that could spike my blood pressure. She wouldn't even let me put pickles on my turkey burger last week. Just a little mustard, plus all the other

veggies that I wanted. It feels like everyone in the Heights is here for my baby shower. Well, maybe not everyone, but I'm surprised at how many people showed up. Momma invited a lot of folks from her job, our apartments, and the little family we do have.

Momma announces that the cotton game is about to start. A group of my cousins I barely talk to and some women who live in our complex rush over to get started. I'm still grossed out from the last game. Everybody was given a diaper with some kinda melted chocolate in it that's supposed to look like baby poop. If you guessed what kind of chocolate bar it was, you won a prize. Let me just say that I'm praying my baby's poop never looks like a melted Snickers, because that mess looks so nasty.

I sit near a table that is lined with gift bags. I'm so grateful that the community came together to help Momma give me the best experience before I have my baby. People provided decorations and a sound system, and Mr. Ross, who owns the party rental store, even set up one of those jumping houses for the kids to play in outside. KO stopped by earlier with a large glittery bag that was heavy as hell, but he said he couldn't stay long because he's starting his new job at Forever 21 today.

I posted my invitation on social media last week for anyone who wanted to come, but not too many people my age RSVP'd, including Miguel. If he doesn't show up today, I don't think I even want him in my baby's life. As much as I hate to admit it, Kelly has been right about him all along. It would've been dope to have Kelly around. She's so competitive, I know she'd have

more clothespins than Ms. Benita and probably would have all the cotton balls scooped into that big-ass bowl Graciela, who lives two buildings down, is struggling with.

Even though the argument that me and Kelly had was the worst, I still can't help thinking about how she's going through a scary time all by herself. It was scary enough for me just to show up to the clinic, so I can only imagine what it's like to actually go through with the procedure. Maybe I should've canceled my baby shower so that I could've been with her. Maybe I *was* being insensitive. All she wanted was for me to be there, like she's been here for me. And when I really think about it, she *was* there for me. It wasn't right how I said she wasn't. My cousin Kiara is scooping a bunch of nothing into the bowl as she crawls around on the large blanket. Everyone's hyping her up, making her think she's doing something, but she's gonna be mad as hell when she sees there's only two cotton balls in the bowl.

"Tilt the bowl, KiKi! Tilt it," my cousin Resee yells.

"Now don't try to cheat." Ms. Benita places her hands on her hips. "Let her be. She's doing a good job."

She's only saying that cause Kiara aint got nothing in the bowl now. Ms. Benita is competitive as hell. Everyone starts to count down from ten, laughing and cheering. R & B songs are bumpin' from the tall speakers, the kids are having a blast, and folks keep going back for seconds and thirds of Momma's barbecue meatballs. I don't care what nobody says, but a baby shower aint complete without a pan of meatballs. Momma notices me

sitting all by myself. I hear her telling Ms. Benita to take over while she makes her way toward me.

"Erykah, what are you doing way over here? You feeling okay?" Momma's voice is calm.

Her eyes are a bright amber when she's in a good mood. She smooths her dark pink shirt that says NANA TO BE and scoots close to me.

"I'm just a li'l tired. The baby is all up on my left side, and she's killing my ribs." I rub my side.

"Well, we can start wrapping things up if you want to go home and rest. Have you heard from Kelly?"

I hesitate before giving Momma a response. I can't tell her the real reason why Kelly isn't here.

"I don't think Kelly's coming," I mumble. "She's mad at me."

Momma moves her chair closer and strokes my hair gently.

"Mad about what, baby?"

"We had a big fight and she's not even talking to me. We both said some things we shouldn't have, but . . . it's just stupid," I say under my breath.

"Well, have you tried to apologize?"

I probably should, but I don't even know what to say. I don't even think Kelly wants to hear from me. I think for a second before saying something.

"Momma, I don't think Kelly will even accept my apology."

"That's because you haven't tried."

I look outside of the sliding doors, watching Jayden and some other kids bounce in the inflated castle. It makes me think about when me and Kelly were little and how much fun we would have. Back then, we never got into fights, but lately it seems like that's all we do. I feel so lonely and empty inside. It's like I'm on a deserted island, sitting there all day, stuck. Wishing I could find a way out, but my pride is making me incapable of doing so.

"Erykah, doing the right thing aint always easy," Momma adds.

I take a deep breath. Even though now is not the time I wanted to share it, I decide that I need to tell her about Miguel's other daughter.

"Momma, I haven't told you everything about Miguel." I look down at my pink sandals.

"Everything like what?" Momma leans toward me.

"He's got a daughter. I didn't tell you because I already knew how you felt about him and I just was hoping he'd prove you wrong," I say.

Momma folds her arms, shaking her head as she stares straight ahead.

"I knew it was something about that boy, but you know what, Erykah, I don't even care. Miguel is not my child. You are. All I can do is pray that he does right by you and the baby." She pats my thigh.

I let out a sigh of relief. That went way different from what I expected, but I'm just glad that Momma knows the truth.

"Momma, do you think I did the right thing by choosing to have my baby?" I look down at my stomach.

Momma gently grabs my chin and turns my face toward hers.

"It don't matter what me or anybody else thinks. Stop looking for validation so damn much. Did you follow your heart?"

"Yeah," I say.

"Then you did the right thing."

Momma smiles so hard, her dimples sink in.

"Thank you, Momma. And you're right. I do need to fix things between Kelly and me. I just hope she'll hear me out."

"She will. Just be the loving, caring person that you already are and don't wait too long to reach out." She pokes her lips out.

"I won't," I laugh.

Momma kisses me on my cheek before starting to wrap things up.

I feel like a celebrity the way everyone is going out of their way to help out. The trunk is so filled with gifts, Momma can't even close it, so we stuff some in the back seat with Jayden. One of the women from Momma's job made a pretty pink blanket with my baby's name, Sierra, embroidered on it. At first I wanted to name her Michaela—Miguel thought it was the closest name to his— but I just don't think he deserves that honor, so I'm naming my baby after my momma instead. Sierra is Momma's middle name, and when I told Momma that's what I decided, she was so happy.

After we get home, I wipe off my makeup, take a long shower, and change into a large T-shirt. I keep thinking about what Momma said at the shower. She's right. I can't keep beefing with my best friend. I pull out my phone and dial her number, but Momma is standing halfway in my bedroom door with an irritated look on her face.

"Miguel's outside," she huffs.

I feel my body tense. I slip on some joggers and go out the front door. Miguel is standing there with a heavy down jacket and two big purple gift bags stuffed with silver tissue paper. That wasn't even the baby shower colors. He could've at least gotten that right.

"What's up?" I stuff my hands in my pockets.

"Damn, bae, you looking more and more beautiful every day." He leans in for a kiss, but I jerk back.

"How would you know? I haven't seen you since you ghosted me at my last doctor's appointment," I scoff.

"Man, I was locked up. Lita was supposed to call and tell you."

"Lita aint called and told me shit. And locked up for what?"

He sucks his teeth, then looks to the side. "Child support."

I raise my eyebrow and give him the ultimate stank face. Since when has he been paying child support? He has his daughter every week and gives his other baby momma money all the time, or so he says. I tilt my head to the side, prompting him to explain more, even though I'm pretty sure he's just making up lies. Matter of fact, I know his ass is lying.

"Trina put me on it when she found out from one of her messy-ass homegirls that you pregnant by me. I had to sit in that dumb-ass cell for almost a week." He shakes his head.

"Okay, but that still doesn't justify why I aint heard from you since then. And why didn't you come to the baby shower?" I say between claps. "You think you can just show up with some gifts, and we back good?"

Before Miguel can answer, Momma swings the door open with a look on her face.

"Erykah, you okay?"

"Fine," I say, looking dead at Miguel.

"We good, Ms. Smith," Miguel adds.

Momma rolls her eyes at him and says she'll take the bags inside. He hands them to her like he really doesn't want to give them up. I can feel the baby shifting to the other side.

"Look, I need to rest. I'm kinda tired from today," I say.

Miguel walks closer to me, wrapping his arms around my large belly.

"Bae, I'm sorry. I promise I'm a be here more from now on."

I just look off to the side with a cold expression. Kelly and my momma were both right. This fool really aint shit.

Miguel leans in for a kiss, but I stop him dead in his tracks. I'm not falling for his bullshit anymore. Him not showing up to his own daughter's celebration was him crossing the line, and usually for me, nobody crosses me once.

"Oh, so you really on that weird shit." He throws his hands up.

I shake my head at him and head for the door.

"Erykah, I said I'm sorry, damn."

I pause with my hand on the doorknob, then slightly turn. I don't know if this is the end for us, but right now I just want him outta my face.

"Bye, Miguel, and thanks for the gifts."

CHAPTER TWENTY-EIGHT

Kelly

I wake up in the recovery room, almost forgetting where I am. There's a flat-screen TV showing images of nature while playing soft music. The room is kind of dim, and there's only one other woman in the room, who looks like she's recovering too. She's balled up with a plush blanket tucked under her chin. Nurse Jill brings me a few shortbread cookies and a bottle of room-temp apple juice.

"How are you feeling?" Nurse Jill whispers.

From the looks of things, I survived. I snuggle into the soft yarn blanket that's up to my neck.

"So-so," I say.

"Any pain?"

My body does feel like it got hit by a semi. I nod at Nurse Jill with a scrunched face.

"On a scale of one to ten, how would you rate the pain?"

"A six, maybe," I moan. I try to sit up a little, but it's painful as hell. "Am I gonna be able to leave soon?"

"How about I get you some Tylenol for the pain and check back with you?" Jill kneels in front of me.

"Wait, what time is it?"

She glances at her watch.

"It's almost eleven fifteen. If you'd like, you can call your parents to let them know you're in recovery. I just need you to try and relax a little longer before I can let you go, okay, love?"

I nod while sipping on some juice.

"As long as the pain isn't getting worse, you should be able to leave soon," she assures me. "I'll bring your clothes and things and you can change in any room over there, when you feel up to it." She points across from my recliner.

"Okay, thank you."

I lean back and try to snack on a cookie. It's really over. Nurse Jill returns with my things and the Tylenol she promised and tells me she sent a prescription for some other pain meds to my local pharmacy. I swallow the two white capsules with my juice, praying that they don't take forever to kick in. Nurse Jill helps me to get settled in the dressing room, then gives me some pain medicine to take home. I stuff the brown bag in my tote and try to get back comfortable. The woman who was balled up in her recliner is now running a comb through her short blond pixie cut. She looks over at me and smiles. I smile back, trying to get more comfortable. After a few minutes, I feel a slight pain in my pelvic area.

"You okay?" The blond lady looks to be in her mid-thirties or a little younger.

"I'm okay," I say as I reach for my juice.

She leans over and hands it to me.

"I'm Eve."

"Kelly." I smile back.

"If you're still in pain, you should let the nurse know. They may have something stronger that can help."

"I probably just need to let the meds kick in," I say.

"I'm guessing you don't have a high tolerance for pain." She sits up a little.

I shake my head in agreement.

"I thought it was gonna be more like period pain," I groan.

"Some of the blogs I read said that too, but this pain is hitting a little differently," she says.

There's an awkward silence before Eve chimes in.

"This was my first time too. I have a boy and a girl already, five and seven. Having a third at this point didn't make sense for my husband and me."

"How did your husband feel about you wanting to have an abortion?"

"He wasn't with it at first, but he understands why it was the right choice for us. The pandemic really took a toll on our family. We went from living the American Dream," she says, "to surviving Lynwood Heights."

"Hey, I'm from the Heights," I say, sitting up a little.

"Oh yeah? We're originally from Fresno, California. It's sorta like Vegas, except it doesn't get as hot in the summers. I'd do anything to have our old life back," she says. "If we were in a better position, I wouldn't have even thought to have an abortion, but we're barely making it now. "

"I'm sorry to hear that. I was just stupid and irresponsible," I say.

Eve sits up. "Girl, don't say that. You didn't get pregnant just to have an abortion, right?"

"No," I say.

"Then don't talk like that. You keep reminding yourself that you did what was best for you. That's all that matters." She waves her finger at me. "And just be glad your state isn't trying to decide for you. I feel so bad for women who don't have the means to make their own decisions."

"I feel bad for them too. It's so messed up," I say.

"As long as you feel like this was the best choice, nothing else matters." Eve takes a sip of her juice.

"Oh, I know I made the right choice, but . . ." I think about E and Ray. "Was it hard for you to tell your husband that you wanted an abortion?"

Eve thinks for a second. "Me and my husband contemplated for a few days, but this really was the best decision for us."

"I wish me and my boyfriend would have discussed this too," I say.

I don't know if Ray would have been as supportive as Eve's husband, but I would've hoped so. Maybe I should've kept it real with him.

"Why didn't yall?" she asks.

"Well, I broke up with him right after I found out that I was pregnant. I didn't want him to change my mind about having an abortion, but I probably should've just told him the truth, because right now I need him more than anything." I begin to cry.

"Aww, beautiful, stop being so hard on yourself. I can only imagine how scared you were when you found out. I think you should tell him when you're ready. Don't put too much pressure on yourself, Kelly. Who's to say that he'll even be upset?"

I shrug.

Eve twists her body toward me, sitting upright. Her golden skin is glowing, even in this dim room. There's a pretty, little diamond on her ring finger. She shakes a red cup like she's listening for something, then pulls out an ice cube to crunch on.

"Still got the urge to munch on cold things," she says with a laugh.

I laugh too, but I don't have the urge to do the same. Nurse Jill mentioned earlier that most of the symptoms I was experiencing might go away instantly, since my hormone levels are balancing out.

"Do you think it's wrong if I don't tell him?" I ask.

Eve shakes her head from left to right, while sifting for another piece of ice.

"Not at all. There's no law that says you have to, and even if there was, you didn't do this for him, you did this for Kelly, right?"

"Right." I picture Ray's face when I told him we needed to break up. "He's probably still wondering why I just up and ended things, but I felt like I had to at the time. I bet he hates my ass," I say, letting out a deep breath.

"Being in love at your age is hard. Hell, being in love at any age is hard. Relationships have their ups and downs. Sounds like a good guy, so I'm sure he won't hate you."

"He's not the only one I lost," I say.

Eve gently tilts her head.

"Me and my best friend Erykah got into a huge argument. She thought I was gonna keep my baby . . . like she kept hers."

"So, she stopped being your friend because you didn't want to keep the baby?"

"Not exactly. I think it's because she doesn't feel I've been a very good friend since she's been pregnant. And maybe I said some things that hurt her feelings."

"Oh, I've been there before. That's why I don't say too much if I can help it. My mouth gets me in trouble sometimes. How long yall been friends?" she asks.

"Since elementary," I say. "She's like a sister to me. I was hoping she'd at least text to see if I'm okay, but my phone's been dry all day. She probably hates me too."

"And again, why you being so hard on yourself? You gotta put yourself first. That's not to say that you can't care about and love others, but sweetie, I don't think you are this terrible person you're making yourself out to be. Yes, these are two very important people in your life, but disagreements happen. If anything, it makes your friendship stronger once you reconcile."

"I doubt she'll forgive me, though." I look at Eve as I wipe my tears away. "Today was the baby shower—I missed one of the most important days of her life." I can't stop the tears. I can't stop hurting inside. What if Erykah never speaks to me again after this? The thought of riding this out alone just eats me up inside.

"Kelly, if your best friend called you right now and told you that she needed you, what would you do?" Eve asks.

"I'd . . . be there," I say slowly.

"Regardless of everything else?"

"Yes," I say.

"And you don't think your best friend would do the same?"

Erykah *would* do the same. Matter of fact, she'd be wheeling me out of here if she could and making sure that I get the VIP treatment as soon as I get home. I bet Ms. Monica would even help too. Damn. I haven't really thought about that at all. Actually, our argument was more over E feeling like I'm not there for her and about her needing my support, now that I think of it.

Nurse Jill walks in to check on me and Eve. She tells us that we are both cleared to go whenever we're ready. Eve starts to gather her belongings, while telling her husband over the phone that she'll be out in a bit.

"You heading back to the Heights? If you want to ride back with us, you can. My kids might CoComelon you to death, but we have an extra row in our van that you can relax on."

"Oh, thanks, but my parents are waiting for me," I say as I text Mom to let her know I'm in the recovery room.

"That's really nice that you have their support. But if you need someone to talk to, give me a call. Take down my number."

"Really?" I say. I'm grateful that Eve was here with me, someone who just went through the same thing as I did, even if our reasons were different.

Eve tells me her number as she finishes gathering her things. We both make sure we're not leaving anything behind, then head out together.

Once we're home, Mom helps me to get settled as I lay in bed with a huge water bottle by my side and my heating pad on my pelvis. Even though this is only day one, I'm not as miserable as I thought I'd be. The lingering nausea that was overpowering my body is gone and so is the fear and guilt, but I'm not totally healed. I'm happy that I did what my heart was set on, but now I have to make things right with Ray and E, so that my heart can mend.

CHAPTER TWENTY-NINE

Erykah

35 Weeks

I never thought I'd say this, but I have been dying to go back to school. Online school is so damn boring. I felt so isolated and low-key depressed without being able to socialize. Ms. Benita would check on me from time to time since Momma had to work most of the days, and Miguel even came by a few times this past week, but online school isn't as easy as it seems. I've managed to keep my grades up, and since my vitals are getting better, Dr. Taheri said that I could go back to school three days a week until it's time for me to go on what he called a maternity leave. Usually that's for women who have to take time off from their jobs, but he says lots of his patients are students like me, although most are in college.

I can only imagine all the gossip that's been going around about me, but to be honest, I don't care. Darrion even texted me a "congratulations" GIF. I had to tell him that I still have another few weeks before the baby's here. Guess everyone thinks that's why I haven't been in school. I didn't sleep that well last night. A little mix of anxiety and the baby kicking me like crazy. On top of that, my back has been killing me, and my side has been aching since I got up this morning. I told Momma it was no big deal—I'm going to school no matter what. I haven't seen Kelly, which is the longest we've been apart since we were little kids. Momma's advice from the baby shower has stayed with me. I need to see Kelly and tell her I'm sorry.

When I arrive at school, everything's pretty much the same. The quad is packed as usual with kids snapping on their phones, chitchatting in tight huddles, and couples glued to each other. I try to find Kelly before first period, but I don't see her. I feel like all eyes are on me as I squeeze through people. My belly's so big, I can't even wear any of my uniform. Kelly's mom said it would be okay if I just wore the school colors instead. Inside, I want to believe that everyone's staring me down because I'm the only person out of uniform in this light blue blouse and stretchy denim-like leggings, but I know that's not why they're looking. I spot Kelly on a bench reading a book. I call her name a few times, but she doesn't even look up. As I get closer, I notice her AirPods are in. The bell rings and everyone is starting to clear out. I push through a few more people, still trying to get to her, but by the time I get to the bench, she's gone and so is pretty much everyone else.

* * * *

Sitting in Mr. Morgan's class, I'm struggling to pay attention; the longer I sit at this desk, the more the pain grows. Last week at my appointment, Dr. Taheri said it sounded like something called sciatica. It's when the baby is sitting on a nerve that's connected to your spine, and the pain can get really intense. I stand up to stretch, and thankfully, Mr. Morgan doesn't say anything. I feel my phone buzz in my pocket and discreetly give it a look once I sit down.

> Kelly: Hey. Can you meet in the courtyard at lunch?

Tears spring to my eyes. Just seeing her name on my phone is enough to make me emotional. It feels good knowing that she's aware that I'm back at school and wants to see me. This is my chance to make things right between us.

I weave through the crowd with my lunch tray, but the pain that's throbbing in my head is making it almost impossible to get from the lunchroom to outdoors. There's a couple stuck to each other like glue blocking the double doors. I want to tell them so badly that if they're not using a condom, run. I try to move slowly as the tray wobbles in my hands, but I have to stop and take a breath before I can move again. I feel a light tap on my shoulder.

"You need help?"

Darrion is smiling at me with a tray in one hand and a fly-ass Supreme bag in the other. He adjusts the straps of his bag on both arms, then grabs my tray.

"Thanks. I'm trying to find Kelly," I say.

"It's cool. I'll help you find her."

We navigate through the courtyard, and Kelly is sitting at a table in the center of it. She looks in our direction, waving at us to join. I turn to Darrion, causing him to stumble. Two chocolate chip cookies fall from his tray, and he looks like he wants to cry. I mean, those cookies do smack. They almost taste better than the ones from Subway.

"My bad." I grin.

"Nah, you good." He shrugs.

"Do you mind giving me and Kelly some alone time?" I tilt my head.

"Yeah. For sure. Let me just help you carry your tray to the table and then I'll let yall do ya thang," he says.

"Okay. Thanks, Darrion."

"Don't mention it."

After a few more steps, Darrion sets my tray across from Kelly and even helps to pull out my chair. He wanders off, and me and Kelly are awkwardly sharing a space with each other.

"Thanks for meeting me here." She stirs her straw in her berry smoothie.

"Thanks for inviting me." I smile.

"When my mom told me you were returning to school, I was really relieved. I've been thinking about you and the baby so much lately."

"For real?" My heart flutters.

"Yeah. I mean, things have been so fucked up between us, but I still care, E." She lets her chin fall into the palms of her hands. The sun makes her amber-colored eyes twinkle. She's still fly as ever, tapping her Cement 4s against the pavement. Not gone lie. At first I was nervous to sit with Kelly, because there was always a possibility that maybe she wanted to go in on me for not being there with her for her abortion, but I'm glad she didn't. I slide my tray to the side and scoot next to her. There's a ton of shit I want to say, like *I'm sorry* and *I love you* and how much I've been thinking about her too. But my arms fly around her, and she returns the love, squeezing me even tighter.

I want to just hold Kelly in my arms until the bell rings, but I feel something wet dripping from my nose. Probably just allergies, since it is that time of the year, and these wildflowers planted all over the courtyard don't make it better. Kelly leans over and tilts her head at me.

"Oh my God, E, your nose is bleeding." She gathers some napkins from the table and shoves them in my hands.

I press the tips of my fingers against my nose, then hold them out in front of me.

How is this even happening?

"I think I need to go to the nurse," I say, scooting back from the table.

I can feel myself starting to panic, but I don't want to show it. Everyone is trying to help me with my things, but I wish they didn't. It's just causing more of a scene, and that's the last thing I need right now.

"Let me walk with you," Kelly insists.

Her eyes are pleading for me to say yes. Even though we haven't been on good terms, I know that her love for me is not gone. I know that she still cares. She loops her arm through mine with my book bag strapped across her other shoulder. I follow her lead as we head to the office.

"156 over 95," the school nurse says as she loosens the blood pressure cuff from my arm. "Erykah, that's pretty high, and because of your headache and nosebleed, I think you should go to the hospital."

I look over at Kelly, who's just as shocked as I am. I don't even know what could've triggered it. I ate breakfast at home, like usual, and I haven't been snacking on high-sodium foods. I've been trying to get my rest. My stress levels aren't the best, but I'm not at rock bottom. I hate going through this so bad. I just wish that I could have a normal pregnancy without all of the scares.

"Are you going to have to call an ambulance?" I hug myself. Kelly is next to me, rubbing my back. I'm glad she's here to help keep me calm.

"That might be the best option, unless your mom can come get you," the nurse says.

I pull out my phone and dial Momma's number on speakerphone. After a few rings, she answers, exhaustion taking over her tone.

"Erykah? You okay?"

"Momma, my blood pressure is high, and the school nurse says I need to go to the ER," I say.

"How high is it? Baby, you know it will take me a while to get to you. Can Kelly's mom take you and I'll meet you at the hospital?"

"I can ask," I say.

"I'll radio Mrs. Lancaster," the nurse says as she begins to call for Kelly's mom.

Momma tells me to go to the nearest hospital, which is Lynwood Memorial, and text her as soon as I get there. Within a couple of minutes, Auntie is standing in the door, out of breath.

"Erykah, are you okay, baby?" She rushes toward me.

"Her pressure is extremely high. She needs to be taken to the hospital ASAP," the nurse says, looking at Kelly's mom.

"Okay, that's not a problem. Erykah, did you call your momma?"

"Yes. She said she'll meet us there," I say.

"Mom, can I ride with yall, please?" Kelly asks.

"Of course you can. Let me lock up my office and then we can get going," Mrs. Lancaster says.

I feel a queasy feeling in my stomach, but it's not from anything pregnancy related. It's me having a flashback from when I told Kelly I wouldn't be there for her when she asked me to go to the abortion clinic, but I try not to think of it. If Kelly wasn't willing to forgive me, why would she even be here by my side?

"Hey, it's gonna be okay," Kelly whispers to me.

I look at her as I try to blink away tears. She helps me down from the exam table, squeezing my hand tightly. There's so much I want to say to her right now, like how much I love her and how I don't *ever* want to fall out again. The way she's looking at me and holding my hand and rubbing my back, I'm pretty sure she's feeling the same. And even though I haven't gotten a chance to actually say how I feel, I think Kelly already knows and has forgiven me.

CHAPTER THIRTY

Erykah

35 Weeks

How in the hell did I go from starting my first day back to school to laying on a stiff hospital bed in this thin-ass gown? I wish the nurse would've just let me keep my real clothes on, but she said they need to run lots of tests, so staying in my little maternity dress wasn't an option. I must've gotten the itis after devouring that chicken pot pie they gave me a couple of hours ago. The filling was bland as ever, but my ass was hungry. Since I'm on a special diet, I could only choose from that or non-sodium vegetable soup, which I didn't even know existed. The pot-pie crust was buttery and flaky, almost as good as the store-bought ones Momma gets. They really got me eating like I'm somebody's grandmama. Damn, I miss real food.

I turn, and Momma is sitting beside me as she strokes her

fingers through my thick curls. I look into her tired eyes that are screaming with distress.

When I open my mouth to speak, it's so dry, I can't get a word out, just like in my dreams. But I can tell that this is not a dream. I don't feel the need to panic, and there's no doctors rushing in to save me and my baby's lives.

"You were sleeping so good, I didn't wanna wake you." Momma kisses my forehead. She's still in her uniform that she wears so much these days, you'd think that's the only wardrobe she has.

I want to go home. I'm tired of all these complications.

There's a fetal Doppler on the side of my belly that tracks the baby's heartbeat. Lately, Dr. Taheri's office observes me this way too, by strapping the monitor around my stomach. If the baby's heart rate is strong, I don't have to sit at the monitoring station as long.

Kelly comes around the other side of the bed and clenches my hand. She doesn't say anything. Her mouth just trembles as her eyes water.

Why does everybody look so sad?

"Is the baby okay?" I scoot up. "How long have I been here?"

"About three hours, and yes, she's fine. Here, drink you some water." Momma puts a straw up to my lips and tells me to take small sips. The chill from the ice water trickles down my throat, giving me life. I press down on my stomach and it's still firm. I slowly lay back down, feeling somewhat relieved.

"I don't even remember falling asleep." I try to stretch my arms. It's kinda hard to do with a blood pressure cuff strapped to one and an IV tube in my other hand.

"We're just waiting on your blood test results to see if they need to keep you overnight," Momma says.

"I'm sorry that you had to leave work early, Momma," I say.

"Listen, don't you worry about none of that. Aint nothing in this world more important than my kids and my grandbaby." She caresses my forehead.

I look over at Kelly, who's admiring me and Momma's bond. She smiles at Momma, then looks at me.

"I didn't want to leave your side until I knew that you and the baby would be okay," she says.

I want to grab Kelly close to me and thank her a million times, but I don't know how. Momma looks between us, then smiles.

"I'm gonna leave you two alone for a while, so I can fill up on some coffee and see if the café has anything worth a damn." Momma grabs her purse.

"Okay," me and Kelly say at the same time.

Momma looks at me with a gesture, like this is my time to make things right with Kelly. I lift the remote control that's attached to my bed and incline it. Kelly is sitting beside me. We make eye contact, both dying to be heard, but I honestly don't know where to start.

"I heard you got MVP for basketball again," I say, fumbling with the remote.

"Yeah, third year in a row." She bobs her head.

There's a beat.

We sit silently in the cold room, which is split by a tan curtain with a dainty flower pattern.

"Is there anyone in the other bed?" I try to look between the curtains.

"Nah, just us." Kelly shrugs, rubbing her arm.

She bends down and begins to search through her book bag. She takes out a tiny box that's wrapped in light pink.

"I meant to give you this at school today, but everyone was around and then you needed to go to the nurse." She hands it to me.

"Is this for the baby?" I ask, shaking the small, light box.

"It's actually for you." She hunches her shoulders nervously.

"Kelz, thank you." I start to unwrap the box. "You didn't have to get me anything."

Inside, there's a silver bracelet with five charms on it. The letters *K*, *E*, and the numbers one, four, and three. They are each sparkling with light pink rhinestones, my favorite color.

"I hope you like it," she says.

I can't help it, I burst into tears. I reach for my best friend and envelop her in a hug. The bed starts shaking, we're both crying so hard. After a minute, we pull apart and laugh as we wipe away the tears.

"Does that mean you like it?" she asks.

"Girl, I love this. Oh my gosh, Kelly, thank you so much."

"You're welcome. Here, let me put it on for you."

I extend my arm to her, and she fastens the bracelet around my wrist, just above my hospital band.

The room grows quiet again. I shift my wrist around as I admire the charms that are dangling from it. I look over at Kelly as I prepare to pour my heart out.

"I'm sorry," we both say at the same time.

That was awkward as hell.

We both laugh at each other. Kelly snorts and we laugh even harder.

"Kelz." I take a deep breath. "I'm sorry I didn't listen to your feelings. It was wrong of me to tell you not to get an abortion. You've been down for me from the start, and I wish I never said those hurtful things to you that day. I only said that you shouldn't because I wanted us to be moms together, but I realize how selfish that was of me. I support you one hundred percent on your decision. I was so stupid for bailing out on you when you've been the only one that I could really trust." My voice trembles. Kelly passes me a few tissues and uses one to pat her cheeks.

"No, I get it, E. I wasn't the best at being supportive to you, either. I really was trying to be, but I had so much on my plate, and then when I found out I was pregnant, nothing else mattered. I really thought my life was gonna be ruined forever. I never thought I'd be getting an abortion at sixteen. I was so ashamed to tell you at first. I knew you weren't gonna be happy with me not wanting to have a baby, but I know you weren't trying to hurt me. And I didn't mean it to sound like I was looking down on you or judging you for having a baby now."

She looks up at me with a half smile and reaches for my hand.

"How was it?" I ask.

"The abortion?"

"Yeah," I say.

"Honestly, it wasn't so bad," she says. "And after, I met this really nice woman who had gotten one too. She's older than us and has a husband and kids, but they weren't ready to have more. Anyways, she really helped me put things into perspective about our friendship. It helped me realize how I needed to check myself and make things right."

"I've been feeling the same. At the baby shower, I was so mad at first that you weren't there, but after talking to Momma, she made me realize that we can't go on fighting over dumb stuff," I say.

"My parents made me realize some things too," Kelly says.

"Wait. You told them?"

"I had to. You know I suck at lying, and it was eating me up inside. I thought they were gonna finish me, but they supported my decision and even took me to the clinic," she says.

"Really? So they wasn't mad?"

Kelly moves her mouth from side to side.

"I think mad is an understatement. I'm grounded for the rest of the year, had to delete all my social media accounts, can't go nowhere outside of school, and my mom's making me see a therapist over the summer." She looks down at the speckled tile.

"But at least they respected your decision."

"Yeah . . . they said they were mad that I didn't tell them at first. I guess I was expecting them to react differently."

Kelly's parents really are the GOATs. I'm glad she had them to confide in, but Kelly hasn't really said much about Ray. He wasn't even at the lunch table with us today.

"What about Ray?" I ask.

"We broke up." Kelly's voice cracks.

"Wait." I stumble over my words. "Ray dumped you when you told him about the abortion? Hell naw. I cannot believe him right now."

"No, E. *I* broke up with *him*. I still haven't told him anything. He doesn't even know that I was pregnant. I just told him I was going through a lot and needed my space. At first he was really torn, but now he's just giving me my space."

I cannot believe what I'm hearing. I never thought Kelly and Ray would call it quits, EVER.

"Oh. Do you plan on telling him eventually?" I ask.

"I'm still tryna decide," she says.

"Yeah, I understand. I'm glad you did what was best for you."

Maybe she understands why I didn't wanna keep it real with people at the beginning of my pregnancy. It was never about me trying to deceive, but more so cause I didn't want to hear no one's judgments, nagging, or opinions. Everyone's so used to me and Kelly always sharing our accomplishments. I mean, we know what to expect when it comes to sharing good things, but "bad" things? Nah. I think it was worse for Kelly to keep her pregnancy a secret. Imagine being a superstar at all that you do, then boom, you're suddenly the statistic of the month.

Rays of sunlight peek through the large window that over-looks the desert landscape. I try to block it with my hand that's poked with the IV.

"Let me close those blinds." Kelly jumps up.

She turns the long stick a few times, making the room just a little dimmer, but that's better than that annoying-ass sun hitting us in the face. She sits at the edge of my bed, looking as if she wants to trade me places. She doesn't even have her face beat today. Just some shiny lip gloss, lashes, and her hair done up in a cute Afro puff that's sprouted with a few honey-blond highlights.

"Hey, Kelz?"

"What's up?"

"Does Miguel know I'm here?"

"Your mom gave me his number to text him." She rolls her eyes.

"Did he respond?"

Kelly pulls out her phone, then shows me the green message that she sent to his ass four hours ago.

"Nope," with her eyebrow arched.

For some reason, I'm not surprised. Wonder what excuse he's gonna come up with this time? The fact that me and his daughter could be in danger and he's not even tryna text back is really starting to make my blood boil, but I can't let it get to me. I don't need my BP to rise any higher. I lay on the flat pillow, shaking my head.

"I really need to just let go of his fuckboy ass, huh?"

Kelly tilts her head, blinking a few times. "Umm, yeah. Like yesterday. The fact that his ass owns an Android is enough to kick him to the curb."

We both laugh together like old times. It feels so good to have my bestie back.

CHAPTER THIRTY-ONE

Erykah

35 Weeks

Kelly left about an hour ago, since she has school the next day. She promised to visit me tomorrow if I'm still here, which I'm praying that I won't be.

Momma glances at her watch and yawns. Ms. Benita is watching Jayden while Momma stays here with me. We've been watching old reruns of some game show called *Deal or No Deal*. Momma's been yelling at the TV, telling the contestants which briefcase they should pick next. The goal is to save the last pick for a million dollars cash, but so far, everyone we've been watching has been going home with nothing close to a million.

"What would you do if you won a million dollars?" I look over at Momma.

A wide smile appears across her face. "I'd buy us a new house and car and put the rest away for you, Jayden, and the baby." She takes a sip from a half-empty Pepsi bottle.

"For real, Momma? Wait, you wouldn't quit your job?"

"I don't know. Maybe. I wouldn't want to do the job I'm doing, but I could help you open that hair salon you've always dreamed of and then we could have people working for us." There's a gleam in her eyes.

My momma has worked all her life, struggling to make ends meet so that me and Jayden can have somewhat of a chance in society. I know getting pregnant at sixteen wasn't intentional, but I'm glad Momma has forgiven me and we've moved past that. I wouldn't want to call anyone else my momma, and that's real.

"Knock-knock. Dr. Palmer here. Is it okay for me to come behind the curtain?"

"Yeah, it's fine," I say.

I usually only see Dr. Palmer for my monthly checkups. I was hoping to see Dr. Taheri today instead, but Dr. Palmer did tell me that Dr. Taheri's job is to monitor me and the baby from the high-risk office only. When it comes to other stuff like emergencies and my delivery, that's a Dr. Palmer type–thing. He slides behind the curtain, analyzing a chart, before smiling at me and Momma over his rectangular glasses.

"Is it okay for me to discuss your medical condition in front of—"

"It's my momma, and yeah, it's okay."

Momma looks at him strangely.

"I almost was about to suggest that this was your sister," he tries to joke.

Momma sits back, blushing a bit.

"Well, your blood work is not too alarming, but you are showing signs of proteinuria—the levels of protein in your urine are slightly high," he says with a frown. "I think we should consider a cesarean, which is also known as a C-section. This might be the safest delivery method for your condition."

"You're not suggesting that she deliver now?" Momma crosses her arms.

"Oh, no. Not today. I think we should schedule Erykah's C-section at around thirty-seven weeks. That way she doesn't have to worry about further complications that could affect her and the baby."

"But that's like two weeks from now," I say slowly.

"Yes. I can have my scheduler contact you this week," he says eagerly.

We haven't even set up the baby's bassinet or anything. How am I gonna finish third quarter at school if I get a C-section in a few weeks?

"Why a C-section?" I ask.

"Well, most high-risk patients deliver their babies this way," he says matter-of-factly.

"But I don't want a C-section. That can't be my only option," I say, but he doesn't acknowledge me. How come no one has ever mentioned a C-section before? Dr. Taheri told me that I could have a vaginal birth as long as there are no serious emergencies that could risk me or the baby's life. Why is Dr. Palmer acting like this is the only option? I look over at Momma, who doesn't seem too content with Dr. Palmer's suggestion either.

"I don't know." She shakes her head. "I never had to have a C-section, and her little brother had me throwing up from dusk till dawn the whole nine months. And I also had gestational diabetes," Momma says.

"I understand, Ms. Smith, but if we schedule a C-section, it might be safer for Erykah and the baby to bring on delivery more quickly. I've performed many, and they've all turned out to be successful deliveries. We're able to control the situation better and avoid an emergency." He walks to the edge of my bed. "Erykah, it's not as complicated as it may sound. You'll be under a mild anesthesia during the process, and you'll be aware the whole time. And at the end of the procedure, you'll be able to hold your baby in your arms." He smiles.

I mean, it sounds good, not having to worry about crazy contractions, but I really wanted to have a vaginal birth. I don't want to be out of it when my baby comes into this world. I want to be fully present to hear her little cry and watch her take her first breath. Momma leans over and whispers to me.

"You need to talk to Dr. Taheri first, Erykah."

And that's exactly what I plan on doing. I feel like Dr. Palmer's not being honest with me, and Momma's right. I tell him I need time to think about it. At first he gives me this speech about how time isn't on my side, but Momma shuts that down real fast. By the time she's done going in on him, he scurries out the room so fast, he doesn't even say bye. Since I'm free to go, the nurses have unhooked me from those stupid machines and just give me more paperwork on how to care for gestational high blood pressure. First thing tomorrow, I'm calling Dr. Taheri's office so I can run everything by him and make the best choice possible for me and my baby.

CHAPTER THIRTY-TWO

Erykah

35 Weeks, a few days later

Ever since Dr. Palmer suggested that I should have a C-section, I've been researching like hell. You'd think Kelly took over my body or something. When I told her about the convo with him, she was worried too. She sent me hella articles over the weekend about how Black women are presented with C-sections more than white women in America. Seems like the more I research about C-sections, the more livid I become. It's already scary to be Black in America, but being Black and pregnant is starting to give me mad anxiety. One article even said that C-sections can lead to infections, kidney failure, or death. Sometimes they are really necessary. But a lot of times they're not, and patients aren't aware of all their options. Plus, they can cost almost twice as much as a vaginal delivery.

Kelly waves her phone around as the baby wiggles around on

the large monitor in front of us. She's making a digital memory book for me and Sierra, which I think is dope. The nurse moves the probe around my stomach as she checks for measurements, but Sierra is moving around so much, she can barely measure her little bowling-ball head. She definitely gets that feature from her daddy.

"Well, everything is measuring beautifully!" The nurse hands me a couple of towels to clean the gel.

"How much does she weigh now?" I ask.

"About five pounds, despite your strict diet," she says with a laugh.

Dang, already? I look down at my stomach and notice that the top is protruding in and out a little. I can feel Sierra's little foot jabbing me. Kelly starts to record again in awe.

"OMG, is that her foot doing that? I'm gonna have to put this on Snap too," Kelly squeaks.

"Girl, you are so extra," I laugh.

"What?" She pauses with the phone still in her hand.

"Dr. Taheri will be in here soon, ladies," the nurse says as she leaves us.

I struggle to pull my extra-large University of Reno T-shirt over my stomach. Just two weeks ago, it was loose, but now it barely fits. Kelly is editing the last video, sitting in a comfy leather recliner that's next to the exam table.

"Make sure you send those to me," I say.

"On it." She taps a few more times on her phone.

My phone chimes with the videos, plus the videos she's tagged me in on IG and Snapchat. I send them to Momma's phone too. She wanted to be here so badly, but I told her don't worry about it since Kelly was gonna be here with me.

"Thanks for bringing me here." I look over at Kelly.

She gathers the box braids I did for her last week and wraps them into a high bun. She waves me off.

"Of course I was gonna be here. Nobody's gonna force you to do anything with your body that you don't feel is safe. At least not on my watch." She folds her legs.

I'm about to praise her some more, but her sneaker that she's swinging from side to side catches me off guard.

"Your kicks are fire." I stare at her crisp, retro dead stock, all-white Anniversary Jordan 11s. Those had to have cost at least a rack. Damn, I didn't know she was ballin' like that.

"Won these a minute ago. Remember that sneaker vending machine at the mall?"

"Oh yeah, the one that you used to spend like twenty dollars on every single weekend?" I laugh.

"Guess it paid off!" She admires her shoe. "Ray was actually the winner that day, but they didn't have his shoe size, so he let me cop instead."

There's a beat before Dr. Taheri lightly swings open the door.

"Good to see you, Erykah," he cheers.

He pauses in front of Kelly.

"Hello, I'm Dr. Taheri," he says.

Kelly looks up, fixing her posture.

"Kelly. The bestie." She holds out her hand.

"Delighted to meet you, Kelly. Okay, let's see what we have here." Dr. Taheri flips a manila folder open as he sits on his rolling seat. "Vitals aren't too bad, baby's measuring perfectly . . ." he mumbles to himself. "Caitlynn said you had some concerns about a C-section delivery. Looks like Dr. Palmer suggested one due to your hospitalization last week." He flips through some more papers.

I look over at Kelly, then at Dr. Taheri, who's patiently waiting for me to respond.

"Yeah, he said it was the best option, but I don't understand why I can't have a vaginal birth," I say.

"He probably was trying to be cognizant of your condition, but from your labs at the hospital, your protein levels and blood work aren't at eclampsia levels. You might have had a scare that day because your body was more active than usual, or it could've been caused by something you ate, but we don't need to necessarily schedule a C-section. I think a scheduled induction might be a better option." He closes the folder.

Kelly bounces in her seat like she used to do when she wanted to answer questions in our fifth-grade class.

"That's when you schedule the delivery, and you have to receive medical treatment to induce the labor, right?"

How does she know more than me and I'm the one carrying a whole child?

"That's right. It's really just a method to initiate the labor process instead of letting your body do it on its own. It helps us have more control of the situation, but it's not so invasive. Lots of women get induced for different reasons, and it carries less risks than a C-section," Dr. Taheri adds. "As long as you or the baby aren't in a critical state, we can schedule it for thirty-seven weeks."

A wave of relief hits my body.

"Does that sound like something you'd like to do instead?" he asks.

"Yes." I give a nod to show I'm for real.

"I was actually going to suggest an induction before you came to your appointment today. Since you'll be checking in with me every week from now on, the staff and I can monitor you and baby more closely so that you'll have some peace of mind," he says.

"Thanks, Dr. Taheri, and thank you for allowing me to have a choice." My voice cracks a little.

"Absolutely. I would never want you to do something you don't want to do. I'll make sure to connect with your doctor's office to let them know you've elected to have an induction in two weeks—that's when you'll be thirty-seven weeks along." He scoots backward, reaching for the manila folder again. "Any questions for me?"

Too many. I mean, I understand what an induction is, but what exactly will it be like?

"Can you explain the process some more?" I ask.

"There will be a team of nurses who will be there to start the induction. Depending on how many centimeters you've dilated, they will give you medicine through IVs, most likely Pitocin. It'll also cause your uterus to contract. The more your uterus tightens, the more pain you'll start to feel, but you'll have the option to get an epidural if you'd like."

I scrunch my face as if I can already feel the pain. I've been watching pregnancy vlogs on YouTube and stuff, and so far, there's only been one lady who says she didn't feel horrible pain during labor. One lady said that it feels like a mix between period cramps and someone twisting your uterus like a wet towel. That analogy alone makes me just want to order the epidural as soon as they admit me. Dr. Taheri continues.

"Once you've dilated to at least ten centimeters, your doctor will be there to coach you through the pushing process, and then you'll be welcoming your beautiful baby into the world."

Kelly raises her hand like we're in class.

"Go ahead." Dr. Taheri smiles.

"So, you're not going to be the one to deliver Sierra?"

"That's normally the OB's job. I'm licensed to perform deliveries, but it's not so common for a perinatologist to be the first in command. I'm more of a specialist for Erykah and baby Sierra."

"Gotcha." Kelly nods.

"How long is the process?" Kelly is typing notes on her phone. It's like she's about to write a paper on labor and delivery.

"It depends on how fast you are dilating. Some women are

only in labor for eight hours; others can be in labor up to three days." He frowns a little.

"Three?" I ask.

"Yes, but I don't want you to dwell on that time frame. Most likely you'll deliver the same day. And I want to note, depending on how things are going, a C-section might still end up being necessary for your health and the baby's. It's nothing to be afraid of. You're in good hands," he says.

"Can my family be in the room with me?" I ask.

"Sure, but they might have to take turns. We usually suggest no more than two people," he says.

That'll be Momma and Kelly, for sure. If Miguel even shows up, he can bring his sorry ass in after the birth. As far as I'm concerned, he hasn't earned the right to get priority.

"It's a lot to take in, but I think you've chosen the best option. If you happen to think of anything else, you have my after-hours number. Don't hesitate to call. Now, there is one last thing I'd like to discuss." He furrows his brow, causing his thick black eyebrows to touch. He looks so serious. I sit up a little, trying to brace myself for whatever news he has for me.

"Erykah, I understand how important school is for you, and I admire your dedication, but I don't think you should continue going in person," he says.

His tone is very direct. It's almost like he's giving me orders instead.

"I haven't been back to school since I had to go to the hospital. I mean, I was hoping I could go until my last month, but I understand. I'll still be able to finish my classes online," I say.

"And you know I'll help you," Kelly adds.

"Okay, great. I'm glad we could nip that in the bud. So, let's move forward with everything. I'll see you next week. Make sure to stay true to your diet, monitor your pressure, and go to the emergency room if anything feels the slightest bit off, alright?"

"K." I smile.

Kelly stands up and holds out her hand to help me off the exam seat so that I can change back into my clothes. In two weeks, I'll be holding my baby. It's all I can think about at the moment. It's the only thing that matters. Honestly, doctors can be intimidating, and when it's your first pregnancy, there are so many things you just don't know. Just because I'm sixteen doesn't mean I can't make decisions for me and my baby. I'm glad I listened to Momma and Kelly and that Dr. Taheri was so helpful. He actually listened to me and answered my questions—I felt respected. After waddling my way through the parking lot, I slide into the passenger seat of the car. Soon as I latch my seat belt, I can feel Sierra jabbing me again on my side, but it doesn't hurt. It makes me feel even more connected to my precious baby. I wonder if it's her way of saying, *Thank you, Momma, for always doing what's best for me.*

CHAPTER THIRTY-THREE

Erykah

37 Weeks

The alarm on my phone startles me as soon as three a.m. hits. I press the stop button and sit up. I've been wide awake, laying in this bed, waiting for the time to grab my things and head to the hospital. My room doesn't even look like it belongs to me anymore. The baby's bassinet is on the opposite side of my bed. Gifts from my baby shower are stacked in each corner. And Sierra has so many clothes, I don't even own a closet anymore. I went from having the average teenage room to a full-on nursery. I scoot out of bed so I can check to see if Momma is up, but soon as I put my hand on my doorknob, my phone rings. I walk to grab it off of the baby's changing station. A few seconds later, Kelly's face is all on my screen. She looks like she hasn't slept much either. She blinks a few times before readjusting her headscarf.

"Just making sure you're getting ready." She yawns.

"I've been packed and ready since last night." I sit on my bed.

"I can't believe today is the day," she says. The camera is angled toward her wall, which is filled with posters of Kobe Bryant and Lisa Leslie.

"Girl, I can't either. I mean, I'm so ready to have this baby, but I'm a miss my little bump." I rub my stomach.

My door creaks open a little. Momma peeks in, wearing her cheetah-printed bonnet.

"Erykah, I'm gonna fix my hair and then we can go pick up Kelly," she says softly.

"Okay, Momma."

Kelly appears back on my screen in a cute pink fitted tee that says QUEEN TINGZ and two buns that are slicked back. Her edges even look decent.

"Momma said we'll be on the way soon," I say.

"I packed you some good snacks that you can munch on while we ride to the hospital." Kelly holds up a few ziplock bags filled with health bars, unsalted pretzels, and veggies.

"Thanks, bestie. Did you fix all that for me?" I ask.

"No, my mom did." She grins.

I roll my eyes and laugh. "That was so sweet. Tell her I said thanks," I say.

"Where's little dude? Is he coming to the hospital too?" Kelly begins to check for imperfections on her face while she waits for me to answer.

"Nah, girl. His butt is at a sleepover with his little school friends," I say.

"Gotcha. Well, I'm gonna go brush my teeth and stuff so I can be ready by the time yall get here," she says.

"Alright. I'll text you when we get there. 143."

"143." She waves, looking much more alert than she did a few minutes ago.

I lean back on my pillows, relaxing my achy back. It's been bothering me for the last couple of months, since the baby has been growing so much. One of the worst things about pregnancy is that you have all these crazy pains and symptoms and can't even take shit for them. My phone chimes. Probably just Kelly telling me something she forgot to say, but when I pick up the phone, it's a text from Miguel.

> Miguel: I can be at the hospital in a few hours.

> Miguel: Just gotta get a ride.

> Miguel: You think your momz can scoop me?

I feel like deleting his messages and blocking his number. He knows damn well my momma aint finna come get him at no three in the morning. And why wait to ask me two hours before

I'm scheduled to be at the hospital? I click his message off and slip my phone into my hospital bag. He can stay on read like he's been doing me for the longest. It would be nice for him to be there and all, but if Miguel still aint got his shit together by now, that's on him.

"Erykah, you ready?" Momma peeks back into my room.

"I think so." I finally get out of the bed.

She stands there, smiling at me for a few seconds. I never thought my momma would be proud of me being sixteen and pregnant, but by the way she's admiring me, I can tell that she's proud of something.

"You ready to miss all that good sleep you've been getting?" Momma teases.

"Oh, you must've forgotten that we'll only be two doors away. We're in this together." I point between me and Momma. We both laugh. Momma leaves so that I can get dressed.

I'm really about to be a mom.

The time has finally come. In less than twenty-four hours (fingers crossed), I'll be holding my princess, snuggling with her and gazing at her like Momma still looks at me sometimes. But damn, am I really ready? I've never done this before, and unlike everything else, where I can just study or practice to get better, this is different. What if I can't get the baby to stop crying at night or if I'm not that good at tucking her in? What if I'm not good at helping her with her homework? What if she keeps secrets from me when she's in high school?

"Come on so we don't get to the hospital late." Momma motions at me.

I blink back into reality, then follow behind her. The dark sky is speckled with a few stars and a bright crescent moon. The warm air sweeps against my body, bringing calmness to my anxious mind. I let out a deep breath before I get into her car.

This is it.

Today is the day that I get to experience true **motherhood**. I just hope that I can be as great of a mom as the **one I have.**

CHAPTER THIRTY-FOUR

Erykah

37 Weeks

The first two hours have been moving pretty slow. I'm only allowed to eat ice chips or clear liquids, just in case there's a need for an emergency delivery. I've been feeling light cramps, but nothing that's too out of control. Momma and Kelly are on either side of my bed, keeping me company. So far, I've already dilated to four centimeters. The nurse says that's a really good sign, which is all I need to hear.

Fourth Hour

I think I've spoken too soon, because I'm starting to feel some pretty unbearable pain and pressure. Momma tells me to breathe through each one, but all I can do is beg for the pain to go away as soon as it starts. I have to wait for the anesthesiologist to arrive before I can get the epidural. At first my contractions were like ten minutes apart, but now they are gradually getting closer together and becoming more and more intense. I can see the shock on Kelly's face. She's probably glad she's not in my shoes, and to be honest, I'd do anything not to feel this pain. Tears flow as the pain grows deeper. Kelly lets me squeeze her hand with each contraction. It helps a little, but I just want so badly for this to be over.

Sixth Hour

The anesthesiologist performed my epidural about an hour ago, and I can't feel anything past my belly button. If I couldn't see them, I wouldn't even believe that I have legs, because they are numb. One of the nurses comes in to see how far I've dilated. She reaches inside of me, but I still can't feel anything.

"You're seven. Getting close." She smiles, disposing of her gloves. "I'll check again in about an hour, but if you need anything, just press the button, and if you start to feel pain, let us know so we can get the doctor back in here to give you another epidural, okay, sweetie?"

I give a light nod, then look over at Kelly, who's watching some anime show on her phone. Momma's knocked out in the recliner across from me. Kelly looks up and smiles, then leans on my bed. I close my eyes, feeling myself doze off.

Eighth Hour

"I'm never doing this again!"

That's what I yell at everyone around me. I lay on my side, rocking back and forth. I try to breathe through the pain, but it just gets worse, and the contractions are coming faster. Kelly calls for the nurse while Momma soothes me. At least my blood pressure is stable.

"It's okay, baby. You're doing good. Breathe," Momma whispers in my ear, but all I want to do is curse, scream, and shout.

The provider comes in and checks my cervix again.

I'm at nine.

I should be ecstatic, but I'm anything but. I just want this to be over.

"We're going to let Dr. Palmer know that you're almost ready. Soon as he's here, you can start pushing," she says. The nurse and Momma help me to lay on my back. The nurse places my feet into the footrests at the end of the bed as her and another nurse start to prep for my delivery.

"Can I get another epidural, please?" I beg.

"I'm sorry, honey, but you're too far dilated. Don't worry, you're almost about to deliver. Once the baby is born, the pain should subside immediately," the nurse says.

"Here, hold on to my hand again," Kelly says. Her voice is so comforting, it's almost like she's done this before.

I grab her hand and begin to squeeze it. Momma lets me

squeeze her hand too. I feel my body warming up and my forehead starts to sweat. I take deep breaths, trying to fight the pain. The nurse reminds me not to push as her and another nurse coach me. It's so hard to keep from exploding, but I do my best to listen to what they say.

"Please, can I just push?" I moan.

I notice one of the other nurses whispering something to the other. The main nurse who has been helping me rushes over with a smile on her face.

"Dr. Taheri has just parked, and he'll be up shortly," she cheers.

Dr. Taheri? I thought Dr. Palmer was doing my delivery.

"That's good, right, Erykah?" Momma looks at me.

I can barely fix my lips to say anything, because the pain is growing more and more. I don't care if a unicorn is delivering my baby, I just want to get it over with.

"Did something happen to Dr. Palmer?" Kelly asks.

"He's still in a surgery and can't make it, so he asked Dr. Taheri to take his place," the nurse says.

The pain. Is beyond. Unbearable.

The nurse checks my cervix again.

"She's ready," I hear her whisper to Dr. Taheri as he calmly walks in and takes his position.

"Okay, Erykah, the next time you feel a contraction, I want you to take a really deep breath and then slowly push for ten seconds as you breathe out. Can you do that for me?" he asks.

"Yes." My voice shakes.

I start to feel a shattering pain that is the strongest contraction I've felt.

"Alright. Push, push, push, push, push," the nurse says.

Dr. Taheri counts backward from ten.

I do this a couple of times, each breath becoming harder and harder, but everyone is saying that I'm doing a good job. Everyone is coaching and cheering me on. My heart is beating so fast, I can hear each thud.

"Okay, Erykah, you're doing so good. Baby is almost here. I just need you to push one more time for me," Dr. Taheri says.

I look between Kelly and Momma, who are both smiling down at me. Momma has tears in her eyes. She reaches down to kiss my wet forehead, right before I feel another contraction starting. I push as hard as I can. Before Dr. Taheri can finish his count, I hear an innocent cry and feel a wave of emotions.

"She's beautiful," Kelly says in wonder.

Momma can't stop crying.

My chest is heaving as I anxiously wait to see my baby. The nurse lays her tiny body on top of my chest. As her creamy, warm flesh touches mine, I stare down at her silky black hair that covers her head. We lock eyes. I tremble as tears flow, caressing my baby. She's everything I imagined her to be. Momma and Kelly embrace us as we welcome baby Sierra into her new world.

Two
Months Later

CHAPTER THIRTY-FIVE

Erykah

I've never prayed for sleep so much in my life. Don't get me wrong, I love my baby, but being a mom is a lot of work. The good news is that Momma's got a new shift so that she can help me with the baby, but sometimes her job has her on standby, so she has to be prepared to work whenever they need her to. I'm back online with school and only have one more month to go before the school year is over. Momma says she's proud of my 3.8 GPA. I'm proud too.

Miguel has been off and on. He ghosted me again after he first came to see the baby at my house. I guess that's his thing. Coming and going when he pleases, and when I ask him where he's been, he's just like, "I was handling business," and changes the subject. It's sad to say, but I'm used to it now. I remember how I used to get so mad at his ass, but now that my main focus is on Sierra, I don't really allow myself to get too hyped.

To be real, I've noticed that I've been worrying about his

whereabouts less and less. I'll admit, we have had sex again a few times. We both made sure we used condoms. And I got a depo shot at my six-week postpartum checkup. But if I'm being honest, it wasn't the same. It's not wack or anything, but I'm really just not that into him. I'm starting to see more of what Kelly and Momma have been saying.

I change Sierra's diaper, then hand her back to Miguel while I style my hair. We're taking her to see his aunt and sister for a little bit. I run the flat iron past my roots, slick my hair into a back ponytail, and swirl my sideburns. The baby is always pulling my hair, and I aint gone lie, that mess hurts. I watch Miguel play with Sierra while I finish getting ready. She's all giggles and smiles with him. He tickles her with a stuffed Minnie Mouse toy while making a cute voice. She kicks and can't stop laughing in her little car seat.

"I'm gonna make her a bottle and then we can go," I say from the kitchen.

"Yeah, aiight." Miguel focuses on Sierra like he can't take his eyes off of her. It's mad cute. Sometimes I believe we could be the perfect family, but I honestly don't think Miguel is ready for anything like that.

"Alright, I'm ready," I say with Sierra's heavy-ass diaper bag strapped across my chest.

I adjust my pants again, trying to make them fit. I've pretty much lost all my baby weight, and I'm not swollen like a blowfish anymore. I didn't think I would lose so much weight, but that first month of breastfeeding really did take away all my meat. Miguel scoops up Sierra, who, even in her car seat, is probably way lighter than this bag, which feels like it weighs a ton. Momma always says to overpack, because I never wanna be stuck without anything.

"Actually, can you take this bag and I'll get her instead?" I ask.

"Yeah, that's cool."

On the way to Lita's, Miguel is blasting his favorite rappers as usual. I've told him about doing this stupid shit, especially when the baby is in the car, but he doesn't seem to care. He turns the volume down a little bit to say something.

"So, you gone get a job with your moms still or you going back to school?" He looks at me with one hand on the wheel while we sit at a red light.

"I'm not dropping out of school." There's a million ways to get my diploma, and he knows I can't get my cosmetology license if I don't graduate.

He just shrugs me off and turns his music back up. I don't know what that's all about, but I'm not dropping out of school just because I had a baby. I think back to when I was considering dropping out, and I'm so glad I didn't. After spending a few hours at Lita's, Sierra is knocked out. Miguel helps me to carry everything in the house. After I lay her in the bassinet, he comes in the room trying to get all freaky, but I'm tired as hell and just want to sleep while I can.

"Can I stay a little longer?" He kisses me from behind on my neck.

I turn around, almost blinded by his heavy gold chain.

"I'm a take a rain check," I say.

"Damn. For real?"

"Miguel. I'm tired," I say low.

Sierra shifts in her bed but falls back asleep.

"I was just gone stay for a li'l bit."

"Oh, and then leave me to take care of the baby all night?"

"Man, you trippin'."

I grab the baby monitor and walk out the room and motion for him to get out too so we don't wake up the baby. After he steps out, I gently close the door and go into the kitchen. Miguel follows behind me, then stands in the living room with his arms folded, looking foolish.

"Listen. I aint got time to just be laying up with you every other weekend, then wondering when you're gonna come back around. I need help with our daughter, and I'm not tryna get pregnant again anytime soon."

"Who said you was gone get pregnant? I got protection."

I suck my teeth and roll my eyes. He really just missed everything I said.

"Yeah, well, that's cool and all, but I think we should just focus on our daughter." I fold my arms.

"Yo, what you tryna say?"

"That I can't be in no relationship right now. I need a break."

"Yo, Moms got you talking like this or something?"

"First of all, leave my momma out of this. You never around

as it is, and this what we doing is stupid. Look, I don't wanna beef with you, Miguel. I still love you and everything, but I just don't wanna be in no relationship."

He takes a step back and looks me up down.

"Man, whatever. I'll be by sometime next week to see my daughter, then."

"Alright," I say.

Miguel lets himself out, and for some reason, I don't even feel bad. It's like me ending this relationship has been a long time coming. I always thought if me and Miguel ever broke up, I'd be a wreck, but that actually felt good. I go back in the room to check on Sierra, who's sound asleep. I adjust her sleep sack, then kiss her little chubby cheek. This is all the love I could ever need and want right now.

Two More
Months Later

CHAPTER THIRTY-SIX

Erykah

"I should've gone with the pink one," I mumble as I tug at the bottom of my shimmery dress, which barely touches my knees. I'm so glad that I'm starting to fit back into my old clothes since having Sierra, even though I still wear my waist trainer with certain fits. Momma says the waist trainer will help my stomach to suck back in, but I plan on going to the gym and putting in some work, too. I look at my body from different angles, and I feel like ripping the dress off and just rocking some sweats and a baby tee, like most days. I don't know why I picked this dark champagne color. It makes me look like I'm wearing my skin.

"E, for real? I bet you look bomb," Kelly says from the other side of the door. "C'mon, let me see," she whines.

I take a big breath, then unlock it. She yanks it open, then stares at me with her mouth almost to the floor.

"You. Look. So. Bomb," she says between claps. "Like a model. You definitely rocking that V-neck dress."

"Girl, quit playin'. For real?"

"Hell yeah," she says, still checking me out.

Kelly looks amazing too. Her cream-colored maxi-dress and tall heels make her look like she should be on the runway instead of dribbling on the court.

"Ray's gonna get his girl back when he sees you tonight," I say.

We both start laughing before snapping a few selfies.

"Well, I invited a special guest tonight, just for you," Kelly says mysteriously.

"Umm . . . who? It better not be Miguel." I roll my eyes.

"Okay, see now you tripping," Kelly says before we both start laughing again.

"My hair turned out so cute." Kelly looks in the mirror while running her fingers through her wand curls. "Thanks, E."

"Aww, you know I'm a always hook up my bestie."

"C'mon so my mom can quit texting me to come outside." Kelly scrunches her face at her phone. I loop my arm through hers as we walk to the backyard. It's her parents' anniversary, and this year they decided to throw a celebration at their crib. The Lancasters' backyard looks like something you'd see in the movies. Star-shaped string lights and sparkling streamers are hanging from their wooden pergola, and there's even a red carpet laid out. We help ourselves to some of the finger foods, then make our way to the rest of the crew. Everyone is seated at a round table that's decorated in a sparkly black cloth. Kelly sits next to Ray, who is eyeing her like he's starstruck. They've started seeing each other again, but they're not officially back together. And I think a big reason for that is because Kelly hasn't told him about the abortion yet. She says they're not officially back together, but I can tell by the way they can't break eye contact, it won't be long before they are. I slide into a seat between Mama and Jayden.

"This is so nice," I say to Momma, who's rocking an updo I did for her and a cute black cocktail dress. She bounces Sierra while fluffing out the ruffles on her pink-and-navy dress. She looks like a live baby doll with her head full of curls and big brown eyes. Momma hardly ever lets me hold my baby when I'm around. She's so in love and I can't blame her.

"Can I *please* hold her, Ms. Monica?" Kelly stretches her arms out.

"Of course you can," Momma says in baby talk while smiling at Sierra.

She kisses Sierra a few times on her plump cheeks, but before she goes to hand her to Kelly, I motion for Momma to give Sierra to me instead. I kiss Sierra on her soft forehead, then caress her in my arms. I still can't believe she's here. It feels like just yesterday I was rubbing my stomach, trying to envision what this moment would be like. Kelly stands behind me, clearing her throat, still stretching out her arms.

"You wanna go to Tee-Tee?" I snuggle with Sierra, before giving her one more kiss and placing her in Kelly's arms.

"I can't believe my parents have been married for fifteen

years." Kelly's eyes wander over to her parents, who are rocking each other on the dance floor, as she bounces Sierra lightly.

"I can, and one day, yall will be celebrating a moment like this too." Momma tilts her glass at us.

Me and Kelly make faces and burst into laughter.

Michael Jackson's "Billie Jean" starts playing from the speakers, and Jayden darts to the dance floor, joining Kelly's parents.

"That's right, baby. Show them that li'l dance you like to do," Momma yells.

I swear it's the same weird dance that makes him look like a dying squid, but it is kinda cute, though.

"I'm about to go on the dance floor and show Jayden how it's really done. Yall tryna turn up?" Ray looks between me and Kelly.

"We'll be there in a minute." Kelly smiles at me.

"Kelz, what do you have up your sleeve?" I ask.

"I don't have any sleeves." She looks at me, puzzled, then starts playing with Sierra.

"Okay, so you got jokes. Girl, quit playing and tell me," I whine.

"Wait and see," she says with a mischievous twinkle in her eye.

Ray jumps up before I can start interrogating him and hits the dance floor. Momma scoops Sierra from Kelly and starts dancing with everyone else.

"You think we'll be celebrating wedding anniversaries one day?" Kelly asks with her chin in her palm, mesmerized by the bright stars above us. I stare at them too as the warm breeze hits my body. Throughout everything I've endured this year, I'm so thankful for the people who are surrounding me. I don't know how I would've made it without them, and even though I'm not the ideal age to be a mom, it is what it is and I no longer dwell on things like that. Kelly gets up like she's got a plan.

"Let's go dance," she says, pulling me toward the dance floor.

Alicia Keys's "If I Ain't Got You" comes on, and I notice Darrion scoping everyone out from afar. He's looking good too. His straight-leg ankle pants and crisp black top make him look even more fine.

"You made it." Kelly claps, then grins at me.

Darrion waves and walks over to us.

"You set me up," I say from the side of my mouth.

"You can thank me later," Kelly teases.

"This is dope." Darrion looks around while giving us hugs. He even smells expensive. I don't know why, but my heart is racing really fast and my stomach is feeling all queasy, like it did when I first met Miguel.

"You look really nice tonight, E." Darrion's voice trembles a little. He's looking at me like how Ray was looking at Kelly earlier. "You wanna dance?"

Kelly is looking at me, like *bitch you better not say no*, and I kinda want to kick her ass . . . but I'm also tryna play it cool with Darrion.

"Yeah, I'd like that," I say.

He takes my hand and leads me to the floor. We dance to the last few moments of the song. Everybody is a whole mood right now. Even Momma, who's gently swaying Sierra to the melody. They are literally melting my heart.

"Your baby's got your moms wrapped around her finger," Darrion laughs.

"That she does. I can't front, though, because I be spoiling her too. My baby deserves the world." I look up at Darrion. He stares back with a glimmer in his deep brown eyes.

"You deserve the world too." His voice is mellow as his words flow through my ears and into my fluttering heart. My stomach starts to feel funny again. I know this feeling all too well, but I never thought it would be happening again so soon.

The playlist transitions to the next song, and "Electric Slide" comes on. Everyone starts to get in position so they can do all the moves.

"You care if I go and dance with my momma?"

"Nah. You straight. Gone and do your thang," Darrion says.

We finish off the rest of the song rocking and singing the lyrics out loud. I'm surprised the neighbors haven't rung the doorbell. "Cupid Shuffle" comes on next, and everyone is even more hyped. Everyone is living it up, and we're having the time of our lives. Reminds me of old times, even though we're all moving on from the past. And that's okay, because I'm so looking forward to what me and my baby's futures hold.

ACKNOWLEDGMENTS

Since I was around eight years old, I've dreamed of being an author. Although the gifts I have been blessed with brought me to this point, I would be remiss if I didn't share my gratitude with the many beautiful souls who have encouraged me.

First, I'd like to thank God for blessing me with this talent and opportunity. Thank you to my ancestors, who watch over me and my beautiful daughter, keep me in line, and remind me to never give up. I give thanks to my mother, who has always encouraged me in all that I've done and still does to this day. I love you, Mommy. To my father in heaven, who brought big smiles to my face: I hope you can see all that I've accomplished and that you're proud of Mook.

I want to give a huge thank-you to all my former students who have been rockin' with me since day one, from Vegas to the Bay Area. Thank you for reading my work, giving me the best feedback, and bragging about your dope teacher who writes books. Yall are truly my inspiration and one of the main reasons I write.

I want to give a very special shout out to my MFA family at UNR (formerly known as Sierra Nevada University). Brian, thank you for giving me a chance. I will forever be grateful for the space you created. To Jessica Henderson, I love you so much.

Thank you for laughing and crying with me every time I felt like giving up. Christa Martin, my soul sister. Thank you for always checking on me and encouraging me. I can't wait until your big day comes! Joe McGee, thank you for being one of the best writing instructors ever! You and your wife, Jess, are so amazing. Christian Keifer, you were my first mentor, and I will never forget you. I remember that crazy first semester I had with you and how frustrating it was for the both of us, but you didn't give up on me, and I love you for that. To my sis Geri and my mother from another mother, Catherine, I love you two. To everyone who was in the YA track at SNU, thank you for reading my work and giving me honest feedback. To Shaneen, Faylita, and Michelle, yall are the epitome of Black excellence. I'm still trying to get on yall level (lol), but thank you for the long talks, encouragement, and just showing how damn dope educated Black women can be.

And now, Pablo.

Pablo Cartaya is so amazing, he gets his own paragraph, which I am sure he is blushing at. Sé que fuistes enviado a mí por los santos y por eso estoy muy agradecida. Sin ti, no estaría donde estoy hoy. Te has quedado a mi lado en las buenas y en las malas. Eres mucho más que un mentor, sino mi familia. Te tengo mucho cariño y siempre estaré agradecida por las oportunidades que me has brindado. Z y yo te queremos mucho.

I'm indebted to Dr. Raegan McDonald-Mosley, Marisa Nightingale, and the whole team at Power to Decide, for their guidance on this book and everything they do. Cicely Paine and everyone at SisterSong Women of Color Reproductive Justice Collective—I appreciate you and your invaluable feedback. Dr. Shawnita Sealy-Jefferson, I'm so glad I had the chance to talk with you. I'll never forget that conversation.

To my beautiful agent, Jess Regel: You took a chance on me, and I can't thank you enough. I never want to leave your side. You are truly the best agent anyone could ask for. I can't wait to do more projects with you. Next, I want to emphasize, very heavily, that Christian Trimmer is the dopest editor on this planet. I've learned so much from you and admire you like no other. Thank you for believing in me and entrusting me with this story. Thank you, Shirlene Obuobi, for being such an inspiration and so down to earth and for helping me to get rid of my imposter syndrome.

I also want to give flowers to some authors who have inspired me. Reading your work has pushed me to where I am today. To the late Walter Dean Myers, Langston Hughes, and Lorraine Hansberry: Your works are not only classics but beautiful representations of Black excellence. To Angie Thomas, I'll never forget the time you supported my students when your debut novel dropped. You've always been so sweet and kind—I admire you so very much. To Tiffany D. Jackson, Elizabeth Acevedo, Matt De la Peña, and Jason Reynolds, yall are the GOATs. Because of you, I not only discovered more of who I am as a writer, but I also found ways to reach out to my students, who desperately wanted to see themselves in the stories they read. Your books saved so many of my students and motivated me to write more.

I must give a thousand thank-yous to my dear brother, Phillip "B" Thompson. You are my best friend and someone I simply cannot function without. From crazy nights in Vegas to sleeping on your couch in Harlem to random phone calls just because Z wanted to talk gibberish with you. You've been there for me like no other and I appreciate you so much. I want to give a special shoutout to my best friend Janelle, who fangirls me and makes me feel all special. Who would've ever believed we'd be some bomb ass mommas, killin' the game? I love you. To my dear friend Vernon, whom I love so very much. Thank you for always listening to, loving, and understanding me. To my bestie Latrease, thank you for over twenty years of friendship and for watching Z so that I could write. She and I love you and your family so much. You're more like my sister than anything. To my BF, Carla: I love Queens so much because of you. It's so amazing how God introduces us to the people who are meant to be in our lives. Thank you for supporting me and being patient with me. I'm getting better at answering the phone. (I know right about now you're probably thinking, Dang, how many best friends does she have? Hella and I love them all to a million pieces. Without them, I don't know how I would have survived this journey.) To my dear friends Leslie and Jeff, yall are like the big brother and sister I never had, and Z loves you two so much. Thank you for lifting me up when I was at my lowest point. To my daughter's madrina, Miosotis, thank you for your prayers and guidance. We love you so much and will be there with you in Santo Domingo, one way or the other lol. To my homie Dion (who still owes me a drink), I'm so glad I met you. I love our extensive convos and am thankful for the support you have given me.

A very special thank you to my baby girl, AaZariah (Z). Every time I sat down to write, I always thought of you. You inspire me more than anything, and Mommy loves you so much. Everything I do is for you. You've changed my world. I could not ask for a better daughter. I love you a lot, a lot, a lot. You complete me in so many ways. Don't ever forget that you are the light of my life and I want nothing more than to give you the things that I always wished for growing up.

Thank you to Morgan J. Freeman, Dia Sokol Savage, and Lauren Dolgen for creating *16 & Pregnant* and *Teen Mom* and for understanding the importance of telling these stories. To the *16 & Pregnant* fans, thank you for your support. Thank you so, so, so much, MTV Books and Simon & Schuster.

I want to give a shoutout to every person who has purchased my first novel—thank you so much. And to every woman of color in America, just remember that your voice is power and that your heart won't ever lie to you. Always do what you feel is right and never let anyone take that away from you.

RESOURCES

If you or someone you know is in need of reproductive health guidance, please visit:

Bedsider, an online birth control support network that helps young women find the birth control method that's right for them and how to use it correctly. http://bedsider.org/

Black Mamas Matter, a Black women-led cross-sectoral alliance that centers Black mamas and birthing people to advocate, drive research, build power, and shift culture for Black maternal health, rights, and justice. https://blackmamasmatter.org/

Coalition for Positive Sexuality, a site that provides resources and tools for teens to take care of themselves and affirm their decision about sex, sexuality, and reproductive control. http://www.positive.org/

In Our Own Voice: National Black Women's Reproductive Justice Agenda, a national-state partnership focused on lifting up the voices of Black women leaders at the national and regional levels in its fight to secure Reproductive Justice for all women, femmes, and girls. https://blackrj.org/

Mental Health is Health, an MTV Entertainment Group initiative, aims to normalize conversation, create a connection to resources, and inspire action on mental health. https://www.mentalhealthishealth.us/

National Sexual Assault Hotline will connect you with a trained staff member from a sexual assault service provider in your area. Visit https://rainn.org/ to chat or call 800-656-HOPE (4673).

Power to Decide provides research-backed information on sexual health while fighting for access to this information and the full range of contraceptive methods. https://powertodecide.org/

Scarleteen, a website that provides a wealth of information for teens and young adults about sexuality, sex, and relationships, as well as advice and support, and even a safer sex shop. https://www.scarleteen.com/

SisterSong is the largest national multiethnic Reproductive Justice collective that advocates for women's human right to lead fully self-determined lives. https://www.sistersong.net/reproductive-justice

Youth Coalition is an international organization of young people committed to promoting adolescent and youth sexual and reproductive rights at the national, regional, and international levels. https://youthcoalition.org/